Nightmare Noir

ALEX AZAR

Mystery and Horror, LLC
Tarpon Springs, Florida

Nightmare Noir
Copyright © 2015 by Mystery and Horror, LLC

Author Alex Azar
Cover Art by T.J. Halvorsen
Sarah E. Glenn, Editor-in-Chief
Gwen Mayo, Editor

First Trade Paperback Edition

ISBN- 978-0-9915825-7-0
(Mystery and Horror, LLC)

ISBN-10: 0991582578

Library of Congress Control Number: 2015936775

Printed in USA by Mystery and Horror, LLC
Tarpon Springs, FL

This book is dedicated to my nieces;

Maya, Zayna, Talya

Zayna, Talya, Maya

Talya, Maya, Zayna

Table of Contents

Onion Avenue
From the Casebook of Detective James S. Peckman
By Alex Azar

People claim you always remember your first: first kiss, and first time falling in love. A paranormal private detective's life has milestones that are a little different than the average person's. I wish I could forget my first time killing someone, and the first time I was shot. Most of all, I would love to forget how my wife and daughter died, and why I left the police force.

When they were killed under "suspicious circumstances," conventional police investigation methods were a dead end. I was ready to try anything to figure out what happened to them. I started looking closer at the unexplained evidence in their case file and was thrown into the paranormal world. Now there was no turning back.

Work helped. Unfortunately, my first client shared a name with my daughter. That made her a constant reminder of the life taken from me, my family life.

I

"Don't 'Jimmy Peck' me; you can call me that when we're friends. Right now, you can call me James S. Peckman," I shouted into the receiver. After hanging up the phone, I laughed at the absurdity of our argument. There was no way I would let Thaddeus convince me to use our names as the company name. Even if my name went first, "Peckman, Coleman and Gomez" sounded like a law firm, not a paranormal private detective agency.

"What's wrong with Argus Agency?"

Naming our company 'Argus' after the thousand-eyed creature sounded much better. It made sense to me, but Thaddeus didn't like the idea.

I continue the argument with myself while flipping the card that started our argument through my fingers.

The card is a standard sized business card; dark brown with tan letters reading "Peckman, Coleman & Gomez." It might as well have 'LLP' after our names. On the reverse is a light brown drawing of an eye with three pupils meant to represent each of us, and below it reads, "Bumping back in the night". Apparently, we had a new slogan to go with our new name.

Elizabeth, the 'Gomez' of the proposed title, has decided to abstain from the name game. She claims it's because she's only known us for two months, but I suspect she enjoys the back and forth between Thaddeus and me. I have a feeling the slogan was her work. I'll have to ask her when she returns from office shopping. Currently, we're using Thaddeus' one room office--two rooms if you count the jail-cell-sized lobby. I don't.

Being my own secretary doesn't mean much without clients, which is why I was surprised when a female officer walked through the door asking for a Detective Coleman.

"I'm sorry, he's away on a case," I reply. "Perhaps I can be of assistance."

Her vibrant green eyes contain a mix of doubt and contempt. "Who are you? I need someone with Thaddeus' "special talents." She stresses the last word to let me know she means a talent for dealing with the supernatural.

"Me? I'm Detective Peckman, Thaddeus' partner. I can assure you I…"

She cuts me off with a quick show of her palm and asks for my credentials.

"Well I was a police detective for..."

She interrupts me again, implying that I'm just a bored secretary.

What I did next, I know I'll regret for years to come. I hand her the business card in my hand, solidifying the agency's name. "As I was saying, I am a detective. I can assure you that I am more than capable of assisting you."

While not verbal, the look on her face is apology enough. She takes the chair across the desk from me. "I'm Sheriff Sophia O'Conner, of Montezuma, Kansas."

Her pause leads me to believe she heard my gasp at the sound of my daughter's name. Her raised eyebrow confirms my suspicion.

I want to explain about the name and the accident that killed my wife and daughter, but that's no way to gain her trust. We are already on rocky ground. "I'm sorry, please continue," I say.

Her cocked eyebrow tells me she has misread my emotions and discounted my age. She addresses me with contempt, "I'm sorry, I can't rely on some heartbroken kid barely out of college. I've got a dangerous situation developing in Kansas. I need someone with Thaddeus' particular skill set."

Knowing that my age and my experience weren't going to impress clients, I had practiced an answer that I hoped would satisfy the sheriff. "I am young, but I spent several years as a detective on the Newark police force. Admittedly, I have had some recent hardships, but they have prepared me for the type of case you've come to us to solve. So, how can I be of service to you?"

I knew I was pushing it by saying she came to 'us' when she had asked for Thaddeus. I hadn't earned her trust. Her look of doubt had been steadily growing through the whole conversation. To her credit, she's remained seated.

"Montezuma has a vampire problem," she said bluntly.

I knew she would judge me by my reaction. It was my turn to surprise her. "Aren't vampires your town's only claim to fame?"

Seeing her eyebrow attempt to raise even further on her face put a smile on mine.

"I knew Montezuma, Kansas sounded familiar, but I couldn't place it until you mentioned the vampires. I've studied as much supernatural and paranormal lore as time allows. I've had a particular fascination with vampires, especially their mythology through different eras."

Drawing a nod from the sheriff, my confidence grows. What she doesn't know is that if she does happen to hire me, it'll be my first solo case. That thought deflates my confidence and wracks my nerves. I light a cigarette from the pack on the desk to help me calm down. I close my eyes and inhale deeply. A now familiar cocked eyebrow greets me when I open my eyes, "Sorry I hope you don't mind the smoke."

"No, but can I bum one?"

Ashamed for not offering her one sooner, I extend my hand holding the pack, "My mom taught me better than that, sorry again." When she finished her smoke, I ask her to explain the vampire problem.

"Well, you may know Montezuma's history as a land of onions created the fake myth that the townspeople in the 1860's used onions to repel a vampire horde. The popularity of that myth was our town's biggest source of tourism revenue. That is, until the more popular belief of garlic took effect and life returned to normal... almost." She arrived planning on speaking with Thaddeus, someone who surely knew the more intimate history of Montezuma, but is still talking to me as an outsider who needs his hand held through the history lesson. Realizing this herself, she stops for a moment.

She takes half a minute of silence to finish the rest of her cigarette. I can see some of the stress melt off her shoulders as she embraces the smoke in her lungs and runs her free hand through her mocha hair. "Ever since I became sheriff, I've noticed a steady number of disappearances." She explains that in a town of less than a thousand people it's easy to notice a pattern.

"I can understand that. Now, you actually believe this is the work of vampires?" I ask innocently enough. A question I feel is completely in line with the direction of our conversation.

With more venom than I think she intended--at least I hope as much--the sheriff spits back, "It's my job to serve and protect; it's yours to figure this kind of shit out."

We're both silent for a few minutes. Her so she can let what she said sink in, and me so she can realize yelling at me isn't going to aid her cause. Only one of us can win out. I was an officer long enough to know that this stage in a negotiation is too crucial to buckle. I only hope she doesn't know this yet.

After a few more silent moments, she lets out a sigh of acceptance. "I don't know what's going on, but I know it's above my pay grade. Because of the false history the town has, the feds aren't taking the situation seriously." Taking another cigarette from my pack, she says while lighting it that she met Thaddeus years ago. She's vague on the details of the circumstance of their meeting, but I knew better than to inquire further.

As I'm thinking of where to steer the conversation, Elizabeth enters the office with a smile that suggests she found a suitable location. Not giving her time to mention it, I ask her to sit with the sheriff while I take care of something. I hear the sheriff tell Elizabeth that I'm going to call Thaddeus to confirm their relationship.

I want to be upset at her presumption, but I'm cut off by

Thaddeus on the other end of the phone.

"I've got Sheriff O'Conner in the office, she says she knows you."

There's a pause as Thaddeus tries to access his memory. With nothing forthcoming, I add that she's from Montezuma, Kansas.

"Oh yes, Sophia!" I hide my cringe at the name, as he asks why she's here. Explaining her situation, I go to no great length to avoid using her first name. "I trust her enough to take her at her word. Tell her I'm sorry, James, but I've got a solid lead on what killed my wife. I won't be able to make it back for the foreseeable future."

Following his train of thought, I let him know I was more than willing to handle this for him. "The main reason I called was about the payment."

"Listen, I wouldn't charge her, so if you'll do this *pro bono*, I'll take care of all your expenses and hand my next case over to you." I'm disappointed that I won't get paid for this job, but hold out hope that the next one he sends my way will be my first paying solo gig.

Following wishes of luck, I head back to the office where Elizabeth is holding the sheriff's hand.

While many would walk in on this and assume that Elizabeth was comforting the sheriff, a few might think something sexual was involved. Both groups would be wrong. Elizabeth is a psychometrist, meaning that through touch she can glean the history of an object or even a person. Typically she keeps her skin mostly covered, but she's bare-handed. What I need to know is whether or not the sheriff is aware of her abilities.

Sitting back in Thaddeus' seat, I ask what I missed, to which the sheriff answers, "Elizabeth believes me and said she can tell you'll take the case."

Although I still don't know if she knows about Elizabeth, I ignore the fact the sheriff knows I spoke to Thaddeus. "Well I can't make a liar out of her, so it looks like we'll help you out."

Quick to correct me, Elizabeth says, "Actually, I'm off to Canada to find Bigfoot; well, I guess technically there it'll be Sasquatch. Looks like you got your first solo case." Seeing the shock on the sheriff's face, Elizabeth comforts her by lying about the number of cases I had while with the police. The sheriff takes

Elizabeth at her word and instantly looks more relaxed than I was ever able to make her.

II

After a familiar conversation, one that I know will be repeated many times throughout my career, Sheriff O'Conner still questions my insistence that we take a train to Kansas instead of flying.

"I told you, this has nothing to do with fear. It's a matter of convenience. Are you going to ask about this for the rest of the trip? If so, I can sit somewhere else."

Getting my not-so-subtle hint, she changes topic by asking what my plan is. "Whatever it is, do you think the two of us can handle it?"

"No, I can handle it; you need to go about your business. Your town needs you; I've got this." I go on to explain that in the two days since she arrived, I did some research and found legends of goblins that kidnap children from their villages. Before she can interrupt me, I tell her: "I know not only kids are missing, but what stood out is that their weakness is the stench of raw onions. The depictions of these goblins with pointy ears and sharp teeth easily could have been construed as vampires before the Hollywood image became prominent. Maybe this is why onions worked before."

She takes a moment to consider what I just relayed before saying, "That makes sense I guess; either that or the vampires didn't know onions wouldn't hurt them." We share a bigger chuckle than the joke deserved.

Both our smiles vanished as I continue with the bad news. "Just because some of this fits with the case doesn't mean we're on the right track. And worst of all, even if it is goblins, I can't find anything that tells me how to kill them. Onions only repel them, they don't really cause any harm."

Absentmindedly, O'Conner says to no one in particular, "Like a dog whistle." I think of how apt a metaphor that is, but she clearly doesn't want to hear my praise. I've successfully made my client more worried than before she came to me.

Hoping to get her mind off the goblins, I ask the sheriff to go over every detail of the case again, hoping we might find some detail we overlooked in our previous discussion. The way she resettles her weight in the seat before speaking makes it clear that she is still uneasy with me.

"In 1868, Montezuma experienced a steadily increasing number of disappearances; too many for a town the size of ours. The mounting missing person cases went unexplained for months. On one night in November two young lovers were returning from a secret tryst when they came upon a humanoid animal feasting on the local blacksmith. The young man's name differs from different sources, but the girl's name is generally agreed upon. Nancy Cantwell was punished for her unlawful actions, while her lover helped lead the hunt for the animal."

I sat forward, listening to every detail of her story.

"The body of the blacksmith was recovered with garish throat wounds, unfamiliar to any of the hunters. Rumors from Europe began circulating. That's when the term 'vampire' made it to Montezuma for the first time."

She frowned. "Eyewitness reports were rare and varied, but a few details of sightings recalled what the first young couple claimed. The pointed ears, sharp teeth, and other details vaguely corresponded to one aspect or another of the vampire myth. Townspeople began using onions as weapons due to the belief they had purifying abilities that counteracted the 'devil' in these vampires."

"The one common thread all the stories about vampires had was they were scared of the sun. So during the days, life went on as normal, and at night the men would hunt. The hunt went on for several weeks, and it seemed each night there'd be one less member of the hunt returning home."

"Fearing the onions weren't working, the townsfolk decided to cook them in different ways hoping to unlock whatever properties were hidden within. These days of cooking became an event the women dedicated themselves to. One mid-December night, the hunting men came upon the vampires beyond the town border. Many of the hunters were savagely murdered before they were able to react. Fortunately, using the freshly cooked onions, they were able to scare off the creatures, never to return again.

"That day has gone down in history as the day the townspeople warded off the vampires, and is celebrated every year. December 13th is now known as Onion Day. To this day every year the largest onion cook-off in the nation is held in Montezuma.

"Years later, when the myth of vampires were becoming

prevalent, the mayor tried capitalizing on the tourism by renaming Main Street to Onion Avenue. The name remains even if the tourists haven't. Once Hollywood got ahold of the garlic myth, people were less inclined to visit Onion Avenue."

III

We arrive in Kansas noon time and more than anything the sheriff and I want a shower. Although she offered her spare bedroom to me, she wasn't too offended when I opted for a nearby hotel instead.

Cleaned, fed and well rested, I travel to the local precinct in my rental car. Admittedly I splurged on the car more than I would have on my own dime, but since Thaddeus offered to cover all my expenses I decided to enjoy what I could. Parking the convertible next to the two squad cars at the station, I'm greeted by a mixed expression of grief and surprise.

Brushing her hair to the side with one hand while flicking ash off her cigarette with the other, the sheriff questions me. "I didn't know private eyes rode around in top-of-the-line sports cars."

Waving the smoke away between words I let her know, "We do when out partners are footing the bill."

She chuckles before joking that the car is probably more comfortable than our train ride. "My neck is still stiff." Seeing me wave the smoke again, curious, she asks if it's bothering me.

"No, I smoke myself; you saw that back at the office in Jersey. I just try not to smoke while on a case. I used to be a heavy smoker, but when I made detective it was suggested I quit. Even though I did, as soon as I left I started again. Now the urge eats at me, especially after that train ride." Wanting to detour my thought track from the desire to smoke, I ask O'Conner to show me the reports for all missing persons.

Clearly noticing my change in tone O'Conner nods and tosses her half-smoked butt in the general vicinity of the garbage can. "Right this way," she says quietly while leading me inside the brown brick station that's too small even for the limited population it supports.

We spend two hours digging into the files she prepared prior to my arrival and the only clue we can gather is that it seems one adult goes missing every nine days or so. Aside from sharing hometowns the victims have no common traits. In the predominantly white population, race isn't much of a factor, and all victims are from varying occupations leaving us without much to go on.

Noticing that we've each been staring at our respective folders with the covers closed for nearly three minutes, I break the silence. "So we have adult males and females missing with no apparent connections, but that's not getting us anywhere. Let's look at the townspeople that have been spared."

"Kids," she says confidently.

"Why?"

Pausing for a moment, the sheriff says in a voice that reveals she's not too confident in her answer, "They aren't as filling, maybe?" Ignoring the comment, we spitball different possibilities such as future prey, innocence, and some other theories.

Despite each of us getting rest, the hours of staring at files drive us delirious. So much so, our serious thoughts give way to the ridiculous. O'Conner draws a belly rumbling laugh from me by suggesting maybe the monsters have moral objections against human veal.

Wiping tears from my eyes, I agree "Yeah, they prefer the aged Angus human meat." We take a moment from the laughter to catch our breaths. I suggest maybe we're too tired to look at this seriously and she agrees to reconvene after a full night's rest.

IV

So much for a full night's rest. I just closed my eyes at a quarter to twelve and after what feels like five minutes I hear shrieking at my fourth story window. Pulling my revolver from beneath my pillow, I'm in time to see a twisted human face in pain pulling away from the glass.

Approaching the glass warily, yet as hurried as my body will allow, I get there just in time to see a figure moving through the shadows. Without pulling my eyes from the view, I grab my phone and dial the sheriff. "O'Conner, I think I was just visited by our friend. Come to the hotel, I'll be searching the area for a trace. Don't call me, I'll find you."

Knowing it'll take her a minimum of fifteen minutes to get here, possibly even more because of how late it is, I watch the window a minute longer before turning away from the glass. I grab my coat, my other gun, a Glock 9mm, and storm out my room. Even in my hustle, I hear Thaddeus' voice reminding me to secure my base, so I make sure the protection wards I laid are still in place.

Entering a small alley between two garages where I saw the shadow enter, I see nothing of note; no track, signs of escape, or pieces of human flesh. None of the things I was hoping to find. After a few minutes of wandering in random patterns, I hear a quiet shuffling.

Not until I actually hear the noise do I notice the difference in volume from the loud city of Newark, New Jersey and the quiet sticks of Kansas. With pistol in hand, I nervously move towards the noise. Unsure of what I'd find, I'm glad when I see it's Sheriff O'Conner quietly directing one of her deputies.

"You guys might want to keep it down. I haven't found anything, but if this thing is still in the area you're making yourselves easy targets." Seeing O'Conner shoot the deputy a dirty look, I can tell she blames him for the noise. I try to make peace by letting them know whatever it was probably hadn't stayed long after trying to get in my window.

This prompts O'Conner to ask me why it didn't make it through. "To date there have been no eyewitnesses other than from the legend, and now on your first night it comes for you and runs off."

Knowing this was going to come up, I had an explanation prepared; I just didn't know I was going to actually have to defend myself about it. "Thaddeus keeps certain supplies in the office, and he has these five pieces of petrified wood that are enchanted to ward off evil when placed in a certain pattern."

Hoping that her relationship with Thaddeus was extensive enough that she takes what I said for it's worth, I turn the topic to more pressing matters. "The real question is, why did it target me? And how did it know where to find me?" With no answers forthcoming, I decide to take initiative on the hunt and ask if the forest is dense enough for goblins to hide in.

"Have you *seen* Kansas before? There aren't any forests here, James. There's a cropping of trees on the edge of town, but nothing to hide a swarm, or whatever, of goblins. Ain't you heard, we got a vampire problem." The deputy reveals that the sheriff is keeping my working theory under wraps. "Sophia, where'd you find this stranger?"

Frustrated, O'Conner spins around to face her employee. "When we're on the job it's Sheriff, got it, Deputy?" Not even waiting for a response, she answers for him, "Good. Now, Detective Peckman here has a theory why onions worked all those years ago, and it doesn't involve vampires. I for one would love to know that this town wasn't founded by a bunch of ass-backwards yokels that can't tell their vegetables apart." Lowering her voice, she tells this as-of-yet unintroduced deputy that she just wants an answer to what's going on with her town. However, this doesn't answer why she wouldn't have told him the details earlier.

Deflated by being reprimanded in front of me, he lowers his head and says he's going to return to the car to check on any calls that may have come through. He shuffles off so defeated, I half expect him to shove his hands in his pockets with a pout and kick a stone in the gravel.

I take this time to ask O'Conner why she didn't tell him about my theory. "It doesn't show a lot of confidence in me if you can't share it with your deputy."

Her change in expression tells me this is the first time she realized that her secrecy could be interpreted that way, "No, let me assure you: if Thaddeus trusts you, I trust you. I have a hard time communicating with Rick." At least now I know his name. "He and I used to date when we were both deputies but when the last sheriff retired and I was promoted, Rick took it hard. We broke up, but he hasn't found a transfer anywhere else so he's stuck with me."

"Sounds more like you're stuck with him." She cracks a genuine smile that reveals she's been faking it every time before. She sees me admiring her smile and turns red. Trying to avoid an awkward situation, I again ask about any nearby forests. "I didn't have time for extensive research, but what I did find--that wasn't linked to some board game--indicates that goblins live in the cover of dense forests."

I can see the 'no' in her eyes before she says anything, so she opts to answer an unasked question. "I have no idea what's keeping Rick. I should go check on him." She takes a couple steps backwards, just far enough so the street light illuminates her brown and tan uniform. It's the kind of outfit that always reminds me of the guys delivering packages. She pauses long enough for me to think she's going to say something else, but instead she turns and heads towards the squad car. I'm left in the dark wondering if she was waiting for me to say something.

She doesn't give me much time to contemplate as I soon hear her screaming. I run with as much haste as my travel-weary legs will allow, drawing both guns in stride. Before I get to her, I can tell she's saying something but can't make it out. Then I see it. Rick's holster and gun are on the floor and the windshield is cracked, "The blood... there's blood and Rick's gone."

V

Sheriff O'Conner and I searched the surrounding area until the early hours of the morning gave way to dawn. The rest of the police force joined us, all three of them, and with none of us being hunters or trackers, we found nothing. We didn't find any more blood either, which I found the most interesting detail of all. Aside from not leaving a trail to follow, no blood usually means a treated wound. Did the abductor want him alive or did a vampire actually drink him dry?

Well, after the sun has risen, it's become evident that the search is futile--evident to all of us except for O'Conner. "Get off your asses; we don't stop looking until Rick is rescued. Until that happens, you don't get to sit."

The other officers all stand but don't dare walk away from her, even if it were to search for their coworker. They know better than to interrupt her. I, on the other hand, do not. "Listen Sheriff, whether he's alive or not, dragging these three through the mud isn't going to produce results."

Without taking a breath she digs into me. "You don't get to tell me how to do my job. I pay you to do yours, so find out what the hell did this." She then surprisingly storms off towards the town.

After waiting for O'Conner to walk beyond our view, I tell the three officers to get some rest and give them the key to my hotel room. "But don't head home; I don't think your boss would appreciate not having you on hand and I can't blame her. I have a couple of things I want to check out, and I'll meet up with you guys after to discuss my plan." They all walk off, leaving me to actually think of a plan.

I head to the car to investigate. Looking for any clues I can come up with, I find the small splatter of blood, Rick's gun and holster, a cracked windshield, and not much else. There's scattered footprints showing signs of a struggle, but the sheriff and I were only about thirty feet around the corner of a small garage when it must have happened. "You're getting in the car here, so your attacker must have been behind you coming from the hotel; only reason why you didn't call out." My frustration is getting the better of me, and when that happens I start talking to myself. Realizing my voice is getting louder than I intended, I stop talking altogether and inspect the windshield in silence.

Running my fingers over the cracks, I discover they're on the inside of the car. "This must mean you were jumped when you were already at least halfway inside the car. Your head was slammed against the glass, and that's where the blood came from. Your feet were out of the car, causing the shuffle in the dirt." And now I'm talking to myself again.

Taking a few steps back to fully examine the car, I can't help but wonder where the attacker's prints are and how they got in and out of the car with a presumably limp body, leaving no traces. Looking away from the car I turn my head skywards, to see an intriguing sight. There's a clear path made through the branches of the trees directly next to the car. "Since when can goblins fly?"

Returning to the hotel room, I'm thankful the cops were smart enough to prop the door open so I could enter without disturbing them. Carmen, the only other female officer, is asleep on the bed, while Hank is loudly snoring in the desk chair with his feet propped up. Robbie, the rookie, is the only one that's awake and apparently he was expecting me since he greets me without turning from the window with a view directly over the squad car, "What'd you see in the trees?"

Not sure how blunt I can be with this rookie, so I go for broke. "Looks like whatever took Rick can fly; there's a path through the treetops."

VI

"So, are we thinking goblins can fly?" O'Conner asks after about ten minutes of staring at the clearing in the branches. She turns to me with an expression painted on her face that lets me know she wants a legitimate answer.

I remain silent for a few moments hoping she says something else, or even one of the other officers, but with no distraction forthcoming I let her know through stammers that I'm not sure. "All accounts of goblins, both trustworthy and fictional, point to no..." She keeps her eyes locked on mine, unblinking. "At this point we have two options; continue under the belief that we're dealing with goblins who can fly, or assume it's something else altogether, perhaps back to vampires."

Her glaring becomes so intense I find it hard to read what she's hoping for me to say. "No matter what took him, we know which way they went." Knowing she needs to see signs of competence on my part, I order Robbie the rookie and Carman to go to the police station and gather as many weapons as they can, as well as flashlights. They look to the sheriff for confirmation and she nods. "Hank," I add, "you take an inventory of what we've got here, including Rick's gun. O'Conner, come with me, I've got some special tools in my room." As soon as the words are out of my mouth I wonder if it sounded as dirty to everyone else as it did me.

They all know what they've got to do and go about it. The sheriff follows without any words. Once we get in the room, I let her go first and close the door behind me. She turns to me, and now it's my turn to stare intently at her. Stepping towards her I back her into a wall, and then embrace her shoulders with both hands. "I know you and Rick were an item, but I don't care." I close the gap between us by half for emphasis. "You have to get your head in the game. Those three cops are going to rely on you, not me, and I need you to be solid."

She gently shakes the cobwebs out of her head before letting me know they should rely on me. "This is your operation; you've got to lead them."

I assure her that I will, but she'll need to support me, "They don't know me from shit on the wall; you're their boss. Without you, I won't have them." I wait just long enough for her to nod again, letting me know she understands my reasoning before I busy myself collecting all the supplies I took from Thaddeus' 'special' stash. "We should hurry and get back out there." I joke that we don't want the others thinking anything is going on between us. She doesn't find any humor in it.

Remaining silent until we get outside, I'm beginning to think maybe she won't be able to focus, but as soon as all three officers are together she flips a switch. "Okay guys, I know we're dealing with some strange shit we thought were tall tales and rumors our whole lives, but we're about to come face to face with these fables. We're not trained for this and I know it scares each of us, but that's why *he's* here. Detective Peckman and the people he works with specialize in the things under the bed and hiding in the closet."

She pauses long enough for me to suppress the smile at her description of what it is I do for a living. "Sheriff O'Conner is right, together we can save Rick, or God forbid, avenge him. Whether its onions or garlic or something else entirely, we'll get this done."

My inspirational speech wasn't well thought out and ended there, so I was glad when Robbie offered an idea. Pointing to a nearby motorcycle, he says "I was thinking that I could scout ahead on my bike, while you guys follow on foot."

I cut him off while he's explaining how he plans to recon the path to make sure it's safe. "It's too loud; you'll alert them to your presence before you can even get close enough to find them." I let him know I appreciate proactive suggestions but unless they have a horse on the payroll, we should stick together for now. While the rookie laughs at the horse comment, the other three show they aren't amused at my lack of knowledge of their town. Defensively, I remind them that even New York City has police horses. "Also, need I point out that we're standing on an unpaved street?" Robbie the rookie continues to be my only fan at this moment.

Composing myself, I order them to follow behind me in two rows. "Keep your eyes open for anything out of the ordinary. I'll follow the path of broken branches." We move in silence, giving me time to think about what we might be walking into.

Instead, my thoughts are plagued with the looks of uncertainty the cops gave me. They remind me of the looks and backhanded compliments I got when I made detective with the Newark Police Department at the age of twenty-two. I had two big high profile cases that not only caught the attention of my superiors, but the media as well.

With the public support it was hard for my promotion to be overlooked, but most other detectives on the force felt I hadn't earned it. Even my friends said shit like, "Who'd have thought you'd be the first of us to make detective?" Worst of all, my dad, who was a detective with the big NYPD, commented that Newark must have lower standards for the title, with no humor in his voice at all.

The double-edged compliments turned to all-out insults when, on my very first case, my partner, a much loved seasoned vet, died during a car chase while I was driving. My survival was viewed as a sign of my incompetence.

All the doubts that began haunting me made me contemplate turning in my badge. If it weren't for my wife I surely would have. Without Talia I wouldn't have...

"James, is everything OK?"

Snapping out of self-pity, I turn to O'Conner who, along with the others, has a concerned look on her face, "Yeah, why?"

Concern turns to confusion as she explains we've been standing here for nearly two minutes, "You just stopped, and haven't said anything."

I nod and try to re-instill their confidence in me, lying. I tell them I heard something but it stopped. "I know what it's like as a cop, but we're not after your ordinary perp. Whatever these inhuman things are, we can't approach them like they're human. A lot of the things I deal with have heightened senses. From here on out, unless I initiate it, no communication."

Once it looks like they all understand, I resume my walk. Noticing the path in the tree tops takes a slight curve from going east to heading north. "O'Conner, you said the woods go for a couple miles east, what about north?"

After I let her know it's okay to talk, she says the trees break about a quarter mile into farmland, then Cimarron. Before I can even ask of its significance the sheriff says, "It's your average quiet American town. If it has anything of significance I never heard of it."

From the corner of my eye I can see Hank start to say something, but then think better of it. I let him know at this point no detail is too small, which encourages him to talk. "I know this has no real bearing on the case, but I once heard that they had a small church on the outskirts where a priest led a cult that practiced human sacrifice." He looks around and misreading my lack of words defends himself. "This supposedly happened long before Montezuma's vampire story popped up."

Hoping I'd found the break in the case I needed, I ask: "Hank, do you know where this church was?"

"Yeah, it's still there, no one wants to tear down a church no matter its history, plus the townsfolk think it's haunted. Do you think this has anything to do with Rick and the other missing people?"

Trying to keep my excitement in check, I answer that there's only one way to find out. "Sheriff, Hank and I are going to head back and get my car to check out this church. You continue following the path with Carman and Robbie. Keep your eyes open and call me with anything."

VII

I don't like leaving the three of them alone in a potentially dangerous environment, but if we're dealing with vampires after all, they should be safe for several more hours while the sun is still up. Hank shares in my anxiety.

For the 'quiet' one of the group, Hank hasn't stopped talking for twenty minutes. As we approach the church, he asks for the third time if I really believe this is where Rick is. "I mean this church has been here forever, wouldn't someone have noticed vampires?"

"You'd be surprised at what we can overlook if we're not looking for it. Think about any person that snaps and goes crazy, killing a group of people. It's always thought they were the nicest person, until they take a closer look and see all the signs he showed in school or online. Then you've got the 'loving' mothers who drown their kids after years of untreated depression. For a time the whole country specifically associated Montezuma with vampires; in their minds there's no reason to think the monsters could have crossed an imaginative boarder separating land." I remind him that a decommissioned church would be a great place for anyone to hole up.

When we exit the car, it's evident that Cimarron has more dirt roads than Montezuma, and I can't help but wonder if this distinction is what upset the cops at my earlier attempt of a joke. The church is a small one room structure with two entrances, one of which is boarded up, as are the windows preventing any sunlight to enter. It lies in an unkempt field with grass and weeds growing nearly to my knees.

As we get closer it becomes clear that what I thought was brown wood panels making the walls of the church are actually well-faded red painted planks. I don't know why, but the fact that the church was once red seems more menacing to me; something about the nostalgic slice of Americana in a Norman Rockwell painting being used for something so evil.

Standing outside the door, I'm reassured of the notion this is the perfect vampire hideout. While all the visible nails and window latches I can see through the boards are well rusted, the door hinges, although old, appear to be in better condition. This is confirmed when Hank is able to gingerly open the door, as I cover him with my revolver and a flashlight.

Seeing no immediate threat, I take a moment to internally appreciate the fact that Hank is seasoned enough to allow us to penetrate the building with minimal communication. I may not know the guy that well, but he's quickly earned my respect. It's also evident he has similar respect for me, even trust, as he approaches the altar knowing I've got his back.

He stops just short of the two steps that span the breadth of the church, representing the beginning of the altar. There's a smell that I hadn't noticed when we walked in, but is steadily increasing as we near the altar. Waiting for me to join him, Hank motions with a quick tip of his gun towards a curtain sectioning off the back half of the altar from the rest of the room. More specifically he points to the unmistakable flicker of a lit candle, further confirming the place isn't as abandoned as previously thought.

With a nod of the head, I signal for him to mimic me as I turn off my flashlight and head to one end of the curtain, as he goes to the opposite side. At this point the smell has grown offensive, a mix of moldy bread and a fresh placenta. On a count of three fingers, we cross the threshold the curtain provided and emerge in quite a different location.

The cordoned-off area of the altar is littered with the discarded remains of countless humans in all stages of decay, from the freshly departed to bare bones. The sight is enough to turn Hank's stomach. He inadvertently expels his recent eats over a woman's severed head, complete with missing eyes. His meal wasn't recent enough to leave any of the food identifiable, which, oddly enough, makes it easier for me to keep my composure.

Trying as much as I can to ignore the disgusting items all around me I notice two things; first, there's a noticeable lack of blood, which explains the absence of flies and other insects. Second, and more importantly, Rick's hat is near a podium that the candle is on. Circling around I find the hat's owner on the ground gagged, blindfolded, and bloody. "Hank! Rick's here and he seems alive."

At the sound of my voice, Rick painfully turns his head, but attempts no other movement. I see as I approach that his ankles are each in large metal bowls that were probably once used for the baptism of babies. His Achilles tendons are torn, maybe completely removed. Whoever did this wanted to make sure he couldn't escape.

"Rick, it's me Hank and Detective Peckman, I'm going to remove the blindfold and gag, stay calm." Unsure of where else his friend is hurt, Hank carefully removes the constraints.

As soon as the gag is out of his mouth Rick commands us to get out of here, "There are five of them sleeping beneath the church; if they hear you we're all dead."

I grab the curtain and pull it down along with the pole holding it up. This barely lets in any light as the windows are still covered and makes more noise than I hoped. "Hank, I'm going to carry him out of here. I need you to cover us."

He agrees without any hesitance, as we both ignore Rick's orders to leave him behind. Halfway through the pews O'Conner and the other two officers enter the front of the church. Even from this distance I can see the fear on all three of their faces. I let them know he's alive. "But if we all want to stay that way you need to open up these windows."

Robbie props open the doors with stray wood lying on the floor, and O'Conner and Carman work off the boards of two windows. By this time Hank and I have Rick in the back seat of the squad car. "Two of you need to take Rick to the closest hospital while the other two and I will finish off the windows."

Sheriff O'Conner and Hank decide to take Rick, leaving Robbie the rookie and Carmen with me. They need a moment to take in the sight of the desecrated altar. After giving them some time, I figure we better get started. I let them know I want to be done well before the sun sets. "OK, we..." Before I can finish my statement Carmen gets to work prying off boards using a flashlight for leverage. Robbie on the other hand can't seem to peel his eyes from the massacre. Figure I'll give him a bit more time, so I join Carmen.

With three windows left Robbie is still fixed on the altar, when a hidden door in the floor creeps open. "Oh shit!" is all he utters before retreating out of the church backwards. He whispers for us to leave but over the creaking of the windows I barely hear it. "Guys!"

Upon his yell I turn to see a pair of glowing purple eyes creeping through a small opening. Locking eyes with me, the creature hisses as I grab Carmen's arm to lead her out. Stopping in the doorway, I realize the sun is keeping the eye's owner at bay. Confidence building, I draw the PSG1 rifle from my back, and take aim. Not sure why a small town force like Montezuma PD even has this type of firepower but at this point I'm too grateful to question it. I draw a bead on the purple eyes. Before I can pull the trigger, Carmen interrupts my shot by putting her hand where the buttstock meets my shoulder.

She whispers the question in my ear: "Will that kill it?" With a shake of my head, she lowers the front of the gun. "You'll probably only piss them off even more."

The internal struggle of anger and rational waging in my mind is interrupted by the ring of Carmen's phone. "It's Sophia." Following several grunts and sounds of understanding she hangs up the phone. "Rick's in critical condition. Sophia thinks we should head over to see him, just in case." She looks at me and silently pleads with her eyes, it's clear she wants to see her coworker and friend. Who am I to stand in her way?

VIII

I've never been a fan of hospitals. Granted, I don't think anyone is, but my only clear memory of a hospital is seeing my grandfather lying in bed with tubes coming out of his nose, mouth, and what seemed like every other orifice. Here was the man, who to my seven year old mind, was the strongest person in the world reduced to a sickly pale imitation of his former self. It's because of that sight that I was, in a perverse definition of the word, glad that my wife and daughter died in the accident and I didn't have to go to the hospital. Adding to my contempt of these institutions, I missed my daughter's birth because of a case the department was working.

So it's no surprise I'm more than content to smoke by my car while Rick's coworkers show him support. I further justify it be telling myself I only knew the guy's name a few minutes before he was attacked. Vindicating my decision to smoke while on the job took more than a few lies and false promises to myself. I'm halfway through my third cancer stick when my musings are interrupted by what remains of the Montezuma police force.

Leading her crew Sheriff O'Conner scolds me for what I already feel crappy about. "You don't get to relax until each one of these fuckers are dead." To emphasize how earnest she is, the sheriff takes the cigarette out of my mouth and crushes it beneath her heel.

Defiantly, I hold the smoke already in my lungs for a little while longer. "You're right, Sheriff, but first things first. Robbie, I need you back at the station."

"Sure thing, what do you need?"

He responds so enthusiastically I'm almost sorry to crush him. "I need a crew of people who won't freeze up on me." He opens his mouth to protest but stops himself before I have a chance to. "I'm sure you want to make some promise about it not happening again and I appreciate that, but I can't risk anyone's life on your pride."

The sheriff makes an argument for having more people but Carmen supports me. "No, Sheriff, the detective is right." Turning to Robbie: "Listen, you're a good officer, but you didn't make a move when you saw the altar and you barely even warned us of that thing when you saw it." She finishes by squeezing his arm and telling him to take care of the town's real world problems. "They still need us. They need you." Got to admit, she's good.

This whole time Hank's reverted to his quiet self. I'm beginning to think this has been too much for him also. "Hank, do you want to head back with Robbie?" I want to say that there's no shame in it, but that'll do nothing *but* shame him.

He looks at me with what I think is contempt, but instead he points towards the horizon out the window. "No, but I think we're about to run out of time." O'Conner's face mimics his concern, and I realize Carmen didn't tell them.

"Before Carmen and I left, we placed the same protective runes I used in my room around the church. They should be trapped." Seeing the confidence across their faces, I add that come tomorrow morning they'll be easy pickings.

What's that they say of the best laid plans?

IX

Hank, O'Conner and I are going over tomorrow's plan several hours after sundown when the call comes in. Robbie comes into the room saying that a local is reporting a murder. "Abigail is on the line, hysterical, says someone attacked Carl when he was taking out the trash."

I ask if she saw who did it, but his only response is a shake of the head, "We don't know for sure, but it's a safe bet the vampires found a way out. I need someone to take me to this home." O'Conner offers to take me as I explain that it's likely the exit they used is close to the house.

"Hank, call Carmen at the hospital, tell her what happened and let her know I'm taking the detective there now." Grabbing her gun and holster, O'Conner is out the door quicker than I expected. But I really shouldn't be surprised; these are her people after all. She knows everyone in town more intimately than city life allows, even a smaller city like Newark. I have to break my thought of this just being a job and take this as personally as she does. It's the only way to protect anyone else from sharing Carl's fate.

During the short trip to the house, O'Conner is quiet. I decide to keep the silence and check my bag. With only enough time to confirm the holy water and wooden stakes are there, I'm not as prepared for an assault is I'd like to be.

Unfortunately, my fears are confirmed when we're not greeted by a distraught Abigail. Instead, she's nowhere to be seen and we have to assume the worst. Soon the worst is confirmed when we find a beheaded body that O'Conner confirms was once Abigail.

"It seems we… I calculated wrong. The stunt at the church has only seemed to make them angry and desperate." I tell her we can't wait for sunup tomorrow and to call in her squad. "Is there a way to gather the townspeople into an area we can protect?"

She quickly shakes her head no before reconsidering. "Actually, there's the old bomb strike alarm still wired through the town; it's hooked up to a P.A. system, but that'll just alert them to our plans."

I let her know it may come to that and we need as many contingencies as possible. "Until that time we search this area for a possible opening they could have used." With that I follow the trail of blood leading away from the vampires' latest victim.

Abigail's head is resting atop an old boob-tube television with rabbit ears antennae behind her. I suppose it was done for comedic effect, but the humor is lost on me. The decapitation must have been quick, as poor Abigail's rollers are still in place.

It's not until I hear the sheriff call me that I realize how far apart we'd drifted. I'll talk to her about staying close once I figure out what she wanted. Following her voice to the kitchen I find her staring intently out the window when I see what she's looking at.

"Please tell me those aren't the same purple eyes you and Carmen saw."

"I'm afraid so, Sheriff."

She asks why it's just watching and I wish I had an answer. Just then her radio squawks and I hear Robbie inform her that Young Willie called in, says he's got a stranger with purple eyes stalking outside his window.

"That's on the other side of town." O'Conner tells me, then orders Robbie to send Hank and Carmen to check it out.

Weighing all the details available, the vampires' goal becomes apparent: these are scare tactics; it's the only reason they'd waste the energy. "They're spreading us thin. Robbie's going to get another call about another attack away from here." Without time to think of an alternative I ask where the controls for the bomb alarm are.

X

The municipal building with the PA system shares a wall with the police station. As we arrive, Robbie calls with the expected news of another attack. What's unexpected is that there are five vampires waiting for us inside the building with no lights. I reach for my guns before thinking better of it and take hold of the holy water.

The oldest looking vampire steps forward and commands, "Stay thy hand, cattle."

The sheriff looks at me confused, not at the meaning of his words, but from the fact they actually talk like that. Additionally, she seems to have chosen to ignore the command by drawing a bead on his head with her rifle.

One of the other vampires joins the eldest. This one looks about my age, but much larger and dressed in a football jersey for some college team I've never heard of. "Sorry, Janus doesn't get out much. He's still mentally a couple centuries back. But he made this trip out just for you, stranger."

It's obvious he means me with his intense stare, and I let him know I'm thrilled. He replies with his own form of sarcasm, a fanged smile that shows my future if he doesn't like my next answer. He returns his attention to Janus and the two have a brief silent conversation before they bother addressing us again. "We'll give the rest of your crew the opportunity to join this conversation."

A few seconds later Carmen, Hank and Robbie emerge from a darkened hallway, all with their guns trained on a different vampire. Hank lets us know the vampires cut the power, and the only illumination we have are the emergency red lights overhead.

"Now Detective Peckman, Janus didn't appreciate you destroying our home of over two hundred years. A home we've had ever since we allowed the cattle of this town to believe onions granted them the upper hand over us. A false belief that allowed us to feed in secret and unopposed over the decades. That is, until you came along Detective." He stretches out the last syllable of my title, like he's weighing the taste on his tongue. "But Janus understands, you're scared of us, as well you should be. He's willing to forgive you if you return home and not interfere in our affairs again." I guess he didn't like the taste of it too much.

As if that were the end of the conversation, he turns to Sheriff O'Conner and offers: "To avoid any further unnecessary deaths, Janus is willing to place the residents of your town on a lottery program where we'll only kill the elderly and ill often enough to keep the five of us sustained."

I don't take being dismissed well and decide to remind the footballer I'm still here, "Well, since you're done with me, mind letting me know where the other exit from the church's basement is?"

A smaller vampire, the size of a child but still potentially older than the church in question blurts out, "What other exit?"

Footballer scolds the child, ordering him to be silent. With his fake manners shed, he warns me: "Janus offered you a pass; I suggest you take it before the only option you have left is which of us will kill you."

Slowly nodding my head in earnest contemplation, I adjust my stance to get a better look beyond the vampires. "So, Carmen, why'd you betray your own people?"

"What are you talking about, detective?" O'Conner asks as she lowers her gun, but moves her focus to Carmen.

Ignoring her, I stay on topic. "Did they offer to make you a blood sucking whore like them?"

"They're not blood suckers, you ignorant piece of shit!" Carmen directs her gun at me when everyone else turns to her, including all the vampires save one. The only female among the vampires stays on me, with a smile that barely skims the surface of her intentions.

Using the provided distraction, I stab the child-vampire in the chest with a wooden stake while tossing the holy water at Janus. Everyone's attention returns to my direction as we watch Janus scream and melt away before the room is filled with the sounds of gun fire. Just barely audible in between shots, Carmen is screaming. By the time the bullets stop flying, the vampires have disappeared.

The sheriff knocks Carmen out with a solid hit from the butt of her rifle, "You... bitch!" It's clear she wanted to say more but her emotions are interfering with her motor skills.

"You killed my son, Janus." Looking up, I see the female that was watching me. She appears to be barely out of her thirties, but with immortal vampires it's possible she's the mother of an eighty year old. "Prepare all you want; you will not prevent my vengeance." And like that, she's gone.

The three conscious officers each have a different question written on their faces. Unsure what I should focus on, I answer the only question I can. "Carmen must have gone back to the church and messed with the protective runes. It's the only way they could have escaped." And on cue, Hank produces one of the said runes from under her shirt.

XI

O'Conner's anger gets the better of her judgment as she tries to rally the troops. "They weren't that tough to kill; we need to go after them now." She yells at Carmen through several walls, calling her a traitor among other words and names even I would rather not repeat.

Trying to calm her down, I suggest that maybe Carmen was being controlled. Even I don't believe that, and O'Conner calls me on my bullshit. "Okay, honest truth, I was able to catch them by surprise. No way we'll get so lucky again." The bluntness of my words cuts through to the sheriff. "We have until the sun goes down again to protect these people."

We begin discussing plans to gather as much of the town as possible in a defensible location. But Hank has concerns with the idea. "Aside from trying to convince the entire town that vampires are, in fact, real, wouldn't herding them together just make them an easier target if we can't defend them?"

"We'll secure them with the protection runes, and that way we'll only need to keep watch over each piece of petrified wood." The simple math leads to the obvious discussion of the four of us targeting five runes. My shooting skills aren't good enough to instill confidence in myself, so I offer an alternative. "There has to be a local who's good with a gun that we can trust. We need the extra gun and set of eyes."

After the officer's share some sideways glances, the sheriff lets me know that Rick was the best shot in town. "He would go hunting once a season with the rifle you borrowed. He was by far the best shot in town, with Carmen close behind. I want to know why she did this, that bitch!" O'Conner takes a breath to steady herself before continuing, "Beyond them, this town doesn't really have any hunters."

I need a moment to think this through and say as much before walking away. I know we have only so many options, and it's highly unlikely the vampires will return to the church. That meant we might not be able to find them until they came after us. Returning to the cops, who are all intently watching my every move, I instruct them to gather everyone in town inside the school. "I'll be back as soon as I can."

Worried at what I might be planning, O'Conner warns me: "Peckman, don't you dare go to a different precinct for help. Aside from them not believing you, I wouldn't want to risk more lives if they do show up."

I can't help but wonder if she's actually more concerned with becoming a laughingstock by those who don't believe the truth, but I keep this to myself. "No, I've got to search for something. I'll be back before nightfall. You just gather everyone."

Leaving them to their task, I opt to hunt on my own. This whole case was supposed to be my first solo mission, and in my short time here I've gotten a deputy hospitalized, three more citizens killed, and betrayed by a cop looking to play Anne Rice. Not to mention, desecrating a church for the first time. I hope to never have to do that again.

Speaking of the church, despite my doubts, it's the first place I decide to check out. I keep telling myself that even though they probably wouldn't return I might find some clues to point me in the right direction.

Approaching the trap door. my mind is telling me there's

nothing to be worried about, but my instincts are screaming otherwise. Thankfully, I've been trained to always trust my instincts. Before I even have the door fully opened, I'm pulled through by my flashlight holding hand. With my free hand, I swing a stake while still falling. The wild stab goes wide and I see I've hit the silent thin vampire in the shoulder. In this artificially lit dugout my attacker looks like Iggy Pop, complete with bare chest, skinny jeans and shaggy hair. I'll be damned it I'm going down by this wanna-be.

Even though it's only a shoulder wound, Iggy's in pain, and I press the advantage, firing three rounds at his chest. However, his wiry frame and unnatural speed make him virtually impossible to hit.

"Mother always yells at me for playing with my food, but she's not here now," he taunts before sending me flying back with a swift palm thrust to the chest. I get up, with stars in my eyes, in time to see Iggy pull the stake out of his shoulder and toss it to me with a devious smile. "Maybe your aim will be better the second time around."

"I liked you better when you didn't talk." I quip while bending over, reaching for the stake, but before I reach it I draw my gun and empty the remainder of the clip in the wood floor above his head. Four of the holes send beams of sunlight down, one of which hits the small of his back, dropping him to his knees. He rolls out of the light, still reeling in pain.

Taking this opportunity to continue the attack, I grab the stake, move towards him, and stab Iggy. Again, his thin frame causes me to miss his center and hit his other shoulder.

Iggy uses the pain like a shot of adrenaline. He grabs and tosses me upwards through the altar floor, stupidly sending more light down to him. Unfortunately, his lack of shrieking lets me know he's still alive... or undead.

"Hey, you dead down there? Or do you need me to come down and help?" My confidence is building and I'm really starting to believe I can do this.

Just when I think he's not going to answer, I hear him talking on the phone: "Yes, mother, he's right here now."

Worried I'd soon have to deal with two more of them, I jump down with wooden shrapnel in each hand to finish off Iggy. Stupidly, I land out of the sunlight and he's on top of me before I can react.

He grabs my throat from behind and starts choking the life

out of me while pressing me against a wall. Unable to stab him from this position, I drop the wood and place my hands and feet against the wall.

"That's right, I like it when you struggle, but don't worry-- I'm not going to kill you. I'm going to feed on you for days before you breathe your last." The way he says it lets me know he's going to enjoy all the pain he causes me, as if I needed convincing.

He ignores what I'm actually doing, and just before he reapplies the pressure to my neck, I push off the wall with all my remaining strength. Forcing Iggy back into the fully exposed sun, he releases his hold. As he bursts into flames, I see the 'cell phone' he called Mother with was actually the flashlight that I dropped. It was a good way to scare me, and would have worked if there wasn't so much sunlight.

XII

It took me longer than I want to admit to regain the strength to climb out of the cave. It's now too close to sundown for me to continue my search, but I'm happy only two of the vampires are left. Hopefully O'Conner and the others were able to convince the citizens to go along with the plan.

I return to the school to find a little over a hundred residents gathered in the gymnasium. Even I'm not dense enough to think that's the entire town. "Where is everyone else?" I ask, already predicting the answer.

Robbie lets me know they're too scared to leave their homes. "More people than we thought took us for our word, like they were waiting for the myths to be proven true. Unfortunately, after what happened last night to Abigail and Carl they don't trust us to protect them."

Agreeing, the sheriff chimes in, "They're all banking on the myth that vampires need to be invited into a home."

"Did you explain that the old lady was killed in her own house?"

Nodding a yes, O'Conner continues. "The whole town knows Abigail's penchant for taking in strays. She'd welcome the devil himself based off a smile alone."

Running my palms over my face, I begin talking to no one in particular. "This doesn't change the plan; we protect who we can here. I have a feeling they're mad enough at me that they'll come." I can read Hank's face questioning my words. "While I was gone, I ran into the skinny one that didn't say a word."

"Is that why you look like you got your ass kicked?" Robbie asks innocently.

Pressing a finger on a tender spot on my chest, I wince and joke that he should see the other guy. Laughing hurts my ribs even more, and I fear I may have broken one, "We've only got two left to deal with; should make it easier for the four of us to handle them."

As if on cue, the female vampire walks through the main doors of the gym with the football player in a different jersey right behind her. Ignoring everyone in the room, she locks eyes on me. "You've killed another of my kin; do you really expect to live?"

"Your 'kin'?" I question flippantly, "Oh, you mean Iggy Pop? Yeah he…"

Cutting me off the footballer laughs with a dry throat. "I called him that too. Now you die." The change in his face as the smile turns serious sends shivers from my neck to tailbone.

With all the lights on in the gym, it's easier to get a good look at their faces. While they could pass for humans at a distance, their features differ enough to set them apart. Their noses are sunken in, flush with their foreheads like a bat's, furthering the vampire association with the flying rodents. But in stark contrast, their jaws jut out, elongated slightly. I imagine this makes it easier to reach their victim's neck.

As I move my attention to their abnormally small ears, the female approaches closer. "You've grown quiet. Has the severity of your situation finally dawned on you?"

"Who, me? No, I just realized how ugly you are."

Not even giving me a chance to defiantly laugh in pain, the football player charges and slams me into the bleachers, assuring me if I didn't have a broken rib before, I sure as hell did now. With the room spinning around me like after drinking too much Jägermeister in college, I hear O'Conner ask, "Now?"

Unable to concentrate on her location, I just tell her to wait, as I try to get to my feet. After successfully failing twice, Hank helps me up and to the center of the boxes forming the points of a pentagram.

Following my line of sight, Footballer focuses on a box. Putting two-and-two together, he cautiously nudges the box to the side with his foot. Once he feels it's far enough out of sync with the others he picks it up and tosses it out a window high overhead. He confidently breaches the broken pentagram unharmed and looks me square in the eyes with a wicked smile of jagged teeth, "Did you think it'd be that easy?"

Standing on my own accord, I look past him and focus on his mother before answering, "Yeah, I did." I weakly toss a bottle of holy water at him, but I knew he'd easily dodge it.

Thankfully, Robbie was quick to follow up the attack with a stab of a stake. Unfortunately, Footballer was faster still and dismissed Robbie with a swift boot to the chest. He crashes hard against a matted gym wall that I'm sure he wished had better padding.

Apparently, Footballer isn't done with dishing out the violence as he easily tosses Hank like a sack of wet feathers into the still hunched-over Robbie.

The gathered crowd is more than a little frightened, and I'm sure they're beginning to wish they stayed home like the rest of their neighbors. Footballer returns to me and roars, during which fur sprouts over all his exposed skin and wings grow out of his back, tearing his jersey apart. What started out as a roar ends in an ear-piercing screech causing many of the citizens to flee the gym.

Once again I hear the sheriff ask "Now?" Again I tell her to wait. Our plan hinges on one simple detail that, of course, won't fall into place. Trying to help things along, I slide my last bottle of holy water to Robbie, who's helping Hank into a seat. Robbie readies his arm to throw the bottle at Footballer, but I shake my head as I receive a quick knee to the gut.

It takes more than a few moments to catch my breath, and I don't think I've chosen to use it wisely, "You hit like a girl." I'm sure I coughed up blood, but I don't need to look at my hand for confirmation; the copper taste is enough. "Speaking of which, why don't you give Old Ugly a chance?" She sneers at me as Footballer backhands a tooth out of my mouth.

Unable to take my eyes off the floor, I begin to think I'll die before the plan is fully realized. With my mortality about to come to its culmination, I try to motion for O'Conner, wherever she is.

Fortunately, I'm cut off by Mother. "For all your false bravado, you've accomplished nothing. Jerry, stop playing with your food. Kill him."

I raise my head expecting to meet the face of my death. Instead, I'm greeted by the backs of heads. Each of the dozen or so townspeople that remain have placed themselves in between Jerry and me. A female voice I haven't heard before says, "You plan on killing us one-by-one to suit your needs, draining us each so you can live longer, but we're not going to let you slaughter the one person who tried to protect us. You're going to have to kill us all, ruining your food supply, to get to him."

I'm proud to hear them defend me but can't help to think how futile their display is. The female vampire mimics my thoughts, "You dare presume your show of unity will prevent his or your own deaths? Whether it's all at once, or drawn out over time, you will all die by our hands and our clan will thrive." She steps through the doorway, pointing at her son. "Jerry, kill them all. It appears we've overstayed our welcome in Montezuma."

Jerry closes in on them as I make my way through the people with a bloody smile on my face, and finally give the command O'Conner has been waiting for. "Now!"

Robbie tosses the holy water behind Mother, forcing her to further enter the room. Simultaneously, Sheriff O'Conner, high in the rafters, walks three steps to her right. Holding one of the runes in her arms, her motion completes the pentagram with the other pieces of petrified wood throughout the rafters and supports.

With the connection made and the protection spell now activated, the presence of evil is expelled in a most unexpected fashion; Jerry and his mother explode in a shower of thick blood and brittle bones.

The citizens that remain are too shocked to react, but Hank and Robbie jump and holler in joy, ignoring their respective injuries. From overhead, I can hear Sheriff O'Conner do the same. I simply collapse out of a combination of exhaustion, blood loss, and my own fright finally catching up to me.

XIII

I wake up blurry-eyed in a soothing taupe room surrounded by more people than I thought I knew. Trying to focus, I can make out O'Conner and Robbie. Hank is in a bed next to mine. It's at this point that I realize I'm in a hospital room.

Trying to get up, I only remind myself that I have broken

ribs. The pain drowns out the various voices in the room. I focus again on the people around me. I no longer see the local cops, but Elizabeth and Thaddeus standing next to me, but maybe I'm just looking at the other side.

The excruciating sensations I'm feeling in my chest force me to close my eyes, but I can hear Thaddeus talking. "Sophia called me as soon as you were hospitalized. Elizabeth and I tried to get here sooner, but we're glad to make it in time for you to wake up."

Keeping my eyes closed, I weakly ask how long I've been here. When they tell me three days, my eyes shoot open and find O'Conner standing next to Hank's bed. "Carmen?" I ask with most of my remaining strength.

Robbie noticeably shifts his weight, and with a low voice whispers, "She fell for the promise of becoming one of them." Apparently it was always something she had fantasizes about. "She became cooperative after Rick..." Hank stops talking, to look at O'Conner.

She tries to talk, but her tears overwhelm her. Hank shifts in his bed, placing a hand on her arm, and he lets me know what I just figured out. "He didn't make it. Doctors said he fought, but the injuries were too much." He pauses to suppress his emotions long enough to let me know Rick died the day after I got in.

Wiping the tears from her eyes, the sheriff puts on a tough exterior. "Don't you worry about him, though; you made those sons of bitches pay and gave this town the peace it deserves." She finishes her words by sweeping her arms wide.

That's when I recognize the other people in the room; they're the people in the gym that stood up for me. They all had large smiles on their faces; some were holding flowers and candy. And at that moment with acid fire in my lungs and images of purple eyes in my mind I thought: I could get used to this.

Beauty is Only Stone Deep
From the Casebook of Detective James S. Peckman
By Alex Azar

I've had an issue with flying since early on in my life, and because of this all family vacations with my wife and daughter, Talia and Sophia, were within driving distance. On these trips, we often passed roadside tourist traps that caught the attention of my daughter, and Talia, God rest her soul, always found a way of convincing me to indulge Sophia's curiosity. Admittedly, it didn't take too much to convince me. I loved seeing the look on Sophia's face when she saw the world's largest ketchup bottle or the world's largest driller statue.

I was a police detective for her entire life. That means I didn't get the chance to see my daughter as often as I wanted and definitely not as often as she would have liked to see me. But on those car trips, being with her for days at a time, I was able to be the father she needed.

Driving cross-country, I told her fantastic stories of how wizards from hundreds of years ago kept running out of ketchup. I somehow managed to keep a straight face while explaining that they created a bottle big enough to insure they had a supply on hand forever. Till the time she and my wife died, she'd ask me about different foods the wizards would use the endless bottle of ketchup on.

This case happened early in my paranormal career. To this day it acts as a reminder of how my family was taken from me. Their absence still causes me great pain. The giant concrete tourist traps, with billboards announcing a world's largest this and that, and that endless bottle of ketchup are now the world's most painful reminders of all I've lost.

I

There's no better start to a workday than being greeted by a smiling face, so I am disappointed to see the distress slapped across Sarah's face when she greets me in her daily manner.

"Hello, James," she says, handing me a cup of coffee with two sugars, no cream, "There are some gentlemen here to see you."

"Clients?" I ask.

She shakes her head saying that these 'gentlemen' didn't give her any information, only that they'd wait for me inside.

I thank her and enter my office to see two large men dressed in similar black suits and the same black-tinted sunglasses. If they're not Feds, they sure as hell are trying to look the part. Fed number one, a beast of an Asian man, gives me a dirty look and sneers at me before Fed number two, a white man big enough to dwarf me while sitting, tells me I'm late.

Ignoring his statement, I take my seat and light a cigarette. After a good long drag, I look Fed number two in the eyes, or where they should be, behind his glasses. "You weren't invited here, but I'd like to invite you to get the hell out of my office."

"Do you know who we are?" asks Fed Number two.

Tapping the ash off my cancer stick, I reply while looking at Fed number one, who hasn't moved or said anything beyond his sneer: "By the looks of it you're Feds, but the truth of the matter is I don't give a shit who you are. You don't come into my office, intimidate my secretary, and try to pull this tough guy crap with me. Now I'm not inviting or asking, I'm telling you to go back to whoever you report to, and tell them to send someone who understands respect."

I spin my chair around to look out the window as they leave, but in my anger I didn't realize that I wasn't sitting in front of it. Instead of facing the window, I'm stuck staring at a blank wall until I'm sure they've left.

"Hey Jimmy, did someone put you in time out?" I turn back around to see Thaddeus standing close to where Fed Number one was just a moment ago. "Who were the Feds, and why'd they leave so fast?"

Explaining that they were just some muscle heads who didn't have any manners, I resume smoking my cigarette, which hits the spot in a way only a good smoke can. Knowing me like no one else, Thaddeus understands what I mean, and warns me that they'll be back.

II

Sure enough, an hour and a half later two more suits walk into the office lobby. In a complete departure from my earlier exchange with these people, they now wait for Sarah to send them in, they knock and, most dramatically, one is a female and an attractive one at that. The shock only lasts a moment, and after I've regained my composure, I deliver the introduction that Elizabeth, a partner in the agency, has driven into my head: "Hello, I'm Detective James S. Peckman, how may I be of service to you?"

Without missing a beat the female replies, "We know who you are Mr. Peckman; there's a reason my associates and I have come to you."

Elizabeth stressed that having an opening line that flowed out of me would help instill confidence with potential clients; it even works at bars. But this Fed was so stoic that instead of instilling confidence in her, she sapped all of mine.

In an attempt to regain my ground I remind myself that this is *my* office, and that she came to *me*. "Excuse me, Miss No Name."

Showing the palm of my hand to her, I call Thaddeus and Elizabeth into my office. "I'm sure you already know who they are, but these are my partners, Elizabeth Gomez and Thaddeus Coleman. I'm also certain you're aware that we'll be talking about you and discussing whatever conversation we have once you leave, so why not skip the middle step?"

The female officer shakes Elizabeth's hand, saying that she's heard a lot about her and in particular her abilities.

Elizabeth is a psychometrist; she can divine the history of something through physical contact. The barehanded handshake was a display of honor and honesty. After Elizabeth gives Thaddeus and I a nod of approval, the female officer begins to fill us in on what Elizabeth has already found out.

"I apologize for the actions of my associates earlier; however, my employer felt a show of force would work better than reason. I'm Master Patrol Officer Beck, and this is MPO Adams. We're here on behalf of Congresswoman Christie Woods."

We'd each seen the news in recent weeks that Congresswoman Woods' parents went missing while on vacation in Illinois, but nothing about the case had hinted at any paranormal or supernatural involvement, making me curious as to why Beck and Adams are here.

She explains that several days ago the congresswoman, on her way to a meeting in New York City, had come across two statues flanking an elevator bank that she believed to have been modeled after her parents. "The male figure had the congresswoman's father's fanny pack that he took with him on every road trip. Additionally, both statues are in the same clothes as in a picture they had sent the congresswoman two hours before they were reported missing."

"The congresswoman had scheduled a web chat with them for 3 pm that they did not make. They haven't answered their cell phones or emails since this picture was sent." Beck produces a glossy print of said picture, showing the missing couple beside the world's largest penguin.

Thaddeus asks the first question that comes to my mind. "Why hasn't this picture been used in the press coverage? It's clearly the most recent…"

Understanding his logic, MPO Beck cuts him off, "The congresswoman has become sentimentally attached, feeling the photo is the last personal communication from her parents and would like you to keep the picture, and the investigation entirely, from the public."

Taken aback from the forwardness of the conversation, I remind the officers that we haven't agreed to the case, and aside from needing to discuss payment, I'm still not sure why we're needed for this, "This all seems very interesting, but replica statues don't really warrant our particular skills."

"It's not your skills we're particularly interested in." With that MPO Beck looks at Elizabeth.

"So you believe if I were to make contact with the statues, I'll be able to divine their origins, thus aiding you in the investigation." Elizabeth turns to me for approval.

I hate to admit it, but it's a sound strategy. "After Elizabeth investigates the statues, what are her and our roles to be?"

The two officers get up and prepare to leave. Before she turns MPO Beck places a large manila folder on my desk, and with a wink, "I'm sure you can make yourself useful."

III

At five foot six and 150 pounds, Thaddeus doesn't have an imposing frame, but his demeanor is another matter entirely. Wearing his signature brown turtleneck sweater, he proclaims: "I don't like it. Who are they to demand us to do anything? They're not even FBI like we thought, they're Capitol Police. Do they even have jurisdiction here?" He slams his copper snake-head cane onto the ground as punctuation to his question. The action jostles his glasses to the tip of his nose, and loosens a strand of his slicked-back, jet-black hair.

Elizabeth, on the other hand, has a personality much more subdued than her appearance. She rises to her feet to display the entirety of her frame, extending just beyond five foot even. Flipping over all of her dark blue hair from the right to left side of her head, she reveals the dark brown skin of her shaved sides and back of her head as she responds to Thaddeus. "I understand you have issues with authority…"

Trying to lighten the mood, I ask if that's because he's black.

Receiving equally angry looks from the two, Elizabeth answers me. "No, it's because he, like you, was a police detective before the nightmare below the sheets inducted you both to this world."

Overdramatic much? I ask myself, but they're clearly not in the mood for my charm. Elizabeth replaced the black studded glove that extends past her elbows before resuming the conversation she was trying to have without me. She says that these officers clearly did their homework on us and are more than likely aware that we haven't had a job since our vampire case two months ago.

Unfortunately, she's right, and she doesn't even bother mentioning that it was also our only case since opening the doors of "Peckman, Coleman, and Gomez".

Deciding to end this conversation before it can turn into an argument, I declare, "The truth of the matter is this: we need the case, the money and the possible exposure such a high profile job can produce." I explain what we all know: that too many people in the world are still ignorant of what's going on in the shadows. Realizing I'm the one being overdramatic now, I add, "Besides, we're being offered full pay for consultation only. Elizabeth only needs to briefly assist in the investigation, and we can focus on a real case after cashing the check."

Thaddeus knows I'm right, but instead of agreeing, he leaves with a huff and a puff. Elizabeth and I decide that she shouldn't go by herself. With Thaddeus still being sour over recent revelations, she asks me to escort her.

The nature of Elizabeth's powers creates a strong bind to all she comes into contact with, especially romantically. This causes her to be somewhat more open than society views as the norm. She and I have been romantically involved for some time now; however, unbeknownst to me, she was also intimate with Thaddeus for much of that time. Elizabeth acknowledges the delicacy of the situation, but her unique view of life and the supernatural connections to everything in the world around her doesn't allow her to fully understand the feelings involved.

In fact, Elizabeth is the only other person Thaddeus has slept with aside from his wife, who passed away several years ago. I fully believe this has caused him to fall in love with her. Unfortunately, the nature of Elizabeth's powers make a similar connection impossible for her. Sadly, he was probably aware of this before he started anything with her, but the loneliness he felt was overwhelming; a feeling I'm all too well aware of.

I've had several partners before and even after my wife passed, and it's likely that this is the reason why I hadn't fallen for Elizabeth the way Thaddeus has, but that's not to say the feelings I have for her are dismissive. The fact that I've allowed myself to have any feelings worries me that I've betrayed the memory of my wife, but even more, the daughter we shared. It's those contradicting feelings that force me to keep Elizabeth at arm's length, while also wanting to pull her close.

After several moments of silence following Thaddeus' departure, we agree to leave first thing in the morning for New York. Elizabeth removes her glove once again and moves close to stroke my cheek, and although I may be more relaxed with the situation than Thaddeus, I move away from her touch. "The three of us need to discuss this, but after we get paid."

IV

The ride to New York from Newark can take anywhere from

half an hour to over two hours, depending on traffic at the Lincoln Tunnel. Thankfully, on an early Saturday morning in September there's almost no traffic, but the silence carried over from the previous night has become less comfortable and makes the drive seem absurdly long.

We emerge from the tunnel and enter a world unto itself. The ever-changing city has its own paranormal defenders, but before Thaddeus and I stepped in, New Jersey was mostly unprotected from the horrors that spilled across the river. The congresswoman presumably chose us for a number of reasons: she's from Jersey, we're relatively unknown to the media, and, most importantly, we have Elizabeth.

Elizabeth is at a stage with her powers where she needs to make physical contact to glean the subject's history, but her mentor, Gidious, says with some decades of practice she'll be able to control them further. In time, she should be able to use her powers when she wants and even without contact. He even proclaims there are some psychometrists that can not only read the history of a subject, but also its future. Only time will tell if she'll develop those abilities. Right now I feel she's able to read into me just by her intense stare. I manage to somehow keep my eyes on the road, when she decides to disturb the quiet in the car.

"I don't know if I'll be able to get anything from the statues. My abilities have always worked stronger with living objects."

I tell her that Gidious recommended her to Thaddeus and me for a reason. "He believes in you and what you can do, and while I can't stand that senile old man and his disturbing manner of speech, I trust his judgment in the area of psychometrics. Besides, you've already proven yourself to both Thaddeus and me."

Finding a nearby parking deck, I avoid exposing my inability to parallel park. We exit the deck and immediately Elizabeth wraps her clothing tight, covering any exposed skin. I can tell from her eyes that she's nervous about the surroundings and feels overwhelmed. Lifting her sleeve, I place my bare hand on her skin, just above her glove. Forcing her to focus on her connection to me, she's able to push past everything else around her.

We approach the building and I can see waiting outside are the two 'Feds' that first introduced themselves to my secretary and I so rudely, although I now know they're Capitol Police assigned to Congresswoman Woods after her parents disappeared.

Skipping all pleasantries, I ask 'Fed' one if he's learned his manners yet, and he actually growls at me in response. During our exchange, Elizabeth asks the Asian officer what this building is and what the congresswoman's business was here.

"That's none of your concern. Just go in there, light whatever candles or incense you normally do to fool people, fail and be on your way. Let the non-frauds do the real work."

While responding to Elizabeth, the Asian officer actually takes a threatening step towards her. Placing a hand out towards me, Elizabeth stops me from doing the same. "You hear that, James? Master Patrol Officer Anthony Kim doesn't believe in the supernatural, although he knows a werewolf killed his daughter." He takes more than a few steps back, asking how she could know that. "Oh, I can't right? I'm a fraud, remember?" She turns with a devious smile and enters the building I follow behind.

Once in the lobby, I ask, "How did you know that? You never made contact with him."

She replies that Officer Kim has been sleeping with Officer Beck since his wife left him. She was able to see all this when she shook hands with Officer Beck yesterday.

Impressed with the display of her powers, I follow Elizabeth to the statues: two older lovers torn apart and trying to reconnect with each other past the infinite marble tiled floor between them. Without knowing the origins of the statues, I'd really be impressed with the expressions on the couple ripped from each other's arms. It would honestly be a touching display of art if the statues didn't exactly resemble the subjects in the photo. With hesitation, Elizabeth approaches the statue of the father, extending her bare hand. Touching his leg, her body instantly stiffens and her eyes dilate completely. She falls back, landing in my arms, and looks me in the eyes. "They're not statues."

V

"Those weren't statues; they are the congresswoman's actual parents." Elizabeth and I told the officers the name of the person who sold the statues, but Elizabeth wasn't able to glean too much information beyond that. There was some kind of magic involved blocking her abilities, but she was able to read another name; she says this person was mired in evil and she believes is the person responsible for this.

Ever since I almost died in a plane crash nearly three decades ago, I've refused to fly and have come to embrace the reliability and convenience of trains. They make me feel like Sam Spade, the old school gumshoe of Dashiell Hammett from the *Maltese Falcon*. Spade was a leading inspiration for my becoming a detective, and that feeling helps me further embrace trains while avoiding my fear. Because of this, it's agreed that Thaddeus and Elizabeth will fly to Montana, home of the world's largest penguin, which also appeared briefly in Elizabeth's vision, while I follow behind on the rails.

Most of the time, clients will ask why I don't fly, and instead of admitting that I'm scared, I say the frequent stops make it more convenient. But since we're apparently doing the rest of this case *pro bono*, I don't have to explain that.

VI

...or so I thought. Upon boarding the train, I'm quickly joined by Officers Beck and Kim. They had no luggage with them, so it's likely that following me was a last minute decision. Thankfully, I keep an overnight bag at the office. I may never have been a Boy Scout, but it still makes sense to always be prepared.

"Officer Kim, one would wonder why Detective Peckman would travel to Montana by train."

"Especially when his partners are about to take a plane to the same destination."

"Very curious indeed. So, Detective Peckman, care to explain?"

Not amused with their obviously preplanned exchange: "You sure you two don't want to just keep talking to yourselves?" After a brief pause, it's clear they're as equally unamused with my answer. "I like trains for their isolation and quietness."

Without missing a beat Officer Kim chimes in, "Well that can't be true, not if you're sitting here with us." The skill in his delivery makes me want to believe that their little play wasn't rehearsed.

If it wasn't clear enough that they planned to take the ride with me, them sitting beside me removes all doubt. They begin another conversation among themselves, wondering why I'm on a train, rather than with Thaddeus and Elizabeth on the plane. Trying to block them out, I put on my earphones and play my mp3 player, a gift from Jose, a friend who works security for a local hospital.

Jose claims I'm not in touch with the technology of today, so for Christmas he gave me this, and loaded it with his favorite music, a band called "The Better World" also from Jersey. They're a good rock band, which is a departure of my typical jazz and blues, but most importantly right now, they're loud enough to drown out the officers' conversation.

I wake up several hours later to see that Officer Kim has also fallen asleep, and Officer Beck is watching him. "I wonder how your superiors would react if they knew you two were sleeping together."

The caring eyes on Officer Kim shift to angry orbs of hate. "I wonder why you would allow your fear of flying keep you from joining the woman you're sleeping with, instead leaving her alone for over twenty hours with the other man she's sleeping with? A man who happens to actually love her."

How does she know all this? Is she a mind reader? I've heard that there are some out there in the world, but why would she work for the Capitol Police? She could do so much more with herself. That is, if she is a mind reader.

I know one way to figure out. First, I need her to look at me and lock eyes, and I blatantly fake a cough. Good, she's looking. Now think hard: *I wonder what she's like in bed. She's so uptight while working, she probably likes all kinds of nasty shit. Probably even other chicks, that's why she's with an Asian man who probably has...*

"What are you looking at? Why are you staring at me? You do know that I can kill you in over two dozen ways right here without any weapons, right?"

Officer Kim wakes up during the conversation to let me know he won't be afraid to actually use a weapon on the train.

Well, all I know is *that* backfired. I still have no clue whether she can read minds or not.

The remainder of the day passes with minimal conversation, and the two officers occasionally excusing themselves together. Aside from not figuring out the truth about Officer Beck, I spend much of the trip upset with myself for resorting to such moronic lows and childlike tactics.

VII

Exiting the train in the cold rain, I put on my fedora and pea coat while looking for any signs of Elizabeth and Thaddeus. Throughout the train ride, the officers had a cell phone signal blocker keeping me from notifying my partners. It appears the blocker is still in effect.

"Don't worry about your friends; we're going to take you to them now." Officer Kim explains that they had similar company on their trip and have been waiting for me.

Riding in standard fare black SUV's, we arrive at the local police station, which evidently isn't used to this much traffic in the entire year. Officer Adams, and the previously unnamed Officer Meson, had commandeered much of the empty back offices.

Even driving through the rain, one could get the impression that this was quieter than the average American small town. Being escorted through the halls of the police station only further confirms that assessment. There are no criminals locked up behind bars, only one person who appears to be the local drunk sleeping off the night's festivities in an unlocked cell.

They lead me into a small room holding too many occupants already: Officers Adams and Meson, Thaddeus, and Elizabeth. My partners are sitting on one side of a table, with Adams sitting across, and Meson leaning against the wall. There's a chair between Thaddeus and Elizabeth that's clearly meant for me, so I oblige. "Since you're hosting, mind getting me a cup of coffee?"

"You want coffee?" Officer Adams picks up his own half-drunk, still steaming hot cup of coffee, spits in it and begins to extend it to me, but is cut off by the opening of the door and a fifth MPO escorting Congresswoman Woods into the room. She stands next to Officer Adams, who is still sitting and eyeing me, until the congresswoman clears her throat just over his shoulder. "Oh, Congresswoman, please have a seat."

Stoically, the congresswoman takes her seat, folds her hands in her lap, and composes herself before addressing us. "Your agency was hired to look into the disappearance of my parents against my better judgment, and in direct violation of United States Capitol Police procedures, because I was hoping you three might be successful where others failed. So it's to my surprise that we find your secretary purchasing two plane tickets to Montana, while two of my men were getting ready to board a flight to Illinois." She motions her hand behind her, not caring who she pointed to, or even if she pointed to anyone. The stress and pain of this situation is clearly written on her face. I can tell she's tired and hurting and willing to take it out on anyone around her if it'll get her parents back.

She removes her hands from her lap and places them on the table with a nearly unperceivable tremor. She lights a cigarette before turning her attention to Elizabeth.

I see the smoke billowing out of her lips, and while the congresswoman isn't an attractive woman on her better days, right now she looks like the sexiest woman alive. I never smoke during missions, but the painful train ride with the lovebird officers drove me to my limit, and I can barely hear what's being said over my echoing thoughts of what I'd do for one good drag.

"So missy, what did your little vision tell you that you decided to withhold from me, and brought the three of you here?"

"Before I explain what I saw, you must understand there are things in this world that you don't know about, things that the public consider myths. These things have been kept in the shadows because if knowledge of their existence became public, life as we know it would be thrust into a never-ending nightmare."

Squeezing the bridge of her nose with her thumb and middle finger, the congresswoman takes a few moments with her eyes closed--perhaps an attempt to escape the situation, or, more likely, preparation to deal with what's at hand. "I know there's more than out there than what's believed, and I'm sure you three could spend days telling me all you've seen, but all I need right now is what you know about what happened to my parents."

Elizabeth takes a deep breath, searching for the right way to phrase the truth. Thaddeus places a hand on her shoulder and looks at me with concern. Receiving a nod of approval, he tells Elizabeth to tell her everything.

Locking eyes with the congresswoman, she says, "Ma'am, what you saw were not statues; somehow your parents were turned into stone and sold as art by Robert Kane." Elizabeth pauses, checking to see if the congresswoman wanted her to continue, because she had begun to pace the available space of the room.

Stopping her rhythmic walk after a few more laps, Woods asks, "Why are we in Montana? My parents went missing in Illinois, and the few accounts we have of Robert Kane are from all over the country selling similar 'art'."

"While I'm positive Robert Kane was the seller, I was able to glean someone else's involvement. Not sure of his name, but something to do with a large penguin."

The new officer that walked in with the congresswoman chimes in. "A statue of the world's largest penguin is one hundred miles from here in a town called Cut Bank."

Tired of not hearing my own voice, I take the opportunity to speak. "That's why we came here. It may not be a solid lead, so we didn't want to alert you on a false alarm. Now that we're all on the same page, it'll be best to leave us to do what we do. We'll be in touch."

The three of us rise to leave, when the congresswoman stops us. "I'll admit that I believe you're telling the truth, but I still don't trust you. Officers Beck and Adams will accompany you until this is resolved."

Now knowing where everyone stands, I try to build a positive rapport with the officers, "Congresswoman, if it's all the same to you, would you mind assigning Officers Beck and Kim? Over our long train ride, I've come to respect them, and feel somewhat more comfortable with their skills."

Moving from rubbing the bridge of her nose to applying pressure on her temples, she waves her hand in the air, shooing us out with a grunted "I don't care".

VIII

Riding in another standard issue black SUV, Officer Kim turns around in the passenger seat to thank me. Officer Beck, ignoring me, tells Kim that she doesn't want him here. "You've lost too much already, and you're not fully recovered."

"My daughter was killed by something from the same underground world as the thing we're after now. I'm as recovered as I'm going to get, but solving this might give me more... closure."

Following this little tiff, the five of us actually enjoy a pleasant, if brief, conversation before we all fall silent with the severity of the matter weighing on us. I watch as Thaddeus prepares his bandolier in the back seat with all types of magical and mystical items. Thaddeus isn't a particularly good detective, but he's acquired certain tools and weapons of questionable origins that help him fight the things he comes across. He has tele-maggots that psychically link two people, explosive pellets made of grass and a number of other things that I hope we won't need. All this is in addition to his guns that he oddly chose to name after two male comic characters, Bruce and Dick.

Elizabeth and I don't believe in his superstition that going on a mission with an unnamed weapon is bad luck. Nonetheless, he did convince me to name my Glock 9mm. I picked Stacy after the Joyce Meadows character in *Two Faces West*.

I watch them all, and can't help but wonder if I'm the right person to be leading them into such a potentially dangerous situation. Just then I notice Elizabeth. I can practically feel her eyes on me. I sheepishly turn towards her, and she tells me not to worry so much. "The three of us can get through anything."

Thaddeus pats me on the shoulder from behind. "Seriously, Jimmy Peck, we might have some things to work through once we get back home, but this is what we do." For some reason, I find his false bravado assuring, even enough to lighten the forecast of these ominous rain clouds.

Seeing me looking out the window, Officer Kim asks if there's something wrong. I tell him to never trust the rain. "Rain always has evil behind it; that's why I don't use umbrellas. Too much of a disconnect with nature."

IX

Arriving at the Glacier Inn, it's hard to miss the world's largest penguin. Thankfully the speaker is broken, apparently a common occurrence, but that doesn't prevent droves of people lining up to take their picture with the eyesore.

Agreeing that it'd be best to begin the investigation without further delay, we enter the inn to speak to the manager. In practiced fashion, Officers Beck and Kim turn off their smiles and are completely stone-faced.

Following a rude introduction similar to the one I initially received, the manager explains. "There is one guy who rents a room for a month at a time, two or three or times a year. He's got a room now, but I haven't actually seen him for around three weeks." He goes on to say that this guy, Dexter Parker, sets up shop selling cheap trinkets and offering to take pictures of tourists with the penguin, and that he travels around to other tourist traps doing the same.

Flashing their badges a second time, the officers order the innkeeper to show us to the room. Unlocking the door, he steps aside to let us in, and then says he needs to return to the desk.

A quick glance shows that Mr. Parker left in a rush. Thaddeus finds an old style ledger that most people have left behind for electronic versions. Flipping through the pages he sees a number of columns. The first contains dates, followed by two, occasionally four, letters, a city and state, and in the final column dollar amounts, but not in every row.

Taking the ledger from Thaddeus' hand, Officer Beck finds the date the congresswoman's parents went missing, followed by their initials, Cut Bank, Montana, and finally a dollar amount of three quarters of a million dollars. "Holy shit! This is a listing of all the people this sick bastard made into statues and how much he sold them for."

I ask why he would leave something like this behind, Officer Kim answers that this guy is probably so confident in his scheme that he didn't think anyone would locate him.

Taking the book in her bare hand, Elizabeth corrects the officer, "Actually, it's quite the opposite. When he took Mr. and Mrs. Woods he was unaware that they were the congresswoman's parents. His M.O. has been to take people no one would miss, and now he's fled this location because he's afraid of the vengeance coming his way." It brings a smile to my face to see that she's really embracing overselling the ominousness of her abilities.

Embarrassed for being put in his place as effectively as he's used to doing to others, Officer Kim asks, "If you know so much, why don't you figure out where this guy's hiding?"

"Unfortunately, there's still some force at work blocking my abilities."

"Shush, does anyone else hear that?" I thought I'd heard something coming from the bathroom earlier, but we got caught up with the ledger. Now I hear it again. "Something is in the bathroom."

"That's the great hiding spot your mind powers couldn't figure out? Samantha, get this guy out of there so we can get back to the city and civilization." Before I could protest, Officer Beck has turned the knob and pushed the door in. Faster than anyone can respond, Samantha is knocked several feet backwards from the swipe of a paw larger than her head connecting with her shoulder.

His reflexes returning, Officer Kim draws his Glock 9 and unloads the entire clip before he realizes the bullets aren't doing anything. "What the hell kind of dog is that?"

Standing at over five feet tall while on all fours, I'd think it was apparent it's not a dog. "Officer Kim, that's a hellhound, and clearly your bullets won't work." I order him to get Officer Beck to safety and leave this to us. From across the room, he's locked eyes on the beast, staring into its jet-black globes; the hound licks a snout as long as an alligator's mouth with teeth sharper than a shark's.

Having finally taken the entire image of the beast in, I realize Officer Kim won't be able to move on his own accord anytime soon. Thaddeus tosses a small burlap sack over the hound and yells, "Wolfsbane!" Shooting the sack with Stacy, I send a cloud of ground wolfsbane over the beast. Hellhounds can't bark, but when they're in pain they let out a low growl that sounds like a shotgun going off in a pile of sand bags. Using its pain as a distraction, Thaddeus pulls a knife coated in the oil of mistletoe and stabs the beast in the throat, killing it instantly.

Trusting in our abilities to stop the hound, Elizabeth continues searching the ledger. Officer Kim finally snaps out of it and checks on Beck. She's bled badly from the wound in her shoulder, but something in the hound's claws also cauterized the cuts, keeping her from bleeding out. Coming around several minutes later, she tells Officer Kim that this is too dangerous; he shouldn't have come. Thinking she's joking, he laughs while helping her to her feet.

Searching the bathroom for clues as to why there'd be a hellhound here, there appear to be small shimmering shreds of snakeskin in the sink. I turn around and, after seeing what's in the shower, I call Thaddeus over and show him the three statues of small children awkwardly stacked atop each other. Not wanting to alert Elizabeth, fearing that she would want to make contact and that she wouldn't be able to take the pain, I tell Thaddeus not to say anything. I rush him out of the room and close the door behind me.

X

Reconvening at the police station, the officers discovered in

Dexter's ledger that he had a particular pattern of cities he visits. More to the point, he frequents Virginia Beach, Virginia after every other city. We come to the conclusion that he has some kind of base of operations there. We make arrangements for Thaddeus, Elizabeth and Officer Kim, while Officer Beck and I take the train. But four hours later, I find myself waking up from a drug induced sleep, literally being dragged off of an airplane.

XI

Not even an hour later and we're in an identical black SUV. If I didn't know better, I'd swear it was the same, but I'm not dwelling on that. I'm still upset for what they did to me, and even more embarrassed that I allowed it to happen.

I'm so lost in my thoughts, I only barely notice the conversation going on, like a fly on the opposite side of a wall. Officer Kim is telling Officer Beck he's not comfortable with her being in the field after she suffered that injury from the hellhound.

I didn't really catch her response, but I assume it's along the lines of 'this is my job, what I live for'. Whatever her response, my thoughts have settled and focused: these officers are too self-concerned. They're a danger to us, and I can't trust them being here. I won't allow them to be the death of another of my partners.

Snapping me out of my thought process, Thaddeus lets me know he's going to need to pick up more wolfsbane. "I know a reliable supplier on the outskirts of town. He keeps his ears to the ground about these kinds of things; maybe he has some info."

The trip to this supplier is filled with more protests from each officer to the other that this assignment is too dangerous. Neither one gains ground in the argument, and we're stuck with them, it seems.

Unfortunately for Thaddeus, it's evident that tragedy has struck his supplier and whatever inventory he may have had. Meryll's backwater paranormal trinket shop is in shambles, and much of the product has been destroyed.

It's easy to see an abundance of claw marks tearing into the shelves and walls. What's less noticeable is a large round stone beneath the counter. Retrieving it, I hand it to Thaddeus after realizing it's a head, one that he quickly identifies as Meryll.

Sculpted in Meryll's ear is the tail end of a tele-maggot. Thaddeus places one of his own from his satchel in his ear. "Oh my

God, he's still alive! I can hear his thoughts. He's begging me to kill him."

Raising the head above his own, with tears in his eyes, Thaddeus hesitates, "I'm sorry Meryll. I should have been able to help you. I wish I was able to undo this." After lowering the head to look Meryll in the eyes, "Forgive me."

Once again lifting the head, he's stopped from smashing it by Officer Kim. "Before you do that, find out who did this."

"He's in too much pain, it's not making sense. All he keeps repeating is 'hellhounds' and 'snakes' but I don't see any signs of snake bite marks anywhere." Thaddeus puts his friend to rest instead of delaying it any longer, smashing the head against the ground.

Following a quick prayer for the deceased, Thaddeus informs us that the crap that was on display up here was for the tourists. "The real stuff is down through a trap door in the back office. From the looks of it, we're going to need to gather all we can."

Scanning over the wreckage, I have to agree. Thankfully, all of the items in this hidden area remain untouched. I lose track of all the things Thaddeus takes, but I do notice a box of bullets loaded with wolfsbane.

Just as we're preparing to leave, Elizabeth, who's stayed above, tells us she hears police sirens. Thaddeus, Elizabeth and I quietly jump into the black SUV, leaving the two officers to deal with the local force, and the ensuing jurisdiction tug-of-war. The last thing I hear of the argument is Officer Kim saying that he doesn't care where this happened, but it has direct connections to a Capitol case.

"So Jimmy, why did you rush Elizabeth and me out of there so fast? Why ditch the cops?"

I tell him that I think their concern for each other is going to get in the way of what needs to be done. "Not to mention, the way Officer Kim froze up with the hellhound, I don't think he can handle whatever we're going up against." As the rain continues to caress the truck like a heavy fog, I can see Elizabeth's uneasiness with my opinion of the officers, although Thaddeus is nodding in agreement.

When we arrive at Virginia Beach and the world's largest sea serpent, I say, "Thaddeus, let me see the photo of the congresswoman's parents." Reviewing it briefly, my suspicions are confirmed. I point out a large RV behind the parents. "Look familiar?"

Elizabeth looks up noticing the same RV parked close to the statue, "Do you think it's his?"

Thaddeus and I agree there's only one way to be sure, and we make our way with haste, while trying to avoid any unwanted attention. Fortunately, whoever the culprit is has no defenses set up around the RV. I make quick work of the small lock on the door and we enter, prepared for whatever horrors await us. What we were not prepared for was the laughter of a child.

Before we can find the source of the laughter, we're ambushed by another hellhound, presumably the same that was unleashed on Meryll and his shop. In fear of causing a panic outside, I refrain from shooting the beast. Thankfully, Thaddeus has his special tools to pick up the slack. He lights a piece of paper with a match and tosses it into the air. It quickly flares up, blinding Rover. Fortunately, Elizabeth and I know about this tactic and are prepared. Before the beast blindly causes a ruckus, Elizabeth tosses two handfuls of powdered wolfsbane, dropping the creature flat. I grab the hound by the mouth, forcing it open until I hear a pop from its jaw, and Thaddeus pushes an explosive grass pellet in its maw. The hound's bulky frame absorbs the noise, but it dies quickly and painfully.

Working as a team, we were able to subdue the monster before the occupants in the back heard anything. Emerging into the rear room, we walk into a photo session of a family on the count of 'cheese' and are forced to watch as the husband and wife slowly solidify into stone. Thankfully, the owner of the laughter we heard was distracted by our interruption and was not affected.

Regretfully, Officers Beck and Kim had caught up to us just in time for the photographer to turn his attention to us. Coming to the same realization as I did, Thaddeus joins me in tackling Elizabeth and Officer Beck, leaving Officer Kim on his feet, "Look out! It's…" Sadly, Officer Kim's ears sculpted into marble, and the sound was unable to enter. He never heard me finish saying "It's Medusa's head". With unsure footing, his unarticulated body can't hold his weight and he crashes to the ground, shattering into dozens of pieces much like the remains of Thaddeus' supplier friend.

Dexter had kept the head under a black cloth like he was using an old-type camera. When he lifted the cloth, he revealed the Gorgon's head and turned his subjects into statues, like the congresswoman's parents and now this little girl's parents. The snakeskin scales finally make sense. I only wish I'd been able to figure this out sooner, more so when I hear the scream of Officer Beck's realization of what has happened to her lover.

Looking at the floor, I can see from my peripheral vision that Office Beck draws her guns and starts to turn towards Dexter, but Thaddeus holds her down, explaining the situation and our inability to look directly at the head.

Thaddeus asks me something about fighting something we can't look at, but my concerns are elsewhere. "Little girl, can you hear me?" In between sobs, I hear her say 'yes'. "Okay, I need you to keep your eyes closed and curl into a ball until I tell you it's all right. Can you do that for me?"

"No, Daddy's holding me too tight. He won't move, and his hands are cold. What happened to my mommy and daddy?"

"I… I'm sorry, I don't know. Keep your eyes closed and I'll find out, okay?" She mumbles 'mm-hmm' through her cries.

"I don't know who you people are, but you'll all be immortalized in the beauty of cold everlasting marble. I'm a Privileged of Orre, the ancient god of stone and earth, long before this age of man came."

"Explain this to me, Mr. Parker Privileged, why are you doing this? Why use Medusa's head to turn people into…" Thinking of the little girl and her parents holding her, I modify my words. "…why do this?"

"My god needs new followers in this modern age, so I've been tasked with making them and selling them as fine art to inspire others. Who you call Medusa, Orre considered a mistress, one of many, but her love and devotion rose above all others. And only those bearing the mark of Orre are immune to her stone cold glare."

"Are Mommy and Daddy statues?" The little girl's ensuing scream is cut off as her lungs harden and solidify; halted as the inside of her throat constricts and the rest of her is marbleized.

The girl was too smart for her own good, realizing what was being said and understanding what that meant for her parents.

Thaddeus, no longer afraid of injuring the girl, rises and turns with eyes closed and guns drawn, shooting in wide arcs, allowing Elizabeth, Officer Beck and myself to climb through the rubble that once was Officer Kim, and into the relative safety of the front cabin. Thaddeus soon stumbles behind us. "I don't think I hit him; we've got to figure a way back in there and finish this."

Looking in the rearview mirror of the RV, a plan forms. "If myth holds true, we should be able to use reflections." Ripping off the mirror, I tell the females to get the two side mirrors while Thaddeus and I get whatever's in the bathroom.

Lining up at the door, I say, "Listen, we don't know how accurate the myth and movies are, so I'll go in first. Only follow if I tell you it's safe." Before any arguments could be made, I enter the room once again, but backwards, using the mirror as my guide. Positioning it so my view settles on Medusa's head on a pedestal with dozens of eyes following my every movement, but no sign of Dexter.

Deciding to cover the head before calling the others in, I slowly make my way closer when Elizabeth calls through the door. "James, are you okay?" Telling her to give me a moment, I get the cloth to conceal the writhing snakes while managing to avoid getting bitten.

The rest enter and immediately notice the missing presence of Dexter. "Mr. Coleman, look at this, a trail of blood. Apparently you did hit him."

"She's right, must be why he left without the head. The trail leads out the window." Elizabeth motions to the cloth rippling like a mound of flexing muscles, "What are we going to do with this?"

Without a word, Thaddeus unloads an entire clip into the head, stopping all movement beneath. Nearly immediately after, the silence is interrupted by the synchronized screams of the once statuesque parents. We all turn to see them clutching the now bleeding form of their daughter. Not only had Thaddeus shot Dexter earlier, but one of his stray bullets had hit the marble girl in her gut. Once again flesh, the wound now proved more fatal than the actual transformation.

Pointing at Thaddeus, Officer Beck blames him. "You did this, that's your fault."

"I didn't know they'd all turn back, I didn't know." He says it a second time, so quiet I'm not sure anyone else heard him. Then again, I don't think even I was supposed to hear it. The tears in his eyes and tremble in his hands are enough of a sign to Officer Beck to lay off him for the time being. He falls to his knees as Officer Beck's back step causes her to slip on the free flowing blood of Officer Kim.

She looks down, and I prepare myself for her to mimic the

scream of the parents, but she remains silent. Tears do fall from her face, but no noise escapes her pursed lips. Wiping the tears from her cheeks, she unintentionally stains her face with streaks of her lover's blood.

Still silent, Officer Beck rises to her feet, now with gun in hand and leaves the room. Elizabeth asks her where she's going, "Someone needs to make sure that son of a bitch is dead." Turning and aiming her gun at Thaddeus, she warns him: "You better be gone before I get back, or I'll have you arrested for the murder of that little girl."

While I agree that he was a bit careless in his effort, I don't believe the girl's death could be blamed on him. The look on his face, though, shows that he blamed himself before Beck admonished him. "Listen Thaddeus, she's wrong, and she's upset over Officer Kim's death, and she has no right to blame you." But I fear my words fall on deaf ears.

Shortly after the RV door closes behind Officer Beck, we hear the screams of civilians followed by the report of two gunshots echoing through the window. That's the last we hear of Officer Samantha Beck; she never comes back to the RV to follow up on her threat to Thaddeus.

Unable to deal with the pain in the room, I step out of the RV to examine Dexter's body, mostly out of curiosity to see where Thaddeus had shot him. I find his body slumped against the vehicle. In this position, I can see the nape of his neck, and a tattoo with an ethereal shimmer. The tattoo is of an eye with an asymmetrical rock as its pupil. I quickly wonder what kind of ink was used for the effect, before I continue to the reason I was even looking at him. Pushing his head against the RV, exposing the front of his body, I see two gunshot wounds in the center of his chest and a third on his leg.

Noticing a complete lack of blood, I call Thaddeus and Elizabeth to weigh in their thoughts, but before they can come, we're interrupted by the sound of police sirens. We flee the scene before I can explain what I saw, but I'll have plenty of time to inform them on the train ride back to New Jersey.

XII

Two weeks later, we received payment in the mail for many

times the agreed amount, with a personal letter written by Congresswoman Woods. In it she thanked us for our dedication, sacrifice, and most of all the result of our work. She's happy to report that her parents were returned to their normal state, with no ill side effects present. She goes on to say that Officer Beck requested, and has been granted, her release of service. The congresswoman goes on to warn us, especially Thaddeus, to be sure to stay clear of her. Even though the congresswoman understands the situation we were in and doesn't hold him responsible, Officer Beck views the little girl's and Officer Kim's deaths our fault.

The most important revelation to come from this case is that my secretary and researcher, Sarah, has been able to dig up some information about these so called 'Privilegeds'. They're apparently the equivalent of prophets for these old gods, like this Orre character Dexter was going on about. Apparently the tattoo Dexter had of the eye is Orre's mark, worn by all of his Privilegeds as a symbol of their loyalty to him over any of the other old gods.

Thaddeus is still devastated over killing the little girl, and, coupled with the revelation of us both sleeping with Elizabeth, he's been almost impossible to contact. When he does answer his phone, it's only to tell me to leave him alone. I can't blame him. For those two weeks all I could think about were the deaths this case resulted in, from the little girl, to Merryl and Officer Kim, but we saved the three little kids in the bathtub in Montana, and the congresswoman's parents, which is what we had set out to do. So why am I finding it so hard to put this case in the win column?

Idle Musing
From the Casebook of Detective James S. Peckman
By Alex Azar

Talent fades, skills dull, and that's why I've survived long enough to tell you my story. Had I remained at the peak of my abilities, I would have died long ago. Being able to understand that I'm not as quick or strong or even as clever as I once was allowed me to bow out gracefully, not something that could be said about many who take up my line of work. I'm barely able to hold my drink steady, but I can remember every powerful punch and unearthly hit that's wrecked my body over the years. Physical abuse is expected in my line of work, but there's only so much the human body can take before your own limbs reject you.

People who've read about the things that beat the crap out of me on a case by case basis will tell you the most damaging thing is the mental toll taken on a human mind not built to comprehend these otherworldly beings. To them I say, survive a fight with a vampire coven or a zombie Viking sea creature and tell me which hurts more, if you survive. In some cases I'm lucky to walk away without bumps or bruises, but often I'm put through a gauntlet of pain where I'm just lucky enough to survive, let alone continue. Such was the case when I decided to pick up and play the saxophone again.

I

I walk into the offices of Peckman, Coleman, & Gomez at five to nine, and it's already a whirlwind of commotion. Thaddeus' office door is closed, which only happens when he's with a potential client. Judging by the fact that I can hear the client plead his case through the door, it doesn't seem likely Thaddeus is taking the job.

On the opposite side of the lobby from Thaddeus' office Elizabeth is being cornered by Sid who, since joining the team over a year ago, has made his case for becoming a full-fledged partner at least once a week. The sad truth is, since his acquisition there hasn't been much work for the three of us. Thaddeus was the only one of us to start this agency with an existing client list, so the cases have predominately been his. Occasionally, one or more of us would assist him on the larger jobs, but he's quick to remind us who's the lead.

I'm standing at the front of the lobby with five rapidly cooling coffees, when Carl gets my attention. "Good morning, Mr. Peckman. Do you need help with these?" He doesn't wait for my answer before taking the four coffees that aren't mine. "I'm sorry, but there've been no messages for you."

I tell him I'd be more surprised if there were any messages for me, then remind him, "It's James. Only clients call me Mr. Peckman."

He hands Elizabeth and Sid their coffees and says to me over his shoulder, "You'll never know when I'll need to retain your services." Carl's a good guy, way too smart to be our receptionist. He used to be a librarian for Columbia University, but came to work for us after Sarah had to take a leave of absence. She's the one who recommended him, and he's completely immersed himself into our world.

As Carl places Thaddeus' coffee on a stand outside his office, the door opens and Thaddeus is showing the potential client out to the lobby. He says loud enough for all of us to hear, "I'm sorry, but this is a business and I can't take any *pro bono* jobs."

Just then Elizabeth does something I've only ever seen her do once before. She removes her glove and apologizes to the man, shaking his hand. "I'm sorry Mr..." She uses the pause before he tells her his name, 'Lou Green', to read his history and reason for seeking out a paranormal detective.

Thaddeus can see what she's doing and from his expression it's clear he doesn't approve, but he doesn't say anything. Instead, he picks up his coffee and tilts it to me in lieu of actually saying thanks. He retreats to his office to enjoy his java before it cools.

Having shown Mr. Lou Green out the office, Elizabeth tells

me I'm going to take the case, if for no other reason than to build my own clientele. She puts her glove back on and explains that for about a decade Lou has lived in a boarding house for artists, and is concerned that the constant murders of residents and owners is a pattern of something more sinister. She was able to sense an unnatural evil on him, but it emanated from an external force, not from him. "He might not be able to pay, but this is a legitimate case. Besides, it's not like you have much to do otherwise."

Of course she's right; she's always right. Elizabeth is a psychometrist, which basically means she can read the history of any subject simply by touching it, or in the case of living beings, she'll get a mix of memories and emotions. Apparently, what she read from Lou was enough to warrant our attention. Because of her inability to control her talent, she never takes on a case by herself, and because of our brief romantic history, she sends most cases my way.

As Sid resumes his petition for partnership, Carl asks the question I wasn't bright enough to think of earlier on my own: "What the hell is a boarding house for artists?"

II

I find Lou Green across the street, waiting at the bus stop. When choosing the location of our office, it was important for it to be accessible by bus and near the major highways to ensure that anyone who wanted to seek us out was able to do so.

Having been in the office for nearly three years, I've come to know the bus schedule, and while I cross the street I inform Lou that the next bus won't arrive for another twenty-five minutes. "Why don't I give you a ride? It'll give us time to talk about your case. And maybe I can learn a bit about this boarding house."

We head to my car and he asks me if this means I'll take the case. I tell him that Elizabeth is a good judge of character and she trusts him. Stopping at the entrance of the parking lot my car is in, Lou asks, concerned, "You know I can't pay, right? I don't make too much, but we need your help."

I smile as warmly as possible to convince him of my sincerity. "It's no big deal; maybe you can repay me with some art piece you're working on." Not having my desired effect, he instead frowns even deeper and lets me know he's an author. "Perfect, just write me into your breakout work, and we'll call it even."

Entering the car on my cue, he's smiling from ear to ear. "Thank you Mr..."

"Detective, actually, "I correct him, "Detective James S. Peckman. Happy to be of service to you." Not my typical introduction, but it'll do this one time.

We head over to the boarding house in Union City, and while not giving me directions, Lou fills me in on the missing details of the house. "The rules for living there are pretty simple. First and foremost, you can't have been published, commissioned, or basically paid for your art in any official capacity. People come and try to scam their way in, but the owners always find out the truth. I guess the Internet makes it hard to hide any modicum of success."

He interrupts himself to tell me to take I-95 North with a point of the finger to the corresponding sign. Before he can continue, I ask him about the owners he mentioned. "Oh, they're great. Only family I've had since I got kicked out as a teen, when my parents caught me shooting heroin with my boyfriend." Lou pauses to judge my reaction to the info he just gave me.

I'm not sure which bit of news was supposed to shock me, but I assure him I've seen it all in my field. "I appreciate your candor, Lou, but I need to know what I'm getting into by taking this case for you. Please, you were saying about the owners."

"Right, sorry." He scratches his arm, a phantom itch of where he used to inject himself, maybe, but I know he's clean now because Elizabeth wouldn't have been able to take the pain of any drugs currently in his system. "The house is owned and operated by six people, all friends. Originally there was a seventh, but he died a long time ago. He was a tattoo artist. Each of them is an artist in their own right, and each in a different medium. All of them gained considerable notoriety at some point in their careers, and the house is their way of giving back."

He paused to tell me to merge onto 495 East. "The only other rules are: twice a month, you have to provide a progress report of your current project, and once you do succeed, you have sixty days to move out. And best of all, with their connections, they help each of us get published or commissioned."

After giving me a series of rights and lefts, he points. "That's the house." I keep driving and turn off onto the next street. "You passed it."

Double parking, I give him a look to mean that I did it on purpose. "If I'm going to do this, I'll have to get close, but more importantly, I'm going to need to know a lot more. Let's meet at the bar we passed on JFK Boulevard, Angelo's. What time works for you?" He tells me he works at the White Castle by the house, but he can be at the bar by nine.

"Sounds good, Lou. I promise, I'll do what I can to get to the bottom of this." Reminding him not to tell anyone about me, I unlock the doors to let him know it's time to get out.

I drive back to the office without turning the radio on, needing the silence to think about the case. It doesn't take me long to realize I have no idea what crime has supposedly been committed, or how any of it is related to something paranormal or supernatural. I trust Elizabeth's judgment, but it's that trust that took me out of my element with Lou. This is going to be an interesting conversation with Thaddeus when I get back to Newark.

III

"So let me get this straight. After I turned this guy away because he couldn't pay, you decide to take the case based on Elizabeth's word, which admittedly is normally enough, but for free? You offer to give him a ride so you can get more info on the case, then forget to ask him anything relevant about the job you're doing for free?" Thaddeus laughs at me for a good three minutes before he decides he's not done. He continues laughing as I leave his office.

As far as best friends go, Thaddeus Coleman leaves a lot to be desired, but as a detective, hunter, and general business partner, I couldn't ask for better. The majority of paying jobs I've received were because of him. It was a dumb move on my part, but I know he'll understand how something like this can happen, I just need to let him work through the humor of the situation.

I find Elizabeth in her office, meditating. I interrupt her with a gentle knock on her door frame.

"Come in, James." She doesn't even need to open her eyes to know it's me. This has nothing to do with her special abilities; she knows I'm the only one comfortable enough with her to encroach on her meditation time. Even Thaddeus, who also has a romantic history with her, would simply wait Elizabeth out or leave her a note.

"What information did you get from this guy exactly?" I tell her I have no info to plan by, and I need something for when I meet him tomorrow.

Thaddeus announces his presence behind me by asking, "Should he be called a client if he's not actually paying?" The cheap shot reignites his laughter; Elizabeth even joins in with a few giggles of her own.

Waiting for their laughter to subside, I inform them that in fact Scott is paying. "We set up a barter exchange for my services."

His curiosity piqued, Thaddeus asks what I could possibly be getting in return. I casually tell him that it's none of his concern.

"If the payment has any effect on our business, it absolutely is my concern."

Since the deal isn't a secret, I tell him. "He's an author, and he's promised to work me into his next story."

Although Elizabeth takes the news for what it is, and doesn't laugh, Thaddeus must be in a particularly jovial mood, letting out some stray chuckles. However, he does provide some useful information. "For the past eleven years or so, your client has noticed a pattern of success and murder of two residents six months apart."

Elizabeth elaborates by adding that all the deaths occur away from the house. "I'm not sure how much to believe, but there is definitely something evil lurking around him."

Thaddeus' change in expression explains he wishes he had been privy to this information earlier.

IV

Knowing I have a late appointment, I don't bother getting to the office until noon. When I do arrive, Carl informs me that Sid caught a paying case early in the morning. He said it cautiously, as if the news was supposed to upset me. Typically, I might have been slightly jealous, but today I'm happy for him.

"I already have a job, Carl. And sure, it isn't paying, but after sleeping on it I think some real good will come of this." Carl optimistically agrees like he always does. There's something special about this case, and I let him know it. He just continues nodding, never one to disagree with any of us.

Carl is so affable and likeable to the four of us, Elizabeth, Thaddeus, Sid and me, that it always surprises me when I hear him raise his voice or say no to a potential client who oversteps their bounds. I would have loved to hear him shush a noisy guest at the library. In any case, once he's done agreeing with me, he lets me know Thaddeus and Elizabeth are waiting for me so they could grab lunch.

I often wonder if the two of them haven't actually gotten back together, but I've learned when it comes to Elizabeth, it's best not to ask. Besides, I know it's none of my business anymore. Letting them know I'm in, they go of on the eternal hunt of sustenance. I, on the other hand, sit myself in front of my computer to do some research.

Finding every bit of information I can on the boarding house, the current residents, the success stories, and most importantly the murders going all the way back to the original owner's death, it takes me hours to sift through it all. I recruit Carl, who's better with computers than I am, to look up the police reports and any investigation notes on the murders of the nine doomed artists.

V

I arrive at Angelo's at a quarter to nine to reserve an isolated pair of seats for Lou and me, but quickly realize the folly in my reasoning. There's less than a handful of people in the place, including the bartender and myself.

Ordering a pitcher of whatever's on tap and two cups, I sit in a booth at the rear of the bar. Lou arrives shortly later, still in his work clothes, reeking of the stench only found in a fast food restaurant. I'm by no means a healthy eater, but I steer clear of that kind of food; there's enough things out there trying to kill me; I don't need my food added to the list.

"Hey, Detective, wasn't sure if you ate dinner yet, so I brought you a sack of burgers." Of course he did. I thank him, and place the bag next to me, not even bothering to open it.

"Lou, I've done some research on the issue at the boarding house, and it seems you may be onto something." I tell him that although there doesn't seem to be any pattern to the tie frame of the various residents that reached stardom, a different resident is murdered exactly six months later every time. "If the cops ever did make a connection between the success and deaths, they dismiss it because none of the murders take place within a five mile radius to the house, and all drastically different in methodology. My question to you is, why come to paranormal detective agency?"

It takes Lou a few moments to build to build his answer, during which he helps himself to the beer in front of him. When he finally does speak, he says he agrees. "At first I thought it was a serial killer of something like that, but now I know it's a cult." He must see the doubt creep into my face because his explanation becomes more animated. "I'm telling you, I don't know how the successful people are all related, but it's clear the murdered residents are sacrifices for the other's success. It's got to be a cult, the only thing that makes sense."

Now it's my turn to take a long drink. I can't believe Elizabeth got me to go along with this. Maybe she is back with Thaddeus and this is just an elaborate joke at my expense. Then I think about how she made contact, shaking Lou's hand; she'd never do that for something so lighthearted. "Let's leave the speculation till we have a few more drinks, okay? I'm here because I'm a detective, I work with facts, first and foremost." I ask him to tell me about the house.

"Like I said yesterday, it's owned by a group of friends, only six of them now. After each reached some measure of fame, they came together to open the house. It's got room for ten residents, and rent is cheap, real cheap, only two hundred a month and that includes utilities. They're thorough with background and credit checks to make sure they aren't being taken advantage of." He tells me how every few months there's stories of applicants being rejected for already being published, earning or having too much money, or even a history of violent crimes. "They let us know any time they reject someone, even burning their application in front of us. I think it's a scare tactic, but it's the only thing they do that isn't from their hearts. They review our work, give us pointers to improve ourselves, and when one of them thinks we have something worthy, they make the effort to get us published or whatever."

After another fifteen minutes telling me how great the house has been for him, he gets to the info I've been waiting for--the other residents. He starts with the ones he considers "safe" and in no way related to the murders. "First, there's Aaron, not because his name starts with 'aa' but because he's the nicest guy in the house. He works as a caricature artist, mostly works Times Square in New York, but also hits the Boardwalk by the shore during the summer. His real goal is to be a comic artist, and he's good, but for some reason he can't draw hands or feet. Aaron moved in about two years ago, long after the killings started. Like I said, can't be him."

I listen to him talk about each resident while trying to stay objective, ignoring Lou's personal opinions. Then he gets to his list of four suspects. "There's Mark, who's been here almost as long as I have. He's nice, and even pretty outgoing, but he's weird." I ask Lou to elaborate what he means by weird, but he can't explain it so he reiterates more emphatically, "He's just really weird, man, and what's worse is he keeps changing his field. When he moved in, it was the piano, then he switched to guitar, which is fine, it's still music. Then he started painting, dropped that and is now doing sculptures made out of discarded electronics." He says although the owners do a good job of weeding out scam artists, Lou thinks this one got through.

He then moves on to his next suspect without letting me know. "I used to think Shaunna was cute, mind you this is on a boarding house scale. We don't get models bunking with us, so take that as you will, but yeah she was cute until I found out her "art"." He says the last word with such loathing, I expect to hear she kills babies or some other detestable act, not something potentially cool like cryptozoology taxidermy. "She takes different parts of dead animals and makes monstrous anomalies out of them. I don't understand how anyone can consider that art. Clearly someone like that has the capability of murder, am I right?"

I choose not to answer his question, and allow him to continue onto his next 'suspect' but he lingers, waiting for confirmation. After a second prompt, I respond with a meek, "Maybe."

By the time he gets to the third person on his lineup, he's finished half the pitcher, and the alcohol is taking effect. "The next guy, that guy Justin, he's just an asshole. He thinks he's so smart; well if he is why's he working at White Castle with me, huh?"

It's clear Lou's going to wait for my answer before continuing, so I tell him I'm not sure. "Why don't you tell me more about him? What's Justin's art?" He scoffs at me and says he isn't an artist; he just plays with Legos, "What do you mean 'he plays with Legos'?"

"He tries to make life-size replicas of famous robots, but he never uses the right colors. If you thought C3PO was gay before, wait till you see him made of rainbow colored bricks." Lou drunkenly remember his joke and chortles, "Gay robot, he's gay, Justin's an asshole."

I'm scared to even ask but I do anyway, and inquire about the last guy on his list.

"What guy, Justin? He's an asshole."

With no options left, I agree but remind Lou he had another potential suspect.

"Yeah, Dick, look out for him." Frustrated, I ask if he's calling him a dick or if that's his name. He chuckles and says, "Both. Guy never leaves his room during the day, no one has any idea what he does and even though I haven't seen it, I believe it." Instead of explaining what it is he believes, Lou finishes the pitcher forcing me to ask what he hasn't seen. "Drink blood. The rumors are he drinks blood, blood like a vampire. Should probably start by throwing holy water at him."

Having more than enough notes in front of me, I part ways with Lou, making a mental note to never meet him at a bar again.

VI

"Welcome to Sheol, the boarding home of tomorrow's greatest artists." A week after accepting Lou's *pro bono* case, I'm sitting in front of three of the owners of this place, begging them to take my money. "We've gone over your application, and although the process is typically a much longer one, we feel you'll be a great fit here at Sheol." The one talking is Michele Halwaji, a pastry chef who won a nationally televised baking competition. She put most of her winnings into this house, and even turned down her own show on the Food Channel because it would have moved her away from here. It must be my Old World mentality, but I wouldn't have expected someone so altruistic to have gauged ears, a bull hoop nose piercing, and half her head shaved.

But that's the way it is with this group. They're all from different backgrounds, with varying interests and they still are able to come together to do something great for people that are going through the same struggles they did. I tell them it's my honor to be able to live here and that I won't let them down. "By the way," I ask, "What's the name 'Sheol' mean, anyway?"

Kris Randazzo, an Internet drumming sensation whose viral video of him drumming while strapped into the bucket of an excavator that turned him upside down, had gained him enough fame to begin performing trick gigs on the late night talk show circuit. He even had a DVD/CD combo of his greatest stunts. This guy played for the President of the USA with his drums linked as the controls for a fireworks show on the White House lawn on the Fourth of July, but he's casually joking with me, "It's the initials of our high school name rearranged, 'East OakLand High School'. We had to take liberties with the 'L'." He laughs in a way you can tell that he never takes life too seriously, like every laugh is genuine. While his laugh may have been genuine, his explanation was not. I had Kelly and Arnold do some research before coming to the house, and we'd learned that Sheol is basically an antiquated Hebrew word for Hell.

Unfortunately, I realize it was a mistake getting the musician involved in the conversation, because now he wants to hear me play. The lie I used to get in the house was that I'm a struggling jazz saxophonist. The truth is, I haven't played since before I was married, but that helps me sell the 'struggling' part. I was never that good, though, even at my best.

Grabbing my sax, I remind them that I'm here because I need the help. They laugh it off saying that no matter how bad I may be, they've heard worse. I play a verse and bridge of Earl Bostic's "Sweet Lorraine", and judging by their faces if I'm not the worst, I'm not that far off.

"Like we said, we've certainly heard worse, and Sheol is the perfect environment to let your creative juices flow," Jeanette Vazquez assures me. She's a *Time Magazine* and *National Geographic* published photographer, with a voice and face so soothing, it's impossible to imagine her ever lying.

She offers to show me to my room when Scott Nossen walks in. He's a standup comedian who gained his fame while opening on a national tour for a washed up comic from the Eighties. He was unanimously considered the star of the show despite the placement of his name on the marquee. He asks if I've paid yet, and I can't say that I'm surprised he's the one to ask.

I've never been the type to get star-struck, but I figured Jimmy Peck, my undercover alias would be, and honestly I had seen him perform live. Jersey pride dictated that I had to go see a local boy who'd made it big. He's a wiry Irish-looking Jew with a beard that matched his shoulder length hair. Most of his act was making fun of his Jewish upbringing. A Jewish comedian, yeah he wants to get paid.

I get up and shake his hand. "It's such an honor to meet you. Always wanted to see your show, but had to settle for watching it on the library computer." I congratulate myself for the well-constructed lie. He thanks me, and I tell him I've got the money. Reaching into my jeans pocket, I hand him a crumpled up wad of tens and fives.

Scott laughs and surmises I must be a musician. The others give a quick chuckle, but I overplay my role and belly laugh, even go so far as to slap my thigh. They all look at me like I've suddenly grown an extra nose, which is good. The less they know about the real me, the easier it'll be to blend in.

They dismiss me, and Jeanette shows me to my room. "Once you get settled in, I'll come back to introduce you to the other residents." She's so likable, even undercover it takes all my willpower not to ask her out. But as it stands she's currently a suspect, along with all the other owners and every resident in here.

She leaves and I begin to unpack my duffel bag, when I realize I can't remember the last time I wore jeans. The job calls for me to be dressed up while working, and when I'm off the clock, I'm the type of guy who like to wear as little clothes as possible. Since my wife and daughter died, and my relationship with Elizabeth ended poorly, I haven't felt like impressing anyone. Well, maybe the photographer I just met, but since that'll never happen I put it out of my mind.

My train of thought, though, was derailed by the nosy resident who walks into my room uninvited. He's about to go through my duffel when I turn from the drawer and catch him. Trying to remain calm, I ask what he's doing.

"I'm the real welcoming committee, and you're not allowed to bring any food into the house. So it's my job to confiscate whatever I find." As if I actually believed him, he resumes looking in my bag. It makes me glad I listened to Thaddeus and didn't pack my guns, which would have been too difficult to explain to whoever this clown is. Instead I let him riffle through. All he'll find are clothes and music paraphernalia. "You're not an artist, who are you? You here to solve the murders?"

Beyond shocked at the discovery, and so soon, I play dumb until I can get my bearings. "What? What murders? I thought the person in this room had her own gallery in New York now." Apparently, not the best course of action.

"What murders? Are you serious, bro? Bad act bro, bad act." He tells me everyone knows about the murders, and that only an undercover cop would pretend not to know. And he calls me 'bro' about six more times.

Caught, I concede to the truth, "You're right, I know about the murders. I just didn't think it'd be cool to talk about them." Some of the truth. I ask him what he meant about me not being an artist.

He closes my door, I guess for the sake of privacy, and explains that he heard me play. "No one that bad has been playing for long enough to have the passion to live here." I try showing him the picture of me from years ago with the sax when I was still on the force, but he ignores it and moves to his next piece of damning evidence. "Bro, you got no food, no drink, no smokes, and no drugs, bro. Something ain't right with you."

"Well because of the sax I don't smoke or do drugs. I'm in AA, so no booze for me." I have no explanation for the lack of food. I stammer for a moment too long.

"Chill bro, I'm only messing with you, unless you really are a narc or some shit. Then you need a warrant to go in my room, right, bro?" Now it's his turn to become nervous and sweat the possibilities.

But I don't leave him waiting long; doesn't look like his fragile mind could take too much of it. "I'm no narc, man, and I got no idea if they need a warrant or anything else to search your shit." Try as I might, I'm not comfortable speaking in the vernacular of a poor artist.

I think he can hear the struggle in my voice, because he gives me an awkward look as he finally introduces himself. "A'ight bro, if you say so. Name's Jamil Nazy, but my tag name is Jamz. If you decide you need some herbal relaxation, I'm in 3B, but my shit ain't free." He walks out without giving me a chance to introduce myself, which is fine by me.

After I finish unpacking my duffel bag, I lock my door to unpack my other bag. The leather drawstring pouch I've kept hidden in the front of my pants is filled with goodies from Thaddeus. While he convinced me not to bring my guns, he wasn't about to let me come here defenseless.

The important thing to know about Thaddeus is that, despite his title of paranormal detective and past life as a police officer, he's not that good of an investigator. And secondly, he's able to do what he does because of the plethora of paranormal and supernatural tools and tricks he's gathered over the years. I, on the other hand, was made detective at the age of 22 with the Newark Police Department for good reason.

Thaddeus filled the pouch with various items to help me on this case, and spent an excruciating amount of time explaining what each one does and how to use them. Not that I'm not thankful, but when he's teaching someone anything, he feels the need to talk down, as if him possessing this knowledge puts everyone else beneath him, which I'm sure is exactly how he sees it.

VII

Although we've run into each other a few times, it's not until a week after I move in that Lou and I can talk in private. During the intermittent time, I'd had the chance to meet most everyone else in the house, including two more owners: Melanie Lewis, a seamstress whose work was featured on *America Thinks You Can Dance*, and, most notably, she'd made Jennifer Lopez's tenth wedding dress. The last of the owners is Pete Hernandez, a horror author, whose breakout young adult novel, *"The Legend of the Summer Thief,"* was optioned for a movie starring Benicio Del Toro as the 'Summer Thief'.

They were as amiable as the others, but Melanie stares at my clothing for an uncomfortable amount of time, causing me to wonder whether I should have purchased ragged clothes from a thrift shop. It's been a week, and I'm still feeling like I don't fit in, which only hurts my cover.

Each of the owners, and Jeanette, had checked to see if I was getting used to my new surroundings. All three of them even asked if Jamil paid me a visit, none of them calling him Jamz. Knowing that they're aware of him does nothing to ease my suspicions. At this stage, he's my top suspect. His routine of going through everyone's bags might be a search for information on potential victims. Not to mention his drug dealing habits didn't help, but none of that is incriminating enough for me to move forward with him.

My biggest concern of this case, and I tell Lou as much when I finally get the chance, is that nothing about this case or anyone in the house reads as a supernatural phenomenon. He asks about the pattern he found, but I deflate that theory, "Most serial killers follow a time table. There's nothing otherworldly about a punctual killer."

Every time I begin to doubt the nature of the case, I remember Elizabeth assuring me of the truth. Although I've only been here a week, I should have been able to find the nature of the evil that Lou was 'covered in' when she made her connection with him. The only thing I've learned so far, though, is how bad I really am at the sax.

Lou asks me in quick succession if I've met each of his top five suspects. He's upset I haven't met the resident at the top of his list. "What do you mean you haven't met Dick, the blood drinker?" He becomes very animated in his displeasure of my progress and says he's glad he's not paying me.

His disrespect and lack of faith in me, combined with the stench of alcohol on his breath send me over the edge. I grab him by his shirt and slam him against a door. Whispering in his ear, I try to sound as menacing as possible, "That's right; you're not paying me, which means I'm doing this out of the kindness of my damned heart. So show some respect and let me do this my way, or I'm out the door and you might be the one to die in five months." Letting go, I ask him if he understands. He nods in response, saving me from a point blank nose full of his foul breath had he verbally answered. I look down at the floor as he stumbles out the room.

VIII

Once I realized that without payment, Lou was technically not a client, I stopped our regular visits, only occasionally asking for details I might have missed. That had been about a month ago, meaning I only had four months remaining to figure out what was going on before someone, possibly me, was scheduled to die.

Since moving into the house, I've fallen into a routine; mornings after breakfast are spent going over my notes on the case, reading and rereading everything in hopes of uncovering some as-of-yet undiscovered clue. Then around noon, I'll have lunch with someone from the agency, usually Carl or Elizabeth, sometimes both if their schedules allow. I'll bounce ideas off of them, unsuccessfully at this point. Then, after returning to the house, I practice my music with the door open so everyone can hear, justifying my presence in the home. Following a couple hours of what could pass as a tortured cat choking on a canary with lung cancer, I mingle among the residents.

When there isn't any pressing business, like the arrival of a new resident, or, I'd assume, the death of one of us, the owners never arrive in groups or even pairs. One will stop by once or twice a day to check on things, and I make it a point to spend as much time with them as possible, especially on the days Jeanette arrives.

Last week on more than one occasion I ran into the taxidermy artist, Shaunna, and I had to agree with Lou: she's weird. But after spending time with her, I've crossed her off my list of potential suspects. While she does play with dead animals for a living, the notion of death in the present, the actual *act* of dying, is repulsive to her. Besides, by all accounts and reports she's a recluse who hasn't left the house in the few years she's lived here, paying her rent with a rapidly dwindling trust fund.

The rumor mill is that Lou had expressed more than platonic feelings for her, but she had coldly rejected him. This could explain her ranking so high on his suspect list--well, that and her odd choice of 'art'.

Today, however, seems like a real break in terms of the case. As I'm doing my rounds, no one seems to be active at all, but just as I'm about to call it a night, I find the door to room 2D open for the first time. This is the room belonging to Dick, who not only tops Lou's list because he reportedly drinks blood, but who has also piqued my curiosity due to his prolonged absence.

Taking a cue from Jamil, I decide to let myself in unannounced and find him sitting at a laptop, typing away. I'm not exactly sure what I was expecting, but it surely wasn't an Asian man in glasses with the build of a young Bolo Yeung. Standing in the doorway, I feel a nice breeze flowing with the scent of lavender brushing past me. I clear my throat to announce my presence, and without looking away from the screen, he addresses me by name. "Detective Peckman. I was wondering when you'd pay me a visit."

Startled, I close the door behind me, and ask how he knows who I am. He laughs and repeats my name, "Detective James S. Peckman. Jimmy Peck? Wasn't too hard." Both of my names. He explains he's from Newark and saw me on the news a few times during my police days. "Seriously, if you're going undercover you'd think you can come up with a better name. Regardless, your secret's safe with me."

Admittedly my 'stage name' isn't very imaginative, but I

haven't been a detective for the police in years. Didn't think anyone would even remember me. Dick, however, thinks I'm still on the force, so I play along.

"It's good to see the cops finally getting involved, but this is bigger than you could imagine." I ask what he means, but instead he warns me. He says I should leave for my own safety. And just like that, this guy goes from the top of Lou's list to suspect number one on mine.

He returns to his laptop, dismissing me. "Now, if you'll excuse me, my review is tomorrow and I need to show sufficient progress if I want to keep living in this love nest."

I try to continue my side of the investigation, but he ignores me completely. I leave him be, for now, to consider the new information I have.

IX

The day after meeting Dick, I'm at his door trying to pry more information from him. Unsurprisingly, it's locked shut. Knocking on the door with more force than I normally would have, but short of actually banging, I speak to the wooden barricade. "I know you're in there, open up." I'm corrected by a voice from behind.

"Actually, he's not... I'm not in there." Dick is walking up the stairs with his keys in one hand and a polished metal flask in the other. He pauses, and motions with his keys for me to let him through.

I step aside and with confusion tell him I'd heard he never leaves his room, and my observations have confirmed that. Unlocking the door, he turns to me and asks if that's all I've heard or observed. Drinking from the flask, he closes his eyes as he lowers it from his face, clearly enjoying the liquid effects. Then I see it, a dark blotch of red smeared on his lips and teeth. He licks it clean like a milk mustache and smiles.

"They say a lot about you, actually, but I'd rather learn firsthand what's true and what's conjecture." He smiles again, appreciatively, so I ask if I can learn more.

He shakes his head as he enters his room, and calls me a detective in such a demeaning manner, I'm tempted to take him down right here. "This isn't your case. In a few months, there's going to be another murder. For your safety, I recommend you leave now."

Sick of his scare tactics, I withdraw a pencil from my pocket and force him back into his room. "This is the second time you've threatened me, Dick. That's not smart; you know who I am, but you don't know what I'm capable of."

Dick agrees and shoves me across the room with ease, "I may not know what you think you're capable of, but I know you're out of your league." Pointing at the door, he tells me to leave.

For whatever reason, this time when he said it, it sounded more like a plead than a threat. Ready to take advantage of this reprieve, I point the pencil at him and utter the spell Thaddeus drilled into my head: "*Raio*," Portuguese for lightning, and as promised a bolt shoots from the tip, hitting Dick in the shoulder.

The blood-drinker falls to a knee, but doesn't seem as injured as I'd expect. Nor is he as mad as he should be, "Holy shit! You can shoot electricity. Okay, time out, James," he begs, holding his one good arm.

"There's no time outs you child, once I kill you, this will all be over." I remark that he's the oddest vampire I've run into, as I press the pencil to his chest.

"You kill me, and this won't end. That's not a threat, and I'm not a vampire." This gets my attention like he was hoping, so I ease up on the lightning wand disguised as a pencil. He reiterates that he's not a vampire and even points out some garlic cloves on his desk. "I always have the stuff on hand, because of the confusion." He explains that's why he needs to let his room air out occasionally, aided with the scent of lavender. "Yes, I drink blood, but my flask is filled with elk's blood."

Dick goes on to say that drinking blood from any animal heals him and temporarily gives him a strength boost. This explains how he threw me across the room so easily. I allow him to drink from the flask and watch as the hole and burn marks on his shoulder heal themselves.

I step back to allow him to get to his feet and finish his story. "As crazy as this sounds, you have to believe me. Fifteen years ago I was kidnapped by a cult planning to sacrifice me to some god of prophecy. The members of this cult are called The Privileged and they worship this whole race of alien gods. Some of them are regular humans who fell into the life, others are like these half-demon aliens that switch between their forms. Most of those demon Privileged have abilities that are used to aid in the rituals. The human Privileged are usually granted enhanced strength and speed. They wanted to kill me for Tamrrof. They started the blood ritual, which is how I got like this, but they were stopped by an old man, who went on to train me."

His tale was beginning to sound like a waste of time, until he mentioned the old man. "Would this trainer happen to be George Gidious?" Confused, Dicks nods his head yes. Aloud, I ask myself why the Old Man never told me about alien gods before.

The Old Man is a psychometrist, like Elizabeth. In fact, he's the one who suggested I recruit her. He said we could help each other and that he was retiring from active hunting. In his many, many years of experience, George has learned to control his abilities, allowing him to work cases more easily than Elizabeth, but he believes, with us, she can learn that type of control.

Knowing that Dick worked with the Old Man gives me all the reason I need to trust him, and apparently vice versa because he shows me his closet. "Because of the ritual, I can sniff out a Privileged like a hunting dog with a cold. I can narrow down the location, but can't seem to pick them from a crowd."

The back wall of his closet is filled with notes on each resident and owner, including myself. They all have yarn strings leading to clues and notes, except my picture. "So what, Dick, I don't warrant my own investigation?"

He laughs. "Please, you've only been here two months, and I knew you were a cop. And the name's Richard."

"Wait, you give me shit for my undercover name, when yours is Dick?"

Laughing again, he offers me a drink. "Don't worry, not of blood. Besides, I've never been in the news." We sit to compare notes.

Even though I now trust Richard, I still feel possessive of the case, so I have him tell me everything he knows, starting with the Privileged. "There are Privileged for each of the different gods, the Brood as they're called, and each Privileged bears the mark of their patron god."

I have limited experience with a Privileged from a case over a year ago, but was never able to learn more about them. It's shocking, and more than a little upsetting, to know there's someone else out there with more knowledge on them.

From his desk, Richard produces a sketchbook that he's filled with several dozen markings and the gods they represent. "This is the one I was to be sacrificed to." He points to a symbol that resembles two upside down crosses forming an 'X'. "Those are swords, and are the symbol of Tamrrof, their goddess of battle. Her return was to be the spark returning the rest of the Brood."

Hearing all Richard knows about this Brood and their Privileged, I can't help but get upset with the Old Man for not telling me about them. I instead choose to focus on the tangibles before me. "So, if there's a Privileged at play here, then whoever it is will have one of these marks you're showing me?"

He clarifies that it may be for a Brood he's yet to encounter, but agrees with the principle. "They will have some mark somewhere on their body. The problem is, they're almost always covered, and I have no real way of seeing the people here in the nude."

He tells me that he's eliminated Aaron as a suspect. "He was almost kicked out of the house for walking around naked. Not the prettiest of sights, but he's got no markings on him." I let him know, barring any unexpected shenanigans, we could discount Lou since he'd brought me into the mix. Still being cagey, I withhold Elizabeth's role in making me take the case, and her abilities in general.

"Is there no way for you to pinpoint the Privileged if we get you one on one with them?" I ask, grasping at straws.

Richard answers in measured tones, letting me know these are the same frustrations he's been experiencing since moving in. "Normally, I could pick them out of a crowd, but there's something else going on here. I'm confident that whoever the Privileged is, they're a human one. A demon would have a signature different from the rest. Unfortunately, I can't even safely remove suspects from the list without a strip search." He also expresses concern over checking Jamil, since he seems to be covered in tattoos, and a close inspection would be needed.

Not wanting to dance around the question, I forget about Jamil and ask if we could eliminate Riva, the painter, as a suspect. "I understand she's in a wheelchair, but should that really excuse her?"

We spend the next hour discussing Riva's spina bifida, and the likelihood of it not being as severe a case as she claims. We move on to everyone else in our suspect pool, and after another hour end up with twelve swimmers in that pool: the remaining residents, excluding Lou and Aaron, and the six owners. Dividing up the list, Richard and I each take our top suspects and work on them.

He settles on Mark, the chameleon of the group, as the top of his list. Mark seems too eager to blend in, constantly changing his art. I target Jamil, for his habit of encroaching himself on all new arrivals, and the fact he's a drug dealer, albeit less than petty with a dwindling clientele. It's too big a coincidence that most of the deaths are covered up as drug-related murders.

X

Like any good drug dealer, Jamil is invasive when it comes to his customers' lives, as well as any potential customers, while remaining evasive about his own. All attempts at friendship have been met with different sales pitches. I've so far spent close to a week trying to crack his defenses, but have constantly been met with rejection.

In that week, I've barely seen him practice his art of graffiti, and even asked how he plans on parlaying that into a career. He told me not to worry about it, but that the owners understood his potential.

"How do you ever get anything done? You practically put yourself in a drug induced coma every night around eight."

As defensive as he always is, I've never seen him react so suspiciously. "Easy with all the questions, bro. I'm still not sure you ain't a narc, bro, and you really startin' to sound like one. As for that coma you was talking about bro, I need that to block out all the fools in this house. Especially you and that crappy sax."

I've gone as far with him as I could tonight, so I leave his room. About to close the door, I'm struck with inspiration and leave it wide open, hoping he won't bother himself to get off the bed.

I check my watch and assured I still have time, I go to Richard and explain my plan. "I'm going to need you to be my lookout."

At seven thirty, well before the house has to go silent, I start playing my sax as loud and horribly as I can with my door open. Justin, Shaunna, Mark, and even Kris, the drumming owner, check on me wondering why I've regressed, but I play through their distraction.

At a quarter to eight, Jamil yells out of his room, "Shut the fuck up!" and slams his door closed. I continue to play loudly, but actually try to hit the right notes now. After another fifteen minutes, I've worked myself into a groove that I almost wish didn't have to end, but it's time for the next part of my plan.

With Richard as my look out, I pour several drops of a liquid from a medicine dropper into the key hole of Jamil's door. The liquid, one of Thaddeus' favorite tools, expands into a semi-hard foam that triggers the lock, allowing me to open the door. In roughly twenty minutes, the foam will dissolve and evaporate, leaving no traces behind. As expected, Jamil has taken some drug, or combination of drugs, to render himself unconscious for the night.

Having no fear of waking him, I turn on the lights and begin exploring the room for any clues he's a Privileged. Richard abandons his post and enters, closing the door behind him. "Keep searching the room; I'll check his tattoos."

Jamil is sleeping shirtless, so Richard can safely and easily inspect and deduce he doesn't have any Brood symbols on his upper body. "Jimmy, I need you to take his shorts off."

"Why do I have to? You're the one checking him."

"And that's why I shouldn't have to take his pants off also," he whisper-shouts back. "If I have to look, you're going to be the one to touch him."

As much as I want to argue back, he has a valid point. And the longer we discuss it, the greater chance we may be discovered. "Fine," I begrudgingly whisper back. This better be worth it, and I tell Richard as much.

Unfortunately, it's not. I pull down Jamil's shorts and learn that he wasn't wearing any underwear. Richard turns him over twice, but is unable to find any markings related to a Brood god. "It's pretty much all Asian-inspired work. I'll never understand the American appeal of getting words in Chinese tattooed on you. That's like if I got a tattoo that says, 'Pride' in English." We share a laugh, and leave Jamil asleep, naked, and turn out the lights.

XI

Two days later and Richard barges into my room, interrupting my practice. I welcome the disruption, as my mind was more focused on my next target on the suspect list, Stephanie. To date, I've had very little interaction with her, only knowing she's a practicing Wiccan and makes papier-mâché art.

Thus far, I've been unable to make any progress on my investigation of her, so when Richard enters, I'm more than willing to listen. He tells me Mark isn't a Privileged. "He was playing volleyball in the backyard, and wasn't wearing a shirt. Shaunna just so happened to pass by my door so I gave her a fifty to pants him the next time he went for the ball. She was pretty eager, and I'm thinking I probably didn't need to pay her." Apparently, Mark is comfortable with nudity, because Richard says he just stood there with his shorts around his ankles, giving him more than ample time to verify with binoculars that he had no Brood markings. "God, I just realize how creepy that sounds. When this is over, you cannot tell anyone about that." We share a laugh, which seems to be happening less and less frequently.

Before joining up with Richard, I had fourteen suspects, including him. Now after little more than a week, I'm down to ten. That's more progress than the unproductive months prior, but we're less than a month away from someone else dying.

On the high on making his own progress, Richard wants to focus on the topic I'd rather not get into, "Any news on Stephanie?" I let him know there isn't, to which he nods, understandably. "Yeah, her being a Wiccan is going to make this tough for you. She's not unapproachable, she's actually very nice, but also extremely secretive. That's why I didn't want her."

He's wrong about her being a Wiccan being the problem. In college I had dated a Wiccan, at least I think we dated. Whatever we were, there was plenty of sex involved. Her friends, all of whom also practicing Wiccans, were some of the nicest people I ever met. "It's got nothing to do with her beliefs, really. It's her constant isolation, and the fact she's rarely at the house that raised flags for me. As often as she leaves, there's a good chance Stephanie was unaccounted for during some of the previous murders."

Clearly not understanding Wicca as a religion and belief system, Richard takes my word for it. "Well, you should talk with Shaunna. She's into a lot of that hippie shit, and actually used to leave with Stephanie a lot. She would be able to tell you at least something about Stephanie's habits."

Knowing it's as good a plan as any, I decide I'll follow

through in a couple days. "I don't want her getting suspicious with the odd requests back to back."

XII

Taking a cue from Richard, last night I challenged Justin. Had I been 20 years younger, this would have been a dare. In any case, for fifty dollars he accepted to streak a few laps around the dining room during breakfast. Now, eating with Aaron, I'm beginning to grow nervous, because meal time is almost over, and there's no sign of Justin. Four people have already finished, he must have lost his nerve, despite appearing to be eager last night.

As I'm about to finish my western omelet, in comes Justin, running stark naked, while holding a boombox playing Blink 182's "What's my Age Again?". As the chorus kicks in, he begins yelling along, in what must be his poor attempt at singing.

Running several laps around the room as promised, I stare intently hoping to catch a glimpse of a Brood symbol. The others either cheer on in encouragement or look away in horror. Clearly visible is a tattoo of the state of New Jersey made of Lego bricks. Admittedly, I can't remember all the markings in Richard's book, but I'm positive that New Jersey wasn't one of them.

Having completed his rounds, Justin bows to his audience, then to either side, and in an act that could be interpreted as an open deceleration of war in some countries, he bows away from us, granting us an unobstructed view of his bent over ass. Even those who were cheering him moments ago were now booing him.

Thankfully he leaves without much more fanfare, only acknowledging those who cheered the loudest; Aaron, Lou and Shaunna. With the entertainment over, Shaunna exits the dining hall from the opposite end Justin used, and it reminds me of her schedule.

In his room as always, Richard is surprised to see me so early in the day. "Hey Richard, I tried being professional about this, even clinical, but I'm sick of seeing random guys' packages. Not to sound too creepy, I'm going to accidentally walk in on Shaunna in the shower." I even put air-quotes around accidentally.

Richard laughs while shaking his head, "No, that doesn't sound too creepy," he pauses to let me think he actually believes that, before "That is creepy as all hell. Go get your rocks off, you creepster."

I stutter trying to defend myself, before blurting out, "It's not like that. I'm not like that."

He continues to laugh even louder now, and draw's Aaron's attention, who looks confused at the sight of anyone talking to Richard. He whispers, "I'm just messing with you Jimmy." He tells me to go get her, with a pat on my back.

After a few minutes of friendly ribbing with Richard, I decide to wait a little longer, partially to allow Shaunna time to get ready for her shower, but mostly to allow myself to build up the courage to follow through with this spectacularly creepy plan. I'm finally ready to go when Richard pulls me close, and continues to whisper, "At least she's got the best body in the house." I'm not sure if that was meant to be encouraging or not, but it made each step I took more and more confusing.

With much struggle and internal debating, I finally get to the bathroom door. I lean in close and listen as I hear the shower come to life. Assuming, she's going to allow the water to heat up, I wait before using a few drops of the same liquid I used to get into Jamil's room. Ready to enter, I open the door with ease, and take a cautious step in, when Shaunna says hello from the stairs behind me.

Worried I'm caught, I return the greeting and rush into the bathroom, closing the door. Nervous that someone saw me sneaking into to see... Then the realization hits me and her name escapes my lips before I can stop myself, "Shaunna?"

"What the hell!?" Riva naked and standing yells at me, and rightfully so. "Get the hell out, Jimmy, I locked the door for a reason!" She's covering her front despite her back facing me.

That's when I see it, a small spiral symbol on her spine. It looks exactly like one of the Brood symbols Richard showed me in his notebook. Despite the mixup and awkward moment, I slip out of the bathroom, embarrassed but also satisfied I've got the murderer figured out.

XIII

"Yeah, that's the mark she's got on her back." I explain while pointing at a page in the book Richard filled with details about the Brood. "Riva must be the Privileged behind all this." Richard and Elizabeth agree that her pretending to be a cripple is the perfect cover, but still, neither of them are compelled to condemn her yet.

Even I have to agree that the evidence isn't enough to act on.

At a diner table several miles from Sheol, the three of us sift through all the facts we have, when Richard asks, "Are you sure it was this exact pattern? With the spiral going clockwise within the three quarter circle." I tell him that although I didn't have time to study and compare notes, this was it. "James, this is the symbol for Phrypeco, the god of fate. He's like the magic monkey's paw of the Brood. He fulfills predictions but always with a twist, and always for the worse. Thing is, I've never encountered one of his Privileged; only know about him through Gidious."

Offering her unique insight, Elizabeth says it makes sense. "He's granting one person's wish, then Riva kills someone else for it."

"Well, we've only got three days left before Riva kills someone else. Elizabeth, head back to the office and get in touch with the Old Man, I'm sure he knows more about this Phrypeco. Richard and I will head back to the house to see if we can figure out who her next target is. Despite the fact, or maybe because she knows Richard trained with the Old Man, Elizabeth doesn't shake his hand with her bare skin, refusing to take off her glove. I wonder what she would have seen if she had, but I wouldn't ask her to. She doesn't need the added pain, especially if she's going to deal with the Old Man.

Richard and I get back to the house with an unexpected welcoming party for us, more precisely me. Pete and Jeanette are standing in the foyer. He's leaning against the rainbow C-3PO statue; she's a step behind him looking sullen. "Hello Richard. Jimmy, can you come with Jeanette and me? We need to speak to you."

Laughing as he walks past the two owners, Richard makes a comment about being sent to the principal's office. "Check for his hall pass."

In the room where I first met Jeanette and most of the other owners of the house, the atmosphere is infinitely different. Thankfully Jeanette is the one to start the conversation. "Jimmy, while we're happy that you seem to be able to pull Dick out of his isolation, we have some concerns about some recent activities in the house."

Realizing what this is about, I try to get ahead of the conversation and downplay what's going on, hoping they don't ask too many questions. "If this is about the bet with Justin, I really didn't think he'd do it, but I promise I'm done with that. It was a childish attempt to get some laughs." Having to explain the prank makes me feel even more childish, not at all like the adult I thought I was before starting this case.

Pete is apparently in no joking mood, as he's quick to answer, "If it were as simple as that, Mr. Peck. Mere minutes after the streaking incident, Riva reports you walked in on her about to enter the shower, seeing her in the nude. And although we can't prove you had anything to do with this, I'm inclined to believe you were behind Jamil's complaint of waking up naked."

"Oh come on, that guy is blitzed out of his mind twenty four, seven, Pete. You actually believe that someone snuck into his room, stripped him, and left without taking anything? Or is it more likely that he got shitfaced and did God knows what to himself?" I argue that I don't want to see anyone in the house naked.

Jeanette questions, "No one?" and winks at me. Sitting slightly behind Pete, he's oblivious to her gesture. "Well Jimmy, there's been a lot of coincidences, and we're going to have to keep an eye on you. I'll personally check on you every day."

Catching on to her flirtations, Pete adds, "Because of what happened with Riva, you're now placed on probation. One more incident of this nature, and you'll be evicted from Sheol."

I choose to ignore the threat, if that's even what it was, and take the opportunity to dig for more information. "Speaking of Riva, when I accidentally walked in on her," I stare at Pete when I stress the word 'accidentally', "when the door was unlocked, she was standing." I leave the obvious question in the air hoping one of them would answer without forcing me to ask.

No longer flirting, Jeanette defends Riva, "Of course she can stand, Jimmy, she's not paralyzed. Her spina bifida is painful, that doesn't mean she's a paraplegic." The rest of the conversation doesn't go well for me. I learn more than I ever thought I would about spinal conditions, and leave fifteen minutes later with my head hung low.

XIV

Today is six months exactly from when Anthony made it famous as a radio personality on a nationwide broadcast morning talk show. Today is the day someone from the house is to die as penance for that success. Today is the last day I have to stop an ancient alien god. Today is not looking too good.

"Okay, here's where we stand, Lou. I'm working with Richard on this as you know, and we know who is behind it all, but we don't know who the target is yet." I warn him not to leave the house, and that Richard is convincing Aaron to skip work.

"I've got the other agents from my firm tracking anyone who might leave to ensure their safety. Dick is going to try and lure our suspect out by running errands, basically keeping himself out of the house all day."

Lou interrupts asking who we think it is, but I tell him it's best if he doesn't know. "I'm going to follow them if and when they leave Sheol. We'll put an end to this today, and it'll be because you saw the pattern."

I send him away and suggest he stay with other people whenever he's not in his room. "My monthly review is today, but other than that, all I had planned was playing volleyball with some of the other guys."

Before heading out for the day, Richard recommends I track Riva down so he's not caught by surprise. I go to her room with the pretense of apologizing, again, but she's already gone.

Walking away from her room concerned I'm already too late, Kris stops me and asks what I was doing at her room when she wasn't there. "No, it's not like that. I just feel so crappy about what happened I wanted to apologize again."

Clearly not convinced, he shakes his head, "Uh-huh, well maybe it's best if you gave her some space. You know, let this whole thing die down first." More concerned how I could find her now that she's already left, I absentmindedly nod. "How's the sax coming along? Your review is coming up soon."

I tell him I'm getting much better and have been writing my own music, which is true. "I'm not sure what it is, but it all just began to click a couple days ago." I appreciate the one on one time with my mentor, but I really need to warn Richard about Riva.

Kris doesn't make it easy. Once he starts talking about music there's almost no stopping him. "Yeah man, I hear you. Once you get in that groove, there's no telling where the music can take you, almost like it's spiritual. Call it a hunch, but I think you're going to be the next star of house Sheol.

Thankfully, Scott interrupts, wearing as serious a face as I've ever seen on a comedian, and says it's time. Not sure where they're headed, but I assume it's for Lou's review. In any case, I can now let Richard know Riva's already left and he needs to be extra careful.

After warning Richard, I figure my best course of action is to find out if anyone knows where Riva might have gone. I quickly discover there's no inconspicuous way for the man who just walked in on her naked to ask about her whereabouts. I contemplate switching roles with Richard, since he should have better luck on this part of the investigation, when I get a call from Sid saying he's following Stephanie, who just left. Elizabeth and Carl are each following Shaunna and Justin respectively. I would have preferred to have Thaddeus' help, but he got a paying job that took him to Florida late last night.

None of the team saw Riva leave, so there's no telling when she left. I have no idea what my next move is supposed to be and feel completely helpless knowing if I don't get control of the situation, someone is going to die. What I do during this type of crisis probably confuses most people, but I pray. I'm always asked how I can believe in God with all the things I've seen, even now knowing there are alien gods out there, but my answer is always the same: it's because of shit that I've seen that I know there's something better out there.

Holding my rosary in one hand, I begin the Lord's Prayer, the comfort and familiarity of which leads me to what I really want to pray for at the moment. "I know you may not approve of some of the things I do, Lord, but I do them for the good of your flock, so please heed my prayer now. Help us stop this before Riva can kill anyone else."

It's a short prayer, sweet and to the point, but if he were able to listen, the message is clear. This ends today with no more innocent deaths. Although I still don't have a plan, I feel better about the situation.

Then God reveals his humorous side. Jeanette comes into my room crying hard. Judging by her red eyes, she has been for a while. "She's dead. I can't believe this keeps happening." She hugs me and lets her tears soak into my shirt.

Two things go through my head; I have to tell the others that Riva already got to someone, and find out whom. Jeanette said 'she', so it's either Shaunna or Stephanie as far as the residents go. Lou told me that one of the original owners had died, so even they aren't untouchable, so expanding to them, Michele or Melanie could also have been the target.

Unfortunately, with Jeanette here in my room, literally in my arms, I can't call the others. At least with her here with me, I know she's safe and I should be able to get more information on who Riva's killed. Before I can ask any questions, though, Jeanette pulls her head away from my shoulder and looks intently in my eyes. She tells me she's sick of all the death and doesn't want to think about it any more. "Can you keep me distracted, Jimmy?"

Without thinking, I hold her tighter, and kiss her in lieu of a verbal response. We remain standing and enjoy the taste of each other. Finally, the passion I've been suppressing for months has been validated. I lift her, letting her wrap her legs around me, and carry her to my bed.

Using our momentum, Jeanette turns us so we land with her on top. I help her remove her shirt and try not to linger on her beautifully cradled breasts. Despite my best efforts I can't help but think for the briefest of moments of the last time Elizabeth and I had sex, and how long ago it was.

Before she can notice my mental infidelity, I'm brought back into the melting world of ecstasy that Jeanette has created. Bypassing her bra, together we remove her gray slacks. About to be awarded for my months of patience, my heart and libido are crushed when I see what her clothes were hiding. At the highest peak of her inner thigh, partially covered by the lace cloth of her panties, the mark of the twin Brood gods. I can't recall their names, but the symbol stands out because it reminds me of that eye from Lord of the Rings.

Knowing what I just learned about Jeanette doesn't make it any easier to stop myself, and even more difficult to stop her. The most obvious part of me protested every attempt of getting off the bed. I finally succeed in getting to my feet and mutter some excuse involving my stomach and the bathroom. She remains on my bed, exposed and confused. I try to convince myself it's a tattoo from her geek days, but she doesn't have any. I even tell myself that whoever it was is already dead, and I'll have at least six months to put an end to it; no need to stop now, but I couldn't live with myself if I did that. Rushing from my computer desk towards the door, I don't make eye contact as I speak, "Sorry Jeanette, you're like my boss." I close the door before she has a chance to reply.

Not aware of when I started running, I'm just glad my phone

was in my pocket. I wouldn't have the courage to go back to retrieve it. First, I call Richard and tell him about Jeanette and that someone is already dead, a female. Then I get Elizabeth on the line, "There's a new player involved, and the victim was a female. They already got to her." I leave out how I discovered the truth about Jeanette.

I check with the team and everyone confirms their tails are still alive and well. Although this could mean Michele or Melanie could be dead, I'm left with a gut feeling that Riva was somehow the victim. "Sid, I want you to use any connections you have with the police force, alive or dead, and find out all you can about the murder. Remember it could have been covered up as an accident or something medical."

As soon as I get off the phone with Sid, I literally run into Pete Hernandez. I apologize and tell him I heard something bad had happened, but don't really know the details. Instead of offering to fill in the blanks, he is angry with Jeanette. "She shouldn't have told you. This is an active police investigation, and I'm sure they want to keep a lid on this. We've gone through this before, and I know how they think."

I thank him and continue on my way. The thing is, I also know how the police think, and his concerns are misplaced. My biggest concern however, is how he knew it was Jeanette that told me. I send a text to my comrades that there may be more involved than we anticipated.

XV

"Okay everyone, we've got to keep this quick. Sid is still following up with the police, trying to discover who the victim is. All signs point to Riva being the target, no longer a perp. We've got new evidence point to at least one of the owners. According to Richard, we're dealing with Privileged for the twin Brood gods Umosa and Umaso." I pause to go over the plan in my head one more time before verbalizing it and assigning tasks to everyone in Carl's minivan. "Elizabeth, I want you to return to the Old Man and find out what you can about these two. Carl, help Richard discreetly evacuate the residents from the house."

I retrieve my knife and guns from the bag Carl brought me. Petting Stacy, my Glock 9mm, while holstering my unnamed Magnum, I let the others know my intentions of putting an end to this by whatever means necessary.

Also in the bag is a revolver I hand to Richard, hoping he knows how to handle it, and four long range walkie-talkies that I distribute to everyone. "Turn to channel 7, but keep the talk to a minimum."

Elizabeth exits the van and takes her car to pay the old man another visit. Carl also steps out, waiting for Richard, whom I hold back for a quick conversation about something I didn't want to bring up in front of the others, particularly Elizabeth. "So you know how I found out about Jeanette; is there any precedent of an owner having an intimate relationship with a student?"

"Every once in a while Shauna is linked to one of them. I'm pretty sure she's been rumored to have been with each of the guys, even Melanie for a time, but I know most of it is bullshit." I ask if there's anyone else, but he shakes his head no. Changing his demeanor, Richard looks excited to have more to contribute. "Actually, yes. Anthony, the one that died, was seeing a resident when he died. She moved out after that."

"Damn, that's what I was afraid of." I don't waste any more time explaining my theory, but I tell him that I think Jeanette may be innocent. Truth is, I hope she is, but I can't let that get in the way of what needs to be done.

Richard joins Carl on the sidewalk and they immediately head to the house. Because today is one of the two review days of the month, all the owners will be present, and we can hopefully put a stop to this today.

I give the two a ten minute head start that I spend checking and loading my guns. Once I'm ready, I enter the house through the back door, hoping Jeanette's the first owner I see. Instead I find Kris Randazzo in the kitchen and think of a way to get him alone.

"Hey Kris, I know my review isn't up yet, but I was hoping you could give the bridge I'm working on a listen." Of course he agrees, and I lead him to my room. As soon as he enters, I close and lock the door behind me, holding out Stacy.

He sees the gun in my hand, and either he's genuinely afraid, or Kris is as good an actor as he is a drummer. "Take your shirt off." He refuses quietly, so I rip open the short sleeve button up and find the eye symbol on his chest.

When he realizes that I recognize the symbol, he goes from scared to angry. "I knew Jeanette chose wrong. You were going to be the next star at her behest, now you're just going to be another sacrifice to Umosa and Umaso."

Finally putting it all together, I elaborate for Kris. "So you six take turns picking success stories, and the sacrifice that follows six months later. Is that the cost you pay for your own fame?"

He seems hurt by the accusation, "We are each *bona fide* success stories based on our own natural skills. It was later that our gods chose us. They thrive off the pain and misery of dashed dreams and unfettered joy of dreams achieved. And I hope you understand I'm only telling you this because now you're going to die, because I know you won't alarm the others by shooting me." Finishing his statement, he bounds towards me, ricocheting off the ceiling and taking an awkward angle that's hard to keep a bead on.

Instead of shooting him, I draw my knife from its ankle strap. He lands behind me, and easily tosses me the length of the room, sending me crashing into a cabinet. Kris jumps again bouncing off the wall to my right, but instead of landing, he plants both feet into my chest, kicking me back into the cabinet. It breaks under the pressure.

Picking me off the floor, he once again tosses me across the room into my locked door. He follows in the air, taking another detour off the ceiling, but he comes down to me straight on. Before he can attack, I move left, letting him pass me, and slide my knife along his neck. Kris reacts before he can even feel the pain, knocking the knife out of my hand.

He turns to face me, and a red line appears below his chin before he collapses on the ground. Somehow still alive, I'm not sure if it's because of some gift a Privileged has, or he simply hasn't bled out yet. Taking no chances and weaponless, I take one of the drum sticks he always has on him and stab it into the second smile on his neck and pry it open like a crowbar. Blood splatters out of the now gaping wound, and I wonder if I'll have to kill all of them.

XVI

After cleaning off as much of the blood as I can in the brief amount of time I allow myself before resuming the hunt. Moving from room to room on my floor, I find that Richard and Carl have mostly cleared everyone out except Jamil, who's passed out on his couch. Probably coming to the same conclusion as Richard, I figure he's about as safe as anyone in his intoxicated state.

Finished with the two resident floors, I return to the main floor. Before I continue my search, I try to check in with the others to see how they're doing with their tasks. That's when I realize my walkie-talkie and cellphone were broken in the fight with Kris.

Absentmindedly, I walk into the dining room, which doubles as the review room. Michele Halwaji is standing behind a table with some crazy animal amalgams, and I realize she's waiting for Shaunna. Because there are still four other people I have to deal with, I don't bother with the guns yet. "Hey Michele." Briefly startled, she recovers and mentions that she didn't think my review was today. "It's not, just on my way to the kitchen. Isn't it weird how in a house filled with people, you can sometimes feel so alone?"

I ask if she minds if I sit.

"Sure, but Kris and I have a review; besides, I thought you were headed to the kitchen."

Knowing I still have the element of surprise in the sense she's unaware Kris won't be joining her, I sit next to her. "You won't be seeing Kris again, and if you leave this house and return to your own kitchen, you'll never have to see me again, either."

Through the gauged hole in her left ear, I can see the mark of Umosa and Umaso, cleverly hidden in some hieroglyphic tattoos on her neck and behind her ear. "I don't know what's up with the odd threat, but..."

"Yes you do, Privileged. And I know why the twin Brood gods are demanding sacrifices, but what I don't understand is why the seven of you would trade in your fame to serve them." Under the table I draw my knife, hoping she won't notice.

She doesn't react the way I was expecting; in fact, she doesn't react at all. "Hmm, so you know about us Privileged, the Brood and even my cousin, but you're wrong about one thing. Anthony refused the deal with Umosa and Umaso; that's why we had to kill him. What you don't understand is we didn't have a choice, it was either this..." Michele opens her arms wide to indicate the house, "...or the gods would kill each of us. Sure, I miss Anthony, but I wasn't going to die for him. And you know that's why you have to die now."

Not waiting for Michele to attack, I stab at her from under the table, but the high arch of the attack gives her enough time to get mostly out of the way. My knife imbeds itself in her shoulder. She falls back, with the knife still in, backhanding me twenty feet forward through Shaunna's display. She scrambles away. On the floor next to me is a starfish Shaunna built five piranha jaws into. I throw it like a shuriken and, surprisingly, it tears into the back of Michele's right calf, dropping her as she enters the kitchen.

Following the drumstick death of Kris, I think it'd be apropos to finish her off with one of her tools of trade. Dragging her over to the counter top mixer and tangling her hair in it, I turn it on, not sure if it'll work. Hearing her scream, my doubts fade away, and, unable to watch, I look away. Suddenly, a loud wet cracking sound echoes in the kitchen. Curiosity gets the better of me, and I see the machine has ripped off her scalp and it's now slopping around, sloshing something around. My stomach isn't strong enough to see this any longer. I retrieve my knife with my eyes closed.

XVII

Although I've killed monsters and humans before, I'm taken aback at the ease with which I've escalated the violence in a matter of minutes. The image of Michele's brain matter and blood getting tossed around by the same mixer that's made all sorts of pastries I've eaten, is enough to wretch my stomach near the point of vomiting. I hold it at bay, keeping my eyes closed until I exit the kitchen, when I see Melanie Lewis and Pete Hernandez standing by the wreck I caused.

The blood covering me paints a clear picture for the Privileged before me, and they attack without warning. I do the same and am able to draw Stacy and shoot Melanie in the center of her chest before she can ricochet off the ceiling. Unfortunately, that gives Pete enough time to close the distance between us, and he easily relieves me of both my gun and knife.

He tosses me around with the strength that I've come to expect from the Privileged. Learning that they don't go for the quick kill, I protect my head to prevent my brains from getting scrambled before I get a chance to think of a way out of this.

"You would have been the next big thing to come out of House Sheol. All you had to do, Jimmy, was keep your nose clean and out of our business. Now you're just another sacrifice." He finishes his sentence by tossing me into the display case of a former resident who used glass bottles in her art.

"Why can't there have been a marshmallow artist?"

Pete ignores what I consider quick wit and saunters over to

me, swaggering with assured victory.

"What none of you understand is that my success story isn't as a famous musician, it'll be for hunting and killing every last one of you monsters, Privileged or otherwise."

"Monsters?" The question stops Pete in his tracks. "We're humans just like you; we've just been blessed with a higher calling. Still, if you cut us, do we not bleed?" He takes his eyes off of me to point at Melanie for validation of his proclamation.

"Let's find out." I announce defiantly, and hurl a handful of glass shards at his face. Pressing the advantage, I charge him with a pencil from my pocket in hand. Jabbing it into his ear while holding his head still with my left hand, I force him to the ground. Removing my hand from his hand, for some reason I decide to wink as I say "*Raio.*" The bolt of lightning shoots through his skull, practically disintegrating his brain. "I guess, in this case, the pencil is stronger than the sword." Why am I talking to myself?

XVIII

The past hour has taxed me like no other, but my biggest concern right now is the fact that I can't contact Elizabeth or the others. I sit down to check my weapons, when I remember that there's a payphone in the foyer at the front of the house. Cautiously, I make my way, keeping an eye out for Scott Nossen, who I don't imagine will be in a joking mood. Jeanette has yet to resurface, and I'm left hoping the worst hasn't happened. It's possible Scott, or one of the other owners, has killed Jeanette like they did the seventh original owner.

Luckily, as I round the corner of the hallway, I find Jeanette in the foyer standing with Richard. "Jimmy, I've been trying to reach you. Carl and I were able to get everyone out safely. I came back to find you when I ran into Jeanette. Wasn't sure how you wanted me to handle her." He talks about her like she's not even there, and I feel disrespected for her.

Richard doesn't react to my current condition, but the same can't be said for Jeanette. "You're covered in blood, is it yours?" She asks the question, but she knows the answer. "So you know the truth now; that's why you ran out on me?"

I can't bear to answer, let alone look her in the eyes. With my head hung low, I reason with her, "Listen Jeanette, I know you want out of this life. That's why you were protecting me, why you had me lined up to be the next one out, but it's over. You don't have to be a part of this any more, you don't have to kill anyone again."

She doesn't smile, but I know there's hope in her words when she asks if I've killed the rest. I tell her only the comedian is left, and she knows where he'll be. "He likes to practice in the attic, something about the acoustics and isolation. I'm sure he's up there now."

The three of us begin our ascent, but Jeanette suggests Richard stay behind to make sure no one comes into the house.

"I'm not staying behind. Jimmy isn't in the best of condition after getting his ass handed to him by your friends. Besides, you heard Jimmy; there's no one left to worry about."

For some reason she's not satisfied with his reasoning, but she relents with a lack of counterargument. I don't like the bickering, so I make sure to keep my body between the two as we go up the stairs.

Unsure of how to get to the attic, I let Jeanette lead until she gets us to the door. I enter first with Richard directly behind me. Standing in front of us is Scott with a mic and speaker, posing in front of a lamp. The light casts him in a silhouette and awkward shadows cascade over the slanted ceiling of the attic. After everything that's transpired with the rest of his crew, I don't bother trying to sway him like Jeanette has.

With my gun already drawn, I'm about to fire when I hear a dull crack behind me, and Richard howling in pain. I turn to see Jeanette has snapped Richard's gun arm at the humerus. Still holding his arm, she steps forward and kicks me towards Scott.

"You ignorant pompous tool, you think me picking you for succession is some sort of weakness in my dedication to Umosa and Umaso, a falter in my love for them? I see now you were never worthy of their pleasures, only their pain." For good measure, Jeanette smashes Richard's head into a support beam. He coughs up blood before losing consciousness.

Scott's holding me up in a full nelson, with his hands weaved through my arms and clasped behind my head. With the slightest bit of pressure forward from his hands, he sends searing pain down my already injured neck and across my shoulders until I feel it in my arm pits. In an act of overkill, Jeanette drags Richard over and thrusts an open palm deep into my chest.

Air vacates my lungs like a folding accordion and fireworks burst in my eyes. Unable to move my upper body, I raise my knees to get as close to the fetal position as possible. Jeanette must have mistaken the movement as a threat or attack because she repeats her strike, sapping whatever strength my legs had.

Whatever air I had managed to regain was once again expelled along with a generous helping of my blood, some of which lands on Jeanette and Richard. Scott throws me into a wall and helps clean up Jeanette's face.

As they're distracted from me, whom they must now believe is out of commission, I make my way towards them. As quickly as I can, I wrap the cord to Scott's mic around his neck, and before he notices, jump on his back. He easily tosses me off with unnatural strength, but I hold onto the cord. About six feet away the wire goes taught, and his windpipe is crushed saving me from crashing into another wall.

He and I play a game of tug of war, which I'll lose if it goes on too long. Thankfully, Jeanette has other plans and she bum rushes me. The impact of her tackle added to the cord is enough to break Scott's neck.

Realizing what she's done, Jeanette rises, furious at me. As she rushes the now limp body of her cohort, I head over to Richard and pour him a mouthful of the liquid from his flask, hoping he'll be healed rather than drowned. With no plan left, I rush and dropkick Jeanette with both feet square in her back, sending her tumbling forward, tripping over Scott.

Her left leg breaks through the thin flooring of the attic, and I imagine the comical scene anyone would witness if they were on the floor below us. In her thrashing to free herself, Jeanette knocks over the lamp. Although the bulb breaking on the insulation didn't start a fire, like movies taught me it would, it did give me an idea.

I look over my shoulder to make sure Richard is recovering, and when that's confirmed, I take out the lightning pencil and fire a bolt of lightning at the wood and insulation next to Jeanette. This *does* start a fire, and I smile contently at the last remaining Privileged in the house, who's trying to escape even more frantically. The weight of my injuries finally takes my legs out from under me.

Catching me before I fall, Richard helps me down the attic stairs, and sure enough, we find Jeanette's leg kicking wildly. Afraid she may break free before the fire consumes her, I grab the appendage and pull down with whatever strength I have. Silently, Richard unsheathes my knife and stabs it into her thigh, leaving it there. Every time she tries to pull her leg free now, it forces the knife to cut further and further down her once sexy thigh.

As we continue our exit, with Richard's shoulder supporting me, I fire lightning at any object that looks to be particularly flammable. In the foyer again, I blast the phone, mostly out of frustration. Looking up at the general direction of where I last saw Jeanette, I say, "Burn, bitch."

XIX

I'm not entirely sure when I lost consciousness, but I wake up on the couch in my office at the sound of a commotion in the lobby. Before I check to see what's going on, I notice my wastebasket is filled with bloody bandages. Newly hanging on the wall behind my desk is my saxophone. The sight of these two things gives me pause to remember everything that happened over the past six months, and the amount of pain I'm still in. Judging by the number of bandages in the trash, I've been out for a couple of days.

I slowly stumble out of my room to find Elizabeth, Thaddeus, Sid, Carl and now Richard added to the mix, arguing. "If he's joining the agency, my name has to go up on the door. I deserve to be a partner." Sid says emphatically, while pointing at the entrance to the lobby.

Before anyone can counter, Carl notices me and rushes over to help. "Boss, you shouldn't be on your feet yet. You've lost a lot of blood."

The others aren't as motherly, not even Elizabeth; they alternatively congratulate me and ask if I'm OK. "Yeah, I'm fine, just a little loopy. How long was I out?" Richard confirms my earlier theory by saying three days. "Sounds about right. So, is what I heard true? You're joining our little band of ghost hunters?

"Elizabeth and Sid have extended an offer, but I can't." Seeing the look of disappointment on my face, he elaborates. "I've got more work with Gidious. The amount of Privileged in Sheol and the fact the house was literally built in praise to the Brood threw off my ability to detect them. Hopefully, with his training, I can refine that skill."

I can appreciate that, and tell him as much. "If you ever need help on a case, or need to escape the Old Man for a drink, don't hesitate to call."

Richard responds in kind, then adds, "Also, I've given Carl a copy of all my notes on the Brood and Privileged. We're going to exchange updates on a monthly basis. Way I see it, the more people who know about them and how to stop the sons of bitches, the better for all of us."

We shake hands, say our thanks and goodbyes; he does the same with everyone else, and is about to leave when I stop him. "What about Riva? Was she ever a Privileged?"

Sid fields this question. "My connection in the force, who you need to thank for covering up all those deaths as victims of the fire, found the tattoo was actually of a seashell, something about it being a reminder of her favorite walks on the beach."

Thaddeus, back from whatever job took him to Florida, breaks his silence and jokes, "Maybe next time you'll leave the *pro bono* cases to the amateurs." We all share a laugh and Richard leaves.

I know I'll see my new friend again, but I dread the fact that when I do, it'll mean the return of the Brood.

Control
From the Casebook of Detective James S. Peckman
By Alex Azar

Most people don't waste their time thinking about what they believe to be fiction, like unicorns, demons and wizards, and when they do, they never think of cutting edge technology. From the time we're kids we have the images of witches brewing spells in a cast iron cauldron with eye of newt and toe of squirrel.

The reality of the situation, while much more logical if you actually think about it, it also much scarier. Not only are all these things real and living in one way or another on our world, they're beyond the next generation of your cellphone. It's from these 'mythical' beings that we were bequeathed Xbox, Nutella, and WiFi. So the next time you video chat, be sure to thank the monks of Tamrrof.

I

Elizabeth, Thaddeus, and I have been in our current office for over five years. I've walked up and down the three flights of stairs, lit with a dim yellow light, thousands of times. I've crossed the dark wood panel hallway with a countless amount of steps. Opening and closing our lobby door has become second nature. I'm no longer even aware of jiggling the lock to turn the key. Walking this beaten path like it's my religion is the only reason I'm able to make it into the office today.

"Carl, tell the landlord that the final light in the hallway blew." He has my morning coffee in my hand before I finish my cheery greeting. I attempt to thank him, but Carl cuts me off.

He tells me he already has, and before I even part my lips to protest, he says, "Twice."

Carl clearly has something else to say, but he is much too talkative in the morning. Instead, I grumble about clients not being able to find their way to our door. "I guess it's a good thing Mrs. Lorna Whalen made it in before that light went out."

His self-satisfied smile shows that he's aware that I now know I should have let him speak first. My slight tip of my cup is all the acknowledgment he'll receive, or need.

When our original secretary, and web researcher, Sarah took a leave from us two years ago, she recommended Carl. We've yet to be privy to the details of their relationship, but their age difference, with Sarah being the elder, is just big enough that a romantic relationship could be considered taboo by some. However, if it were a blood relationship, Thaddeus and I can't understand the need for secrecy.

In any case, Carl's been a godsend, the perfect substitute for Sarah, whom we considered irreplaceable. His Columbia University education overqualifies him, but the fact he's a supernatural groupie of sorts makes him fit right in as our office assistant-slash-web researcher.

Standing outside my office door, I take a long drink of my coffee and ask Carl if there's anything I need to know.

He shakes his head and holds up his hands in an empty gesture. "Says she wouldn't talk to me about it. Looks like she's got money, but something seemed off." Thanking him, I turn to my door with an audible sigh.

Taking off my pea coat, still wet from the freshly fallen snow, I enter the office and hang up the jacket on the coat rack in my office. From that rack, I transfer a hat to a freestanding rake just outside my door. This is the agency's version of a "do not disturb" sign.

At first glance I see what Carl meant by "off". Mrs. Whalen, who's looking at the pictures on my wall, has her oversized fur coat, probably mink, carelessly draped over one of the chair backs on the client side of my desk. Her shoes are black with silver details, but the belt sewn into her empire waist is brown with a gold buckle. Her ring is platinum, while the watch on the same hand is yellow gold.

At least her earrings and necklace are from a set of white gold with sapphires.

Initial instinct says she's not even new money, but that everything's stolen or bought with dirty money. And while I trust my gut in the field, I tend to give clients the benefit of the doubt during their first meeting. "Hello, Mrs. Whalen, my name is Detective James S. Peckman. How can I be of service to you?"

She doesn't immediately turn to me, or even acknowledge I've entered the room. Instead, Mrs. Whalen inspects a particular photo more closely. With her nose mere inches from the glass of the picture frame, she asks, "Is that a werewolf you're shaking hands with?" Her tone is equal parts skepticism and excitement.

Deciding that is she isn't in a rush to talk about what brings her here, neither am I. I instead take a moment to look her over. If anyone were to catch me, I'd say I was looking over a prospective client. In reality I'd have to admit I'm admiring her five foot eight frame with ample breast and rear, and apparently a lack of body fat anywhere else.

Before I linger too long, I answer that yes, that is in fact a werewolf. "Dean is a good friend of the firm's. We assisted him with an issue several years ago, and he's since provided invaluable insight when dealing with certain... elements."

Looking at me for the first time, Mrs. Whalen asks with complete seriousness, "Does he know about TV remotes?" Seeing the confusion on my face, she cocks her head to one side and plants her hands on her hips to punctuate the sincerity.

Unable to process her question, I sit in my seat behind the desk and motion for her to have a seat as well. She opts to remain standing, supporting herself on the chair back, crushing her coat. "Why don't you start from the beginning? What brings you here today, Mrs. Whalen?" I've gotten better at anticipating the different motives of people entering this office. This case feels like a deadbeat husband having a dramatic change in luck and fortune.

"You can call me Lorna, and it's my boyfriend, Bobby, Bobby Derwin." Not a husband, but close enough. "He bought a magic wand that looks like a TV remote."

Any other client, I would have asked if he paid for the remote with the family cow, but whether it's 'old money', 'new money', or stolen money, women with fur coats don't appreciate my sense of humor. "Why do you believe it's a magic wand?"

"It changes things." She must have seen my internal struggle with the obvious joke because she clarifies, without being prompted to, "And not just channels on the TV."

Either Lorna overestimates my deductive abilities, or underestimates how cryptic she's being, which happens often when clients are embarrassed to admit the reason for their visit. She waits for my request to further explain herself. "Over a year ago, Bobby came home with this remote. He says he got it at some electronics expo. Thing is, he was never into that kind of stuff." She goes on to say for about a month, life went on as normal. Then, slowly, Bobby would bring home brand new expensive toys, but only when she was at work, and she says she never saw any discarded boxes in the trash.

"First it was the TV itself. Suddenly, our thirty-inch boob tube was now a sixty-plus inch LED brand name. Then it was the rest of our entertainment system." I ask Lorna if she confronted Bobby about this. "At first? No, it wasn't the first time he stole things for us. I was even a little impressed with his ambition. I just asked if he knew what he was doing, he said we'll never have another worry, and I believed him. That was the first night he brought the remote to bed." Without asking, she ignites a cigarette with a gold plated lighter that's engraved with her initials. "The next few weeks my jewelry was more expensive, my clothes were fancier, he even moved us to Los Angeles and now we live like celebrities, but we do even less." She says the last part rather proudly as she taps ashes into the tray on my desk, and I decide I deserve a smoke as well.

I get a little token of revenge by taking a cigarette from her case without asking, mostly to gauge her response, but she remains indifferent. "Forgive me, Lorna, but what made you go from thinking he was stealing to coming to a paranormal detective?"

From the inside pocket of her fur coat, she produces three photographs of the same woman. "I don't understand, Mrs. Whalen. Do you think he's cheating on you?" She doesn't say anything, but motions towards the pictures with her chin for me to look again.

Examining the photos more closely, it's remarkable how different the subject's body is from Lorna's, but how similar their facial features are, even down to the beauty mark next to her left eye.

Unconvinced by the similarities within the pictures, "Mrs. Whalen, I'm sorry Lorna, are you implying you're the female in the pictures?"

She cocks her eyebrow and tilts her hip, giving me an attitude that could only have been born in New Jersey. "I'm not implying anything. That's me four months ago, that's me seven months ago, and that was me before Bobby got that stupid magic wand." She points to each picture accordingly. "He changed me to fit this perfect little mold of what he thinks a female should look like, but that was never how he was. He always loved me for me, but now when he says 'I love you' I'm pretty sure he's talking to the wand, not me."

Looking at the progression within the images, I can see where the first small amount of fat on her stomach and thighs were reduced. Then her butt and breasts were increased, substantially. Finally she grew several inches. "I know what you're thinking detective, but I haven't had any surgeries. You can touch them, all natural." She presses her breasts together.

I take her at her word, and opt to remain professional. "Well, a magic wand would certainly explain all the changes. Do you have it with you?"

"The remote?" she asks incredulously. "He never lets it out of his sight." Troubled by this, I ask if he even takes it into the shower with him. "No, but I tried to take it once from its pillow to see if I could change something, but it's like he could tell when I got close to it."

"So right now it's in California with your boyfriend. Where does he think you are?"

"Visiting family," she answers casually. "Tomorrow is my brother's birthday. I fly back the day after."

Figuring it out mentally first, I then add it up out loud. "If I take the next train out, I'll get to LA in about three days, a day after you. That should give you enough time to book me a room at the nearest hotel, quality, good or bad, doesn't matter."

"Why take a train? I can pay for a plane ticket." She asks the question out of curiosity, not with the lack of confidence I've grown used to hearing from clients.

"You can pay for a train ticket as well." I attempt to be charming. "There's less security on a train, so I can bring whatever... tools I may need. And because of the frequent stops, if there's a change in plans, I can reroute quicker." I've become good at hiding my distrust of flying.

Looking the schedule up online, I find the next train out is in three hours. With plenty to do before I leave, I call Carl into the office, "Carl, draft up a contract for Mrs. Whalen, standard fare." Turning my attention back to my client: "Lorna, I'll take the case, but I need you to know my goal isn't to return you to your previous body. I'm going to get that dangerous magical item out of civilian hands. If I can help you in a different way, that'll be an added bonus."

She nods, just barely, and says she understands. "Please, just don't hurt my Bobby."

I take her hand in mine, and say as sympathetically as I can, "This should all go smoothly, and life will be back to normal in no time. Trust me." I wish I were as confident as I sounded.

II

I'm still a little confused at what's going on, but Sid, the only agent we've added full time to our roster since Elizabeth, Thaddeus and I opened up shop, is riding in the cab with me to the Secaucus Train Junction.

"Anabel and Tyson have picked up some chatter of strange paranormal energy fluctuations in Chicago, and since you're switching trains there anyway, Carl thought I could keep you company, at least on the first leg of your trip." Sid's explanation makes more sense than Carl's did.

Anabel and Tyson were Sid's friends and partners when the three of them worked for the NYPD. They worked together when all three of them were still alive. Those three were inseparable before Anabel and Tyson were gunned down and Sid was put in a coma. Apparently, they're still inseparable, because when Sid awoke from his coma roughly six days later, the spirits of Anabel and Tyson stuck around.

Unlike most hauntings we've encountered, they have a healthy relationship. The spirits help Sid solve cases he would otherwise be hard-pressed to do on his own, and he dedicates as much time as he can to tracking down their murderer.

As ghosts Anabel and Tyson are able to communicate with other spirits. Early this morning, they received word of some strange occurrences going on in the Chicago area, so here we are.

Settled in our train seats as we begin our journey, I prefer trying to sleep the first stretch of long trips before my minds gets too busy with thoughts on the case. Sid, of course, has other plans.

"What do you think the situation with the remote is? My instincts say it's along the lines of a Midas Curse. He's going to end up changing everything he looks at, even his food, and he'll eventually die of starvation."

"I thought of that, but all the changes have been upgrades of their original form. If it is a Midas Curse, he'll eat like a king forever. My money is on a variation of the monkey's paw. The guy's got a set number of changes, then everything turns against him. Maybe his girlfriend conspiring against him is the first step in his downfall." Thinking the conversation finished, I nestle into my seat and close my eyes.

Ignoring my desire to sleep, Sid continues unhindered, "If it is a monkey's paw and he's been making changes for a year, he probably has six hundred and sixty six changes." Sid pauses, allowing me to add my feedback, but when he sees none forthcoming, he finishes for me. Says I have to find out how many changes remain.

"Or I could just take out the batteries." Rolling my head and shoulders away from him, showing Sid my back, he finally takes the hint and lets me sleep.

After a few hours' rest, I'm ready to talk with Sid about the case. We've agreed that whether this 'wand' is a monkey's paw or has a Midas Curse, the best course of action is either destruction or containment. "If the remote is able to be destroyed at all, it should be relatively easy. These things are usually all or nothing when it comes to protection." Sid suggests I simply shoot the remote as soon as I see it.

"My concern is that destroying it may release whatever curse or evil is contained within. I'd rather contain it until I'm sure one way or the other." One of the shops that Thaddeus gets his tools from is in Chicago, so Sid and I go there to pick up a Pandora's Box. A Pandora's Box allows you to trap whatever you'd like within, and comes with a key that is imbued with the essence of the person who locks it. If anyone else uses the key to unlock it, whatever evil is inside will be released, but the original key holder can safely unlock it.

Sid nods in approval, "Once you get it safely locked up, you can have Elizabeth inspect the remote. Smart thinking."

With my first steps of the case decided, we turn our attention to Sid's, "Any idea what this 'disturbance' your investigating is?"

Shaking his head, Sid tells me no. "Only thing Anabel and Tyson are hearing from the spirit world is that anyone with half a brain is leaving Chicago, and something evil is coming. Don't know when or how or what, but something." The vagueness of his details doesn't leave much for us to converse about the rest of the trip together.

III

I step foot into Chicago for the first time, and am a little impressed. For one who loves the cold, I never believed Thaddeus when he said this city was too cold, even for me. Wishing I had brought a jacket, even if just for the three hour layover, Sid and I make our way through the whipping wind to Thaddeus' specialty shop.

We enter the underground, windowless, magically hidden store by walking through a wall that would have been solid were it not for the seeds that Thaddeus gave us to put in our shoes. In addition to granting us access through the deceiving entrance, the seeds allow us to see the hidden symbol marking the portal so we aren't randomly crashing into brick walls across Chicago.

Once inside, our setting changes from a dirty Chicago alley to an even filthier windowless thrift shop. The store is cramped with freestanding wooden shelves, which are in turn overpacked with tools and items that are magically enchanted or of some mystical nature; everything an investigator like Thaddeus would ever need.

Sid appears right at home, walking around like he owns the place. While I, on the other hand, couldn't look any more out of place. I'm just wandering about, not focusing on anything, but touching everything. "Sid, what does a Pandora's Box look like?" Thaddeus made the suggestion I pick one up prior to our leaving, but I've never seen one before.

Instead of Sid, the proprietor of the store answers me as he walks away from a muscular giant of a man who looks like he should be on a football field, not in a magically hidden paranormal market. The football player is saying something about evaporating a large body of water. The owner, who doesn't appear to be any taller than five-foot-nothing, explains in a heavy Russian accent. "Nyet, nyet. Ze box doesn't matter, only ze spell." Anticipating my next question, he explains any container can be a Pandora's Box, although he says the name like a cross between 'panda' and 'pander'. "I have Pandor Urn und Pandor Casket for beeg evils."

I ask if he has something smaller and less conspicuous, "And hopefully something less morbid."

He lets out a belly-shaking chortle before saying he has just the thing. "Da, da, I have Pandor Box for you, no questions being asked about zis." He retrieves a rolling step ladder, and hands me a dusty orange shoe box from the top shelf. I turn the box over in my hands, letting the flap top swing open, revealing nothing inside and a small luggage key taped to the bottom of the lid. "Zis what you looking for, da?" I nod confused and hesitant; if Thaddeus didn't trust this place, I'd swear I was being sold snake oil. As it stands, I tell him to add this to Thaddeus Coleman's tab.

At that moment, Sid walks up with two armfuls of supplies and says the same. Sitting atop the pile are tele-maggots in a plastic bag sealed with a thick folded paper label stapled in the center, much like the gummy worms I bought as a kid in the drugstore by my grandparents' house. The difference is, you don't eat these. You place one in your ear and someone else does the same with another. The 'maggots' create a psychic link between the two users, allowing them to communicate telepathically. "Thaddeus asked me to pick up these up for him."

As we're leaving, after all the items were logged under Thaddeus' account, I see the football player from earlier resume his conversation with the shop owner as though no time passed at all. "Like I said, I don't swim."

IV

After a brief lunch at what I think is nine in the morning local time, during which Sid relentlessly asked about my lingering feelings for Elizabeth, and current status with Thaddeus, I'm back on a train headed to LA. Sid stays behind for his investigation. He would never admit it, but he's worried about what's going on in the Windy City. There's something bigger going on that he's keeping to himself. Once I've wrapped up the nonsense with this remote, I'll return and offer some assistance, wanted or not.

Best not to think about that right now. Instead, I redundantly check my bags, and find the same equipment that I packed half a day ago when I left Chicago: my Glock 9mm Stacy, my Magnum, which

I've owned for most of my adult life but has remained unnamed despite the negative luck that's supposed to attract, and, of course, my newly acquired Pandora's Shoe Box.

Whiling away the hours, I take out my notebook to go over the details of other cases that are lingering, waiting for my return. The book easily opens to the pages where photos have been stapled to the sheets. The photos are from an acquaintance's notes on the Brood, an ancient race of evil alien gods that use humans as puppets, or something like that.

The notes are from another investigator, Richard Yu, who I ran into on a recent case that dealt with the Brood and their disciples, called the Privileged. Richard works with Gidious, the old man who directed Thaddeus and Elizabeth into my life. So why wouldn't he have told me about the Brood?

With a day's worth of travel left in my journey, I decide to call the old man, and see if he'll finally answer the questions that he's been avoiding since I first encountered the Brood.

"Hello Ancient Warrior, how kind of you to remember your old friend George Gidious." I'll never get used to his voice. It sounds like gravel in a blender filtered through cancer-riddled lungs. "Let me guess, you're going to once again ask about the Brood." And he tells me again that I know everything I need to know at the moment.

"Listen, old man, I don't know why you admit to knowing more than you're willing to tell me, but stop calling me Ancient Warrior." We've had the same back and forth conversation dozens of times, and will most likely have it many times again in the future. I think it's his irritating voice that just sours my mood every time we talk.

He asks where I am, but I have the feeling he already knows and why. "Elizabeth told me of your case. I caution you not to take this situation lightly. I have a feeling there's more going on than you are aware of."

As if I didn't have enough to worry about with whatever Sid is going to find! But, I've grown to trust Gidious when he's being serious. His psychometric powers are reliable on a level I can only pray Elizabeth will one day match. Now it seems my 'easy' case may turn out to be more than I expected. "Thanks old man, and stop scaring the local kids," I joke to lighten the mood, but hang up before I can tell if it worked on him. I know it didn't for me.

V

My first stop off the train is the hotel... actually it was the train station's restroom, but then I went to the hotel Lorna booked for me, and I find her in my room. If this were a late night cable movie, we'd end up in bed together. However, as reality goes, she loves her boyfriend and as attractive as she is, I've no interest in her. If I keep telling myself that, I just may believe it before the case is over.

She begins to say something about her boyfriend, Bobby, but I hold up my hand to silence her. The way Lorna whips her head around it's obvious she suspects that I'm implying someone may be listening. "Relax, we're not spies." She watches as I make my way to the mini bar and drink an airplane bottle of far-from-top shelf rum. Shaking the sting out of my head, I ask her to continue. To answer her look of irritation, I tell her: "Hey, I saved you money by taking the train."

Lorna gives me a crooked look that reveals her New Jersey roots. "As I was going to say, Bobby is at a golfing range. He always showers right when he gets home; you should be able to get the remote then."

I'm not used to letting the clients dictate so much of my plan of action, but it's a good strategy, and I let her know. "What time will Bobby be getting home?"

Checking her phone for the time, she tells me he should arrive in about half an hour. "Does no one use watches anymore?" I mumble under my breath. When Lorna asks what I said, I clarify, "Cutting it close, aren't we?"

Lorna shrugs her shoulders with a non-committal moan, and announces she's ready to leave by retrieving her keys from her purse.

VI

Lorna and I arrive at her home, or, I should rather say palace. The sheer size of the estate is incredible, even if the design-slash-furnishings are gaudy and heavy-handed. The fleet of cars in the garage, on the other hand, is a mix of modern sleek, vintage muscle, and classic performance that makes me wish my morals would allow me to take advantage of the opportunities I come across.

Instead, I'm hiding in a walk in closet that's bigger than my first apartment. I've no fear of being discovered here; as I look around, I find only female clothing and accessories, leading me to believe there's an equally impressive closet for Bobby also stemming from the master bedroom.

Shortly, I hear two voices enter the room: Lorna's and a male's I can only assume is Bobby's. As they venture deeper into the chamber, the voices become clearer. "Sure thing, babe, we can eat anywhere you want tonight. Let me just shower and clean up. Maybe we'll finally have time to talk about your trip back to Jersey."

Personally, I read no accusation in his voice, but Lorna's guilt puts her on the defensive. "I told you honey, there's nothing to say. We had a big family dinner the night of, then I took my brother out to lunch before flying back home." While I'm sure the details she gave were factual, it's what she didn't say that's making her nervous. Thankfully, Bobby either didn't notice the change in her voice, or he simply didn't care because I hear footfalls going into the master bath.

About three minutes later, Lorna opens the closet door and lets me know Bobby's in the shower. "I swear, he used to take the quickest showers, but now he'll be in there for a minimum of half an hour. It's like he knows he needs to get away from that remote, but can't allow himself to do it."

More relaxed now that I have a time frame, I still choose not to dally any longer than needed. Picking up the Pandora's Box, I exit the closet like a secret lover avoiding attention. Inside the bathroom, just before the frosted glass shower doors, is an ornate white wood stand topped with a cushion that is clearly intended solely for the remote during Bobby's showers. Resting safely atop the silk pillow is the remote, its appearance as unassuming as the shoe box in my hand, but the power emanating from the device gives my arm pause before touching it. My instincts caution me from proceeding any further.

On second thought, I take pictures of the remote with my cellphone, zoomed in as far as it'll go. Suddenly, only after several minutes, the shower turns off. "Lorna, baby, are you messing with my remote? You know how I feel about that."

Answering from the bedroom door, she calls back, "No! I'm just in here getting ready for tonight. What's wrong?" She motions for me, stuck between the two, to grab the remote but as I turn back, I see, through the frosted doors, Bobby reaching for the handle.

I run passed a half dressed Lorna, making a conscious effort not to look at her exposed flesh. Once I'm in, she closes the door.

"That was quick; everything okay Bobby? You don't look as relaxed as you usually do after a nice shower."

I can only assume the sight of his girlfriend half naked, while fully nude himself, has put Bobby in an amorous mood, because he doesn't answer her with words, but instead by throwing her on the bed. In hindsight, I regret not getting a Pandora Box large enough to hold me and block out what I'm hearing.

VII

Back at the hotel and after a shower of my own, I forward the pictures I took of the remote to Carl. There is no brand name, and the logo is nothing I can recall ever seeing. However, between Carl plus Kelly and Arnold, the firm's two archaic researchers, I'm sure we'll get a bead on the thing.

In the meantime, I've got to keep my mind busy, lest I dwell on the dirty talk I overheard between Lorna and Bobby.

"Sid, what's going on with your case?" He's been in Chicago for two days now, and with the extra help of his ghost partners, Sid typically has his cases well in hand before any of us would be able to.

Before he even says a word, I can tell he's frustrated. "I don't know, James. There's some sort of mystical energy building on the edge of the city. Anabel and Tyson haven't heard anything from their typical sources, but the whole supernatural community is concerned. If you're finished in LA I would appreciate some assistance."

I tell him I'll be there as soon as I can, "But I've hit a hiccup here. Wasn't able to grab the remote yet, but I sent the research crew some pics of it."

Sid and I end our call with mutual wishes of luck. I spend the next few hours worrying about Sid in Chicago and checking my phone for any updates from Jersey, when suddenly I'm woken from a sleep I don't recall falling into. Arnold is calling my phone, and that's when I realize, if it's midnight here, it's three in the morning for him.

"Arnold, what are you doing up so late?"

"Oh, you know, partying and drinking till the wee hours of the morning." He pauses to make sure I interpret his sarcasm as an explanation of the stupidity of my question. "I'm sixty-five years old, what else would I be doing awake at this godforsaken hour if not keeping you alive? The picture on that damned clicker is from your friend's notebook."

If I understand Arnold correctly, he mean's Dick's notebook about the Brood and that this case just got a lot more serious. I ask him which Brood, while flipping through my copy of the notes, but he doesn't have any good news for me, and I can't find it.

"Don't know. All he has in the book is the logo, an upside triangle piercing a circle, and about a dozen question marks around it." I remember that page. I hadn't bothered to copy it because it didn't seem to shed any light on what we might come across. Arnold goes on to tell me that in the morning, Kelly is going to meet with George Gidious to see if he has any more information on the Brood, while Carl digs up any info he can find online. "Now let an old man get some sleep, will you?"

All things considered, that was one of the more pleasant phone conversations I've had with Arnold. He's not a fan of phones in general, which goes to show how serious the situation is: not only was he still awake, but that he'd bothered to call.

Knowing how punctual Elizabeth is, I forgo a full night's worth of sleep and call the office at six am; that should be right around when Elizabeth walks in at nine her time.

She answers as if she were expecting the call. "Having trouble, Jimmy?"

Her cavalier attitude leads me to believe she wasn't included in the team's three am conversation; she only calls me Jimmy when she's in a good mood. "Actually, I am. Turns out this case may be Brood related." Her silence is indication enough of her understanding. I ask her to find a printout of the remote picture, probably on Carl's desk. "You know I hate to ask, but I need you to use your ability on it. Tell me something."

Elizabeth is psychometric like Gidious; this means she can sense an object's history through touch. Unlike Gidious, she's still perfecting her control over this. Currently, she has to walk around covered nearly head to toe in clothes she knit herself out of the fear she may accidentally touch someone and get lost in their history. This is why being intimate with her means so much more than with anyone else, and why it feels like such a betrayal to learn she had a similar relationship with Thaddeus.

He and I haven't fully resolved our issues, but I think we're slowly moving beyond them. She and I have been able to remain friends, despite her continued relationship with him. He claims that love has nothing to do with his intimacy with her, while I know part of me will always love her.

"James, are you still there?" Elizabeth asks, her tone a complete one eighty from when she answered the phone. "The connection to the remote isn't strong enough. All I'm getting from the picture is that the stock boy where the photo-paper was bought masturbates in the backroom to mind-control fantasies of female customers."

She already knows, but I proclaim my frustrations. "Not what I was looking for Liz; hopefully Gidious can do better." My fears and anxiety of this case force my words to come out much harsher than intended. "I'm..." My attempt at an apology gets lost in anger. "I've got to go."

Finally, I say it. "I'm sorry." but the dial tone doesn't absolve me, and I wonder if Elizabeth still has the phone to her ear, and despite a lack of connection she somehow heard it.

VIII

Several hours later I'm at a fancy hotel restaurant with Lorna eating brunch, which is apparently a real thing, and not just something the movies made up, like vampires turning into smoke. "Detective Peckman, you have to do something. He came home from his morning run with a pet cheetah." She begs me to find a way to get rid of the magic wand.

It almost seems too obvious, but I ask, "What about when he's asleep?" Lorna says that not only does Bobby sleep with the remote in his hand, he's apparently a light sleeper. I ask my next question sheepishly. Thankfully, Lorna understands my reasoning. "What about during sex?"

"He tried to bring it in once, but I refused to sleep with him. Now he keeps it on a pillow on the nightstand next to our bed. Picks the damn thing up as soon as he's done, though." I ask about sex in the shower, and she says they do that occasionally.

A new plan is forming and I begin telling her the details; those I feel she needs to know. "Tonight, I need you to sneak me back into the house, and initiate shower sex. I'll steal the remote then, but I need to pick something up before." She trusts me enough to not ask what.

IX

It takes longer than I expected to find what I was looking for. In New York, where I typically do my shopping, if I walk into a shop that doesn't have what I'm looking for, the salesman knows of a place, or knows a guy. Here in LA, if the store doesn't have the item, it might as well not exist.

Kelly calls me as I'm headed back to my hotel room, which is not the fancy hotel I had brunch at earlier. "Hey, Mr. P. I'm at Mr. Gidious' place with Mrs. Gonzales; you're on speaker phone." Kelly has a heavy Brooklyn dialect with a vernacular that peaked in the Eighties, and to top it off she always sounds like she's chewing gum, even when she's not.

"Ancient Warrior, it's me, Gidious." As if I couldn't tell. "Listen, you need to get possession of that remote, and not let anyone else have it."

I tell him I've got a plan to steal it in a few hours and a Pandora's Box to lock it in. "I should be on a train back to Jersey tonight."

This time it's Elizabeth talking into the phone, "No. You need to go to Chicago. Thaddeus and I are taking the first flight tomorrow."

I hear through the silence on the other end of the line that they would prefer if I flew also, but that's not an option. Instead, I offer an alternative, "I'll rent a car and drive it. Should take me under..."

The old man cuts me off. "Don't bother; once you've got the remote, things shouldn't get any worse." Finally, he decides to tell me what he's learned so far. Using his psychometric abilities he knows the remote is tied to the Brood and Ibn'Roth, and his attempt to return to Earth. "From talking to Sid, we think Chicago is where it'll happen."

Sid knew there was something big going down, but he didn't tell me--he went to Thaddeus instead. I understand why; much like he did with me, Thaddeus recruited Sid into this world after his partners died, but I thought the similar recruitment had formed a bond between us. Stupid, I know. Instead it seems, just as with Elizabeth, that Sid trusts Thaddeus more, creating this divide between the three other agents and myself. A divide made worse, because I can't get on a damned plane.

All I've got on my side are Carl and Gidious. Speaking of which, "What's Carl doing during this?"

Apparently tired of chewing her non-existent bubble gum in silence, Kelly answers, "He's hitting the web looking for any spells or magic that this 'Roth guy might be usin'. Hasn't left his computer for a minute, poor guy." Through the cloud of her dialect I hear it: she misses him.

Kelly and Carl have a secret relationship, good for them. I, for one, know anyone who can find happiness in this world deserves to have it. "Well someone make sure he doesn't spend the night in the office. Tell him it's an order from me."

X

Once more into the fray, well, closet technically. My part of this plan is fairly simple; I just have to grab the remote while Lorna distracts Bobby... by having sex with him in the shower. Come to think of it, I'm sure Lorna is okay with her part of the plan.

The dueling scents of her plethora of perfumes and litany of lotions from an open cabinet within the closet is proving distracting, but I hear Lorna just on the other side of the door. "I've missed you Bobby. Feels like we haven't had any time together since I got back. Why don't you keep me company... in the shower?"

Either I've been single for too long, or Lorna's laying it on a little thick, because I suddenly feel like I'm on the set of a porno. In any case, it works. I hear Bobby literally bark as he runs towards the bathroom. "You just read my mind, babe."

I wait just long enough that I'm confident Bobby is motivated to stay in the shower before I make my move. Gingerly, I make my way from the closet in the bedroom to the bathroom. My ears are once again assailed by the unique sounds of Lorna and Bobby's love for one another. As I approach the remote, reaching out for it with my one hand, holding open the Pandora's Shoe Box with the other, the noises suddenly stop.

"Hold on babe, there's someone here."

Despite the pleas from Lorna for him to stay with her, I'm standing face to naked and wet face with Bobby. In a throaty rumble I thought was reserved for Lorna, he growls at me and lunges.

Before the soap-covered boyfriend can reach me, I draw my gun and shoot him twice in the chest.

Screaming bloody murder, Lorna's love and fear blind her to the facts before her. Despite the tight walls around us, there was no deafening report of the gun shots. Even though Bobby took two hits to the chest, the floor isn't stained red with his blood.

It isn't until she hears a moan escape from his lips that she realizes I didn't kill him. Waving my gun so she can see: "Tranquilizer gun. Didn't think I'd need it for him, got it for his new pet cheetah."

Holding the remote in my hand, I feel the power within emanating through my arm and out to my whole body. From the corner of my eye, I see Lorna staring at me, concerned the remote already has a hold on me. I assure her, by placing it in the shoe box and sealing it.

I've never used a Pandora's Box before, but I'm a bit disappointed. I was expecting more of a show, some indication that evil was trapped, that I won. A small hole appears on the box, and I lock it, remembering the merchant warning me, stressing the importance of not losing it.

The hole in the trap disappears, and I'm holding an ordinary looking shoebox with an evil magical remote locked within. All in all, a good day's work.

XI

Back at the hotel, I turn my cellphone on, and I'm bombarded with texts and voice messages, never a good sign. I call Elizabeth without checking any of them first.

"James! Thank the gods you're okay, we've been trying to reach you. Started to think they got you too. James, they killed Carl." I think she's waiting for a response, but I can't think of anything to say. She continues anyway. "He was at the office late, researching Ibn'Roth and this attempt to get to our world. Kelly called and told him you didn't want him staying the night. Carl left, but *they* were waiting. Somehow this Brood, Ibn'Roth, and his Privileged found out we were looking into him. The office was protected, so the Privileged, these four thugs, caught Carl as he was leaving the office. Security footage caught the whole thing. I think they wanted to be caught."

I hear Kelly rip the phone out of Elizabeth's hand. The pain in her voice covers the chewing sound. "Mr. P, they weren't men.

I've never seen someone this strong. They threw Carl around like he was nothing. When it looked like they were done, they ripped off his..." She can't finish her sentence, but she doesn't have to.

I now hear her crying, and realize she has been the whole time. Somehow Kelly shedding tears makes this situation all the more real to me. "I never should have made him leave the office." I didn't mean to even say that out loud, let alone loud enough that it could be heard on the other end of the line.

"No James, this isn't on you." Elizabeth takes the phone back from Kelly whose crying has evolved to full-on sobs. "This isn't on anyone but those monsters and their boss." It wasn't my intention, but this got Elizabeth to focus. "Thaddeus doesn't want anyone alone until this is taken care of. Kelly is going to stay at Arnold's, and I'm with Thaddeus since we've got our flight tomorrow morning."

It pains me that I can allow myself to get jealous of Thaddeus at a moment like this, but I know it's the best plan for them. Looking at the tranq gun carelessly thrown on my hotel bed, I make the most courageous decision of my life. "I'll be on the first flight to Chicago."

Elizabeth is too stunned to respond initially. I say goodbye, and this snaps her back, "Oh James, one more thing," I expect her to tell me she loves me, but: "There was a note left on Carl's chest. It read, 'None shall stand in the way of the glorious return of Ibn'Roth.' Then it had some lines in an alien language. George couldn't read it, which scares me even more. It had the triangle circle logo. Jame, these guys are serious; be careful."

XII

No way TSA would allow me on the plane with my tranq gun, but sleeping pills and copious amounts of alcohol have the same effect. I wake up from the jostle of landing. Fear grips me, thinking we're all about to die. The prepubescent child sitting next to me is staring at me with an awkward grin on his face. "You're funny." That's when I notice I've drooled a great deal during my chemically induced coma.

Unable to travel with my tools, I paid a hefty sum to have everything shipped overnight in a discreet box. The only thing I brought with me on board the plane is the Pandora's Shoe Box.

Exiting the airplane, I'm assaulted by the Chicago cold while still in the walkway. The extreme temperature change announces my time in sunny California is at an end, and none too soon. The ice in my blood and chill in my lungs pulls the last of the sleep from my body. I almost begin to relax until I remember why I'm here.

Had the cold not fully woken me from my assisted nap, the faces of Elizabeth and Thaddeus would have. No words are shared between us, but Elizabeth grips me tight in a mournful hug, as Thaddeus rests his hand on my shoulder. The three of us together like this, I can almost forget our history. Almost.

Breaking the hold together, we silently agree it's time to get to work. "So, what's the plan, Thaddeus?"

He nods his head to the shoebox in my hand and says that we need to get the remote to Sid. "Not sure how, but that remote is tied to Ibn'Roth and the sons of bitches that killed Carl. Hopefully, we can find a way to turn its power against them"

I grip the box tighter, creasing the lid as it folds in ever so slightly. "Are you sure that's a smart idea? What if we're delivering the one thing they need to finish the ritual, or spell, or whatever?"

The wheels are turning in Thaddeus' head, I can tell he agrees with me but refuses to admit as much. Elizabeth defuses the tension by wisely suggesting we meet Sid at his motel room.

The cab ride to the motel takes nearly an hour. The driver quickly gives up any attempt at humor after seeing the grim dispositions on all three of us, leaving the majority of the trip silent. I only have one question towards the end of the drive: I wonder why Sid chose to stay so far from the airport. Thaddeus' answer noticeably disturbs the driver. "That's where the world is going to end."

XIII

Sid says he's glad to see me, but the weight of the situation makes him wish it were under better circumstances. He has made it a habit to never initiate a hug with any guy. He's been self-conscious since coming out of the closet. That was before I even met him, but Carl's murder, a death in our family, trumps Sid's awkwardness. Having broken the ice, Elizabeth follows suit as does Thaddeus. We share a moment of silence.

Clearing his throat, Sid breaks the tension by offering to share what he's gathered. "This is what we're dealing with." He shows us pictures on his laptop. "That's Hamlin Park; it's a rundown field that doesn't get much traffic, only the occasional person walking a dog. This whole neighborhood used to be upper middle class, really family oriented. Then kids and pets started disappearing, unsolved murders plagued the area, and the entire power grid began going on the fritz."

To most people, the missing kids and murders would be the most alarming, but when dealing with the paranormal a large-scale electrical disturbance can only mean more death is on the way. "Who are they?" I ask, pointing at several men wearing black.

"I wasn't sure myself," Sid admits, "until I got this photo." He clicks on a picture of one of the men, and blows it up, zooming in on the guy's face. "Look at that." Tattooed around the man's eye and on his cheek is the logo from the remote, the mark of Ibn'Roth. Collectively we take another moment of silence, but for an entirely different reason.

Giving us a moment to absorb the reality of what we're dealing with, Sid continues to the next picture. "It gets worse," Initially it appeared that this photo was in black and white, but now I realize that's just this Privileged's skin tone. "Some of these guys aren't even human. I don't know how we're going to deal with them."

Despite the uniqueness of the situation, we build the case like we would any other. Thaddeus, as the perpetual self-appointed leader, takes point and begins by asking Sid what he knows. "How many Privileged do you count?"

"Numbers change between day and night. They keep a low profile during the day; only have a handful covering the park in plain clothes." He opens a few files on his computer, showing the daytime Privileged. "They're all human, and they all have the same tattoo mark. Their numbers vary between five and eight. As soon as the sun goes down, their numbers jump to twenty, and that's when the demons come out."

Trying to keep the situation manageable, Elizabeth asks if 'demon' isn't a bit of an exaggeration. Sid looks up from his seat and says he wishes he were blowing things out of proportion. He opens a few more pictures. "You tell me." These three photos show a blue-skinned Privileged with fangs peeking between his lips, a Caucasian female with small horns protruding from the forehead, and the final is a beast of a man standing nearly two feet taller than those around him. This Privileged has bright red skin made of snake scales and all three are, of course, marked by Ibn'Roth.

"How did you take these pictures without getting caught?" I tried to hold the question in, but those photos should have been impossible to take.

He points to the empty bed. "Them. Anabel and Tyson quietly jump into the Privileged. They can't control them, because these beasts are too powerful, but they can make them just ignore me for the few moments it takes to get the picture. Can't do that when there's more than two, though. Even just slightly influencing a Privileged takes a toll on them; that's why they're resting now." He turns back to his computer, then does a double take back to the bed. "By the way, they say hi."

Elizabeth, Thaddeus, and I say hi in unison. I always make the mistake of trying to extend the pleasantries and ask, "How are you?" realizing too late, as I always do, that they can't reply to me.

Sid answers for them, "They're worried about this business with Ibn'Roth, and are glad you three joined us." I often wonder how Sid handles having these two constantly with him, especially when having relations, but can never find an appropriate time to ask. Surely, now wouldn't work. I'm starting to think it may never be a good opportunity.

Elizabeth calls my name, bringing me back to the moment. I ask, "Do any of the Privileged you've witnessed seem to be in charge, or are they all just front line?"

Answering my question with a shrug of his shoulders, Sid says there seems to be no power structure. "Human Privileged interacting with... demons." He pauses to look at Elizabeth prior to using that word again.

She nods morosely. "What are we going to do with that?" she points to the Pandora's Box I'd placed next to Sid's computer.

Thaddeus suggests we destroy the box with the remote still inside. "That should eliminate it as a threat while keeping its energy within."

"We can't base our entire strategy on the hope that destroying the box will contain the remote's energy. For all we know that could just release it all negating our only advantage." Perhaps because the Pandora's Box is the first piece of paranormal paraphernalia I bought myself, I feel protective of it.

Thankfully, Elizabeth and Sid agree; destroying the remote is a worst case scenario, ending the discussion. "Next option?"

Thaddeus doesn't like the question, even more so that I asked it.

He doesn't look at me when he answers. "We need to get into that park, find out all we can about the energy field and when everything is supposed to happen."

Elizabeth suggests we also speak to the people who live in the area. "They have to have seen something."

The rest is easy to figure out; Thaddeus and Elizabeth are going to canvas the neighborhood, gathering what information they can from the locals. While we've still got some daylight, Sid and I are going to sneak past the Privileged security detail.

Preparing for our respective missions is the first time Thaddeus and I check our respective equipment shipments. I'm satisfied with the condition of my weapons, secured in a metal lock box. Unfortunately for Thaddeus, the jostling of the delivery broke a vial of a liquid foam that hardens into a rock he uses to pick locks. Typically, the foam dissolves away after roughly twenty minutes, however this much of the foam may take days to fully go away, rendering most of his supplies useless. He's left with his guns, Bruce and Dick, and his last two tele-maggots.

Many times in the past, Thaddeus and I have shared the psychic link they create. Today, however, he gives the other maggot to Sid. I think he did that to upset me, but it's for the better. He wouldn't be able to concentrate on his objective, having to hear what I thought of him right now.

XIV

After doing a perimeter search, Sid and I count a manageable six guards. My concern is how many more Privileged are lurking around, ready to attack if we get caught. We choose an entrance to the park that is only protected by a single sentry. Anabel and Tyson are able to manipulate his mind and keep him from noticing our entry and they direct us to the abandoned baseball field, scattered with doggie landmines atop snow. Sid startles me as he hisses, "One at a time." It takes me a moment to realize what's going on. It must be bad enough when he's already got two additional voices in his head, but to add Thaddeus to the mix must be practically unbearable.

He looks at me and takes the maggot out of his ear. Thinking he and Thaddeus decided I should wear it, I extend my hand, but he places the brownish ear plug into his shirt pocket. "I'll put it back in when there's something to actually report."

Anabel and Tyson lead us to the pitcher's mound, which feels to be about ten degrees colder than the surrounding area. They tell Sid the focus of the energy is coming from here. "What they're saying doesn't make any sense. Something about a singular presence emanating from here, but its source is from hundreds of different dimensions."

I don't even pretend to understand what any of that means. "Is that 'presence' Ibn'Roth? And if so, is this definitely where he's going to return?"

A voice that doesn't belong to Sid corrects me. "Ibn'Roth isn't just going to return here. This is where his reign over humans resumes." Standing behind us is an average looking Hispanic man I'd put in his late thirties, with the mark of Ibn'Roth over his eye.

Hiding the dread creeping up my spine, I flippantly ask, "Human?" indicating himself. The Privileged begins laughing as his skin is hidden by a green thicket of rapidly growing feathers covering his exposed flesh. His mark disappears during the process but reappears upon completion.

As if his transformation weren't enough, he further proves he's not human by speaking in a language I happen to think is actually from an alien planet. *"Cron einnod ayasor toyap senoni dech,"* as the bird man continues to laugh.

Sid begins to panic even more, "James, we've got company." Anabel and Tyson warn Sid that other guards are starting to converge on our location.

"You're coming with us, Detectives." Before the half-breed bird with dialogue from a cheesy 80's action movie can close the four foot gap between us, I draw my Magnum and fire a round in his chest.

The Privileged is dead before he hits the ground. I turn to Sid. "Hopefully they're all that easy to take down."

Sid is too busy fishing the tele-maggot back out of his pocket to respond. As he communicates with Thaddeus, we get surrounded by the five remaining Privileged, and in no way do I trust in my fortune enough to believe there won't be more joining them.

"New game plan; back to the motel and regroup with the others." Sid's obviously talking to me, but he hasn't taken his eyes off the dead Privileged, while my attention is squarely on the nearest live one.

120

I draw a bead on the Privileged with my unnamed gun, but from the corner of my eye I see Sid pluck a handful of feathers from the dead guy, and shove them into his pocket before drawing his own gun. We quickly make our way to the nearest entrance. I'm backpedaling protecting our rear while he leads the way. Trying to limit our exposure, I hold off firing off any more rounds until it's absolutely necessary.

That is until a cat-like Privileged closes the gap and gets too close for comfort. Anyone who claims they can hit a bull's eye with a Magnum while running backwards under duress is either a world class bullshitter or Annie Oakley. My first shot hits the ground in front of our feline pursuer. The second whizzes by its head, clipping a different Privileged in the shoulder. Finally, third time's a charm. I shoot it in the leg, causing it to tumble and taking down the other with it.

Sid and I reach the entrance to the park, and I stop on the other side of the stomach-high chain link fence. Using the fence to steady my hand, I fire off three rounds from Stacy, my Glock 9mm. Two hit Privileged in their chests, while the third drills into the top of the cat's head as it's trying to get to its feet. I leave the remaining two alive, not out of mercy, but for fear that reinforcements will soon arrive.

I follow Sid, who's running a maze through backyards, deserted streets, and the occasional alley. Anabel and Tyson guide him through flawlessly. They're even kind enough to schedule a rest to catch our breaths in an abandoned garage. We're back at the motel quicker than if we had driven. "Hey, Sid, you notice there weren't any cars on the roads?"

"That's because almost no one actually lives here anymore." Thaddeus explains, revealing his and Elizabeth's hiding spot behind the table, scaring the shit out of Sid and me to boot.

After letting us calm our racing hearts, Elizabeth asks Sid if he 'has it'. In response, he removes the feathers from his pocket, and now his reasoning becomes clear. He places them on the table next to his computer in a neat pile. Sitting in front of the feathers, Elizabeth takes off her gloves.

"Holy shit, it's gone!" Just before Elizabeth is about to touch the feathers, I notice what's missing. "Where's the Pandora's Box with the remote?" Sid and Thaddeus begin to scramble for it, but I cut them off. "Here it is." I hold it up from next to the bed, turning it over to show them it's empty. "Sid, can Anabel and Tyson sense the Privileged that broke in?"

"Unfortunately, no," he says, shaking his head. "Something about the nature of the Privileged sends them for a loop when they jump in them. I'm surprised they were even able to help us get home, but I can barely see them right now. Maybe the feathers have something, Elizabeth, if you wouldn't mind."

She nods to Sid, and hovers her hands over the pile of feathers. Her face already announces how difficult this is going to be for her. Elizabeth practically whispers, "Okay," before picking up a feather, avoiding the table. "His name was Jamal Hawkins, his father is Percy."

Thaddeus explains that Percy is one of the people they spoke to. "Jamal has been missing for about five years. Percy gave up hope of ever finding him again."

Elizabeth continues talking over Thaddeus. This deep in a reading, she doesn't even realize we're in the room with her. "Every time the remote makes a change, it also creates a link to one of the 328 different dimensions that pieces of Ibn'Roth have been banished to. The man who had the remote had no idea he was aiding in the resurrection of a demonic interdimensional godlike creature, who apparently has the temperament and abilities to either destroy or enslave Earth, depending on his mood."

I begin pacing the room, still holding the empty shoe box. These Privileged having the remote is scaring me more than I already was. "This isn't like the other time we've gone up against the Brood."

At the mention of the alien race of gods, Thaddeus jumps up excitedly, apparently with some good news. "That reminds me; every time the area lost power, one spot remained lit up. A local dive bar that happens to be called "The Brood".

XV

We've walked to the bar, discussed the situation again, are actually standing outside the place now, and yet we still don't have a plan. Thaddeus, in his typical fashion, dictates that we don't need a plan. "It's a bar, and we know other non-Privileged humans come here. Percy, the guy who told us about this place, admits to frequenting this establishment. We'll figure something out once we get in."

Choiceless, we enter blindly into the unknown, and for the briefest of moments that fear supersedes all others, and I forget we've already delivered to these demons the exact weapon they needed. "What can go wrong?" The others, apparently unable to detect sarcasm, agree and walk into The Brood. That doesn't sound too ominous, but I decide to keep that bit of sarcastic wit to myself.

The interior of the bar looks like your average Irish pub that you'd find in any city, although The Brood is filled with people and there's no music playing. The walls and bar top are a dark wood, with green pleather lining the ridge and a single glass sheet mirror running along the wall behind the counter. I'd love to say all conversations ceased and every pair of eyes were on us the second we walked in, but the only person who pays any attention to us is the bartender.

"Yous look like lost puppies. Ain't ever been to The Brood before, eh? Don't worry, we ain't gonna bite you, unless that's what you're inna." That last part was directed to Elizabeth. Thaddeus and I step closer to her, and she instinctively reaches for his arm, not mine

Thaddeus takes point, and for once I don't mind. "Guess it's that obvious we're not from around here." Closing the gap to the bar he extends his hand, "Name's Chuck."

The bartender meets 'Chuck's' hand with his own. The stretch makes the sleeve of his shirt ride up a bit, and I see a tattoo. I remember it from Dick's notes he left with us; it's the mark of a different Brood god Xordam. The mark is an X dissecting two off center rectangles, one inside the other. "Friends call me Donovan."

"Oh yeah, why's that? What's your real name?"

"...Donovan..."

"Ah, smart friends."

Thaddeus looks at us for help but I'm too busy spotting all the different Privileged markings disguised as tattoos. Worryingly the common one I'm finding is the mark belonging to Ibn'Roth. I wonder if we're the only regular humans here. Well, 'regular' might be a bit of a stretch.

Sid orders whiskey from Donovan. "Double Black if you've got it."

Beer isn't my typical drink of choice, but whiskey relaxes me too much; can't take the chance of being lethargic at a time like this. I instead ask for a brew. "What do you have on tap?"

Donovan gives me the cheesiest, most awkward smile. "Nah, you wouldn't like what's on tap, trust me, it ain't for ya kind."

Before I have a chance to ask what he means by that, I see the answer reflected in the mirror behind him. Gidious had mentioned that Ibn'Roth is possibly the only Brood god to not employ any normal human Privileged. Seems the old man may be right, because all the patrons with the mark over their eyes have now surrounded us and shifted into their 'other' form.

A smaller than average Privileged with paper white skin and yellow jagged teeth like a baby shark, approaches closer than the rest. "Thank you for bringing what we needed; saves us from having to kill any more of your pathetic family."

Thaddeus and Sid catch me as I lunge at him with my blade aimed for his throat. "I'm going to enjoy covering that skin red for what you did to Carl."

He laughs while Elizabeth, Sid, and Thaddeus tell me to stop and calm down. "I'd listen to the others, human."

Thaddeus tries to reason with him. "You've already got the remote, you won, just let us go."

The Privileged stops laughing, but keeps the vicious smile on his face, "Oh you adorable plaything, we could have grabbed the remote anytime we wanted. That's not all you brought us."

All of our eyes follow his as he looks at Elizabeth, who grows three shades paler. They knew that the remote was in that particular motel room; of course they knew who we were before we even walked into this damned bar.

I look at Sid and mouth the word 'now' but he shakes his head. If Anabel and Tyson can't help right now that either means they still don't have the strength after possessing the Privileged earlier, or they can't enter the Brood Bar. Both scenarios concern me.

I knew we shouldn't have walked in here without a plan.

XVI

The sound of a now familiar alien chanting wakes me as I'm being dragged across the baseball field Sid and I visited earlier. The cold snow rushing through my ears helps with wakening my senses. Sid is walking, forced by a large hand on his back. The large hand is attached to an even larger Privileged. Thaddeus is being dragged by the ankle like I am, by one of the Privileged I recognize from the bar.

It makes me happy to see I recovered sooner than he did. Lastly, Elizabeth is being carried over the shoulder of the paper white Privileged. He's making sure not to touch the exposed flesh of her face.

The Privileged dragging me stops abruptly, "You're awake. Start walking."

With my hands bound behind me it takes a moment to get to my feet, but I feel that they didn't relieve me of my weapons. I can't build the faith that this was a simple oversight, it's more reasonable that they're just that confident in what is about to happen.

My Privileged tour guide stops me on the first base of the diamond, while Sid is escorted to second and Thaddeus to third. Elizabeth's hands are tied above her head to a pole erected in the past hour on home plate. The tightening of the knot wakes her up.

We're all trained not to show any external signs of emotion, positive or negative, but I know these three better than anyone else in the world. I know that just like me, they're more angry than anything else. Honestly, how did we get caught with our pants so far down that it ended like this? It's easy for me to look across the field and blame Thaddeus, but it's not all on him.

Before I can find a reason to share the blame, my Privileged captor grabs hold of my hands behind my back in a vise like grip, much like I would have to assume the Privileged behind Sid and Thaddeus are. Then they, along with the almost two dozen other Privileged around us, begin chanting even louder. *"Chinnid regath Ibn'Roth krakako warg chin'ok."* The same line over and over.

"Holy shit!" Thaddeus' exclamation draws my attention to the pitcher's mound where the remote, which must have been there the whole time, begins to spin, hovering a few feet off the rubber. After increasing speed, the remote stops all at once, glowing. A beam of light discharges from the infrared sensor and hits Elizabeth in the chest, causing to her to scream in excruciating pain.

"Elizabeth!" "Liz!" "Lizzie!" I'm not even sure who said what, but Sid, Thaddeus, and I realize we need to get free... five minutes ago.

"Chinnid regath Ibn'Roth krakako warg chin'ok."

As the glow around the remote grows, so does the volume of Elizabeth's screams. "Liz, I will get you of this," I vainly promise.

"No you won't." A voice calls me on my bullshit. The voice originates from the glow around the remote. "You four, along with this entire decaying carcass of a planet, will either worship me or become the shattered spines my empire is built upon."

A face, which logically would have to be Ibn'Roth's, emerges from the glow. Atop his head are spikes like a reptile's, while his cheeks are covered with long thick hair, like antennae that are pulled over his ears and bound like a ponytail behind his head. "I am almost complete." I'm not sure who he said that to, but I hope it wasn't us.

During all this, Elizabeth hasn't even been able to stop screaming to catch her breath. I struggle with my arms, but the Privileged's grip is so tight, I feel the pain in my shoulders. Thaddeus is similarly attempting to thrash about to no avail.

The chanting continues around us. "*Chinnid regath Ibn'Roth krakako warg chin'ok.*" It's almost drowned out by the crackle of energy surrounding the remote and Elizabeth, still in pain.

"Guys, we need a plan," Thaddeus pleads, mimicking my own sentiments.

As serenely as if he were relaxing on a beach, Sid says a single word. "Soon." I'm not sure if I really heard it over the cacophony around us, or if I simply imagined it, but I trust him.

Through the remote's glow, which is not quite six feet in diameter, a hand and shoulder emerges. It's covered in the same spikes as is his head. I hear Thaddeus shout, "Sooner would be better."

Somehow sensing something was about to happen, paper white Privileged stops chanting while the others continue. "*Chinnid regath Ibn'Roth krakako warg chin'ok.*" He instead runs from home plate, where he was watching Elizabeth writhe in pain, towards the pitcher's mound.

Before he reaches the remote, Sid shouts out, "Now!"

The Privileged holding Thaddeus' and my hands suddenly loosen their grips and actually tear the ropes binding us. Thaddeus and I, on the same page for the first time in ages, take the briefest of moments to lock eyes and confirm the obvious choice before us. We draw a gun each and take aim at our target.

Targets...

Seeing Thaddeus' aim, I scream out trying to stop him, as I fire my gun twice. The first bullet rips through one side of Paper White's head, exploding out the side. My second shot shatters the remote, and continues through, almost hitting Thaddeus in the shoulder as he fires his gun with a tear running down his cheek. He mouths the words 'I love you' as his bullet hits Elizabeth in the chest.

Ibn'Roth joins my yell of 'no!' as the energy around him explodes outwards and his visage disappears along with it. The shockwave knocks us on our asses, but does more to the Privileged, who are all lying dead on the snow and patches of orange dirt.

Sid, unable to comprehend what Thaddeus did, much like myself, mumbles to himself, "You two are the better shots. I didn't know. Tyson could have freed me, but you're the better shots."

Thaddeus runs towards Elizabeth, but I tackle him before he reaches her. "What did you do? I had it!"

Fighting me off of him, he rationalizes his murder away like he does all of his questionable actions. "You said it yourself, breaking the remote would probably only help him get here sooner. If they needed her... it was the only way. It was the only way." He continues to repeat himself as I walk away. Sid helps me untie Elizabeth, and we gently rest her on the ground. We spend an impossibly long time over her body, during which Thaddeus has gathered his things and left the park.

Sid is the first to break the silence. "James, your shot, it almost hit Thaddeus."

He leaves the question hanging in the air, allowing me to answer or not. I hope one day I can convince myself that I meant to miss Thaddeus.

Today's not that day.

Under the Hood of Winter
From the Casebook of Detective James S. Peckman
By Alex Azar

I wish I could say I hate winter, and I'd have every right to, what with smoking making my lungs feel like they're caught in a frozen vise. And due to an old football injury, my knee sounds like dead branches being trampled by a horse. Snow and rain are preceded by a dull ache in my arm and chest from a gunshot to the shoulder, but damn I love the cold. Feeling the cold in my bones brings a smile to my face, even if it is occasionally broken with coughing. Hearing the crack of my toes after a night of sleep with no socks is one of the little joys in life.

Unfortunately, those little joys aren't always enough to force away my personal demons. Such is the case waking up one morning in Morton, Washington.

I

I don't know how anyone can handle death well, but you'd think with all the loss in my life I'd be more desensitized. Sadly, that's far from the truth.

Following the death of Elizabeth Gomez, my business partner and former lover, and the resulting fallout with our other partner, Thaddeus Coleman, I closed the doors to our detective agency. Three months later, I've yet to return. I aimlessly traveled the country trying to lose myself, only to find myself here, perhaps even led here subconsciously, to Elizabeth's hometown of Morton.

I haven't been here since the old man sent me to first recruit

Elizabeth. Now I'm back in the very same hotel room, waking up to the cold I love, but unable to appreciate it because of the weight of the task at hand. I must inform Elizabeth's sister, Victoria, of her passing.

With no immediate time frame, I let the urgency of the situation slip as I dawdle in my morning routine, a habit I've found myself in since everything that happened in Chicago. I lose myself in thought with the rhythmic sensation of brushing my teeth. The cascading water flowing from the shower head washes away all desires of completing the very reason for my being here. But eventually reality sets in and, after getting dressed, I prepare a breakfast of instant coffee and a cigarette for the road.

It's not until I'm waiting for Victoria to answer the door that I make the connection of her and Elizabeth being named after British queens. For some odd reason the realization brings a smile to a face. A smile that unfortunately misleads Victoria, who opens the door at this inopportune time, into thinking my presence at her doorstep is for a social visit.

"Hi! Wow James, good to see... Where... Where's my sister? James, where is Elizabeth?" The almost maternal connection she has with her younger sister allows Victoria to understand without words what Elizabeth's absence means.

"You son of a bitch, you promised me you'd take care of her!" she cried, falling to her knees with streams of tears rolling down her cheeks. "I told you this would happen, and you were supposed to protect her."

I reach my hand down to touch her shoulder and open my mouth to apologize. "Don't touch me, and don't you dare say you're sorry. You don't get to be sorry." Once again rising to her feet, Victoria slams her fist against my chest, but emotion has sapped her strength. "You piece of shit, this is your fault. Why did my sister have to die while you're still here?"

I want to answer her rhetorical question with tears of my own, tears that haven't been shed for anyone since my wife and daughter died, but I know Victoria wouldn't accept my pain or my sorrow, so I take a step back and look at my feet. I'll wait here as long as it takes, but Victoria has to make the next move.

The next two minutes of Victoria crying feel like an hour, but I'm determined to wait her out. Eventually, she sits on the steps behind me, and without looking up at me asks, "Did she die helping someone?"

"I can say with no hyperbole that she died saving the entire world." I begin to go into details, but Victoria cuts me off with a wave of her hand, still refusing to make eye contact.

"One more question before I tell you to get the fuck off my steps. You hear about what happened to the miners about a dozen miles from here?"

"Can't say that I have, but if it's about a case, I have to admit, what happened to your sister was a real wakeup call. I don't think I'll be doing any more detective work anytime soon, especially of the supernatural variety."

"Bullshit! You don't take my sister away from me after I practically raised her myself, helping her cope with the side effects of her abilities, and introduce her to this whole new world of horrors. You don't get to decide to back out now that she's gone." Finally turning to look me in the eyes: "You're going to find out what happened to those miners, some of whom we grew up with, for me. Then you're going to go back to New Jersey and do this until you're the one that dies, while thinking of my sister every day. Now get the fuck off my steps."

With that, Victoria reenters the house and, with regained strength, slams the door hard enough to rattle the windows. I'm left to contemplate my next move, standing in the cold I love, so lost in thought I don't even register the temperature.

II

It didn't take me long to discover what Victoria had been talking about. All I had to do was turn on the news or look at a local newspaper. Around ten days ago, an entire coal mining crew working in the mountains was found slaughtered onsite, by unknown assailant or assailants. They were completely mutilated by crude cutting instruments, also of unknown origins. At this point officials have no clues or leads and are finding it difficult to even find plausible motivation.

Thankfully, their cluelessness is making them sloppy; they've left the now vacated caves unguarded, allowing me uninterrupted searching time, or they *would* have if I had come prepared. With no additional source of illumination, my cell phone light won't allow me to venture very far. I can't even get deep enough to locate where the murders took place, which might be for the best. Five minutes alone in those caves can get to a person.

I've become a good judge of which cases require my specialized talents and which are just unexplainable while still within what's considered 'normal' boundaries. Everything I can gather about this case makes my skin crawl like only the paranormal can. Sadly, this could just be another side effect of everything that happened; just me needing to feel useful after Victoria's barrage.

I head back out while making a mental checklist of what I'll need when I return. Topping that list is a thicker jacket. Even as a fan of the cold, those caves are too much. They gather the freezing air for an effect opposite of hot boxing.

III

After completing my shopping list, I decide to grab dinner at a local diner. I'm quickly reminded that New Jersey diners are unparalleled, a fact this Washington diner proves in spades. In need of a pick-me-up, I revert to my standard comfort food, disco fries. Following a blank stare from the waitress, I clarify. "French fries, topped with gravy and mozzarella cheese."

Answering in between open-mouthed chews of her gum: "All we got is uh-jew sauce."

"You mean 'ah jus', no gravy? Never mind, I'll have the chicken fingers with fries and honey mustard." What arrives fifteen minutes later is chicken nuggets drizzled in mustard with a packet of honey.

Finishing my meal, I promise myself not to judge all of this state's eateries on this experience, immediately followed by a vow to finish this case quick enough to never have to eat here again.

I pay for the food and as I'm waiting for the waitress to return with my credit card, another patron approaches me, asking if I'm here to find out what happened in the caves. "I am; how did you know?"

"You look like a cop, but we know all the cops around here." He says 'we' with a shake of his head, motioning towards a table of three other men, all similarly dressed in flannel, jeans, and well-worn boots. I'd imagine in comparison, me dressed in my favorite tan pea coat, black slacks, and newly bought winter cap and scarf covering my shirt and tie, I'd look like an out-of-town cop to most people. "We'd be mighty grateful for anyone who can find out what happened to those guys, even one from the south such as yourself."

It takes me a moment to realize that 'south' here means California, unlike the rest of the country. "I'm Detective James S. Peckman, and I'll get to the bottom of this but I'm not from California; I'm from New Jersey."

Flicking the puff of my cap with a smile, "You're not used to this kind of cold, huh?" I politely chuckle and joke that I thought I liked the cold before spending time here.

Breaking my vow from the previous night, I return to the same diner for breakfast. I'm served by the same waitress and see mostly all the same customers, including the gentleman that approached me and his friends.

Upon noticing me they invite me over to their table. Typically, I'd kindly refuse; however, with virtually no clues about what I might be walking into, I take a seat between Gus and Chuck, the one I spoke with last night. Sitting across from me are Mike and Michael, identical twins.

These guys, along with the rest of the male workforce, mine the caves. More importantly, they've all at one time or another worked with those that were killed. Chuck tells me that the entire community revolves around the caves, and that no one in the area would benefit from this. They just broke new ground deeper within the cave.

Mike chimes in that the whole community gets excited whenever miners explore deeper or a new cave, "It's like clockwork; every five years the foremen choose a new cave to begin work in, or explore previously unmined areas. The town has a festival, and all around it's good for the economy."

"Is there anyone that would benefit from preventing this economic boost?"

Michael argues that "there's no 'Big Business' in these parts that want us failing." He continues to defend his friends' stance, returning me to the conclusion that there is no natural solution to this case, but a supernatural cause.

I announce to the table that I'll be heading to the caves now, and withdraw my wallet when Chuck grabs my hand. "Now you stop right there."

With steel in his eyes, and the grip of a python, he rises to his feet. "We can't have this." Not sure of what he's talking about, I step back defensively. "You come out here to look into the murder of our friends, there's no way we're going to make you pay for your meal with us." He emphasizes the last word with a firm pat on my shoulder while never letting go of my wrist.

After a round of 'goodbyes' and 'good lucks' Gus warns me to be careful up there. "Parts of those mountains are covered with snow year-round, making it easy to get lost. Strangers die out there every year."

IV

Exiting my car at the mouth of the cave, I'm still unsettled by Gus' parting words, unsure if they were a warning or a threat. Is it possible my four new friends are actually responsible for these murders? Upset at not landing the new mining job that's attracted so much local attention? But I also have to wonder why the cops wouldn't have investigated this lead.

I decided that my best course at this point would be to continue searching in the caves for clues the local force hadn't discovered or trampled over. Venturing deep within the cave, I drag along a flatbed hand truck loaded with enough generators, lights and wires to power the Rockefeller Christmas tree and the surrounding city blocks, but the most important things I have are my guns. Stacy, a Glock 9mm, is safely tucked under my arm in a holster, while my unnamed Magnum rests comfortably in my hand. The leather grip has worn and contorted to my hand over the years making it second nature to wield, like a major league catcher and his glove, or an author and his favorite pen.

So comfortable is the gun in my hand that I can almost forget I'm holding it while searching these seemingly endless caves, completely devoid of natural light and all life. I suppose not 'all life'. Something must be making these noises I'm hearing. In fifteen minutes of walking these noises have become rhythmic, so it's easy to notice the break of monotony of a kicked rock. Unfortunately, the openness of the cave wreaks havoc on the acoustics, making it impossible to determine the direction of origin. I spin a full five hundred and twenty degrees before acknowledging the futility of it. "I'm armed and will not hesitate to fire, come out." Even though I will shoot, my threat was so unconvincing. Even I doubt it.

However, it appears to work, "Easy there, James, it's just

us." Chuck says as he comes around a rock formation. Appearing from three different rocks, never can remember stalactite or stalagmite, are the twins and Gus, who has a rifle aimed at my head. "Easy Gus, can't you see that it's our new friend Detective Peckman?"

"So it is. My vision gets blurry sometimes in these caves." I notice behind his slick smile that he never actually apologized for pointing a gun at me after trying to sneak up.

"What are you guys doing here? These caves are closed to civilians." The Magnum rests easily in my hand, but my finger never moves from the trigger.

Following a quick chuckle, Chuck answers "Haven't you been listening, Detective? This is a mining community; we belong in these caves more than most."

"Some would say miners have more power in these parts than the police." Gus quickly adds.

"And who is it that says that, the miners or the police?" I pause a moment before adding a nonthreatening chuckle. I don't like the situation, but I have to stay in control. "Either way it doesn't matter. I work alone and can't allow outside opinions to interfere with my investigation."

"Outside opinion? It doesn't get more…" Gus is cut off by a deep wailing that despite the bouncing echoes is clearly coming from deeper in the caves.

Mike nervously shouts the question on all our minds, "What the fuck was that?" His question is answered with a flint-tipped spear striking the right side of his chest. I know that the spear is tipped with flint because another spear emerges from the shadows, striking my Magnum holding hand with a glancing blow. The gun skids across the floor away from me as I draw Stacy from her holster. I yell for the miners to retreat out of the cave as I reach for my dropped gun. Just as my fingers are about to touch the handle, a tomahawk flies out of the darkness, shattering the trigger and guard before bouncing off. Oddly, the tomahawk bounces perfectly back into the shadows from which it came.

The image of the disappearing weapon is replaced by a Native American in naught but a loincloth and red face paint, running at me at full speed. He must either have had another tomahawk on him, or he caught the one he threw off the bounce, which seems impossible. I don't have much time to ponder the details as he pulls back his arm to throw it again. Not giving him the chance, I fire Stacy three times, hitting him twice in the chest, dropping him on the cold stone ground.

Deciding to check on Michael before looking into the attacker, I find Chuck and Mike about to drive off in their truck with Michael in the backseat. Gus, who's outside the truck, is encouraging Michael, clearly not planning on going with them. The truck starts to pull off, when I shout for them to stop. "Gus, you should go with them. I killed the Indian, just going back to see what I can discover."

Shaking his head, Gus responds, "Uh-huh, there may be more than one of them, and that bastard attacked my friends and my family. Not something I can walk away from."

V

Searching the area where the skirmish occurred, Gus questions if I'm sure I killed the attacker. Looking at the ground where the Native American fell, I can't answer him. "Gus, I'm telling you, I shot that guy twice in the chest. He fell right there."

Following the line from my pointing finger, he says, "There's no blood! How can there be no blood?" Pausing to catch his breath, "And you see how he hit Mike from the shadows? Had to be over thirty feet with a fuckin' spear." Turning his attention to the shadows, "Get out here you piece of shit. Show your face!"

With no response forthcoming, we set up additional lights, extending our area of view by nearly fifty yards. Fifty yards of the same monochrome gray that we've been surrounded by since entering the cave.

After the extra lighting was set up I reexamined the area where I was ambushed twice, first by my questionable new friends, and again by a fur underwear-clad, red face-painted Indian who can apparently see in the dark. I notice that not only is there no blood, but both spears are missing. "Hey Gus, look at this," I say, pointing to long dragged trails moving outward from the general area where he fell. I add that Gus may be right about there being more than one, "Unless he literally dragged himself out of here with two shots in the chest."

Although I'm not familiar with cave mining, I can tell that this area has been recently worked. The cart rails have no dust settlement on them, and there's more footprints than we would have created today alone. "Is this where the new work started? Where the miners were found dead?"

"That's about two hundred yards deeper, halfway down the path splits. We gotta head to the right." I ask what's to the left, and he explains the foremen haven't explored there yet, "That hasn't been reinforced yet." He finishes his sentence by knocking on one of the wooden support beams that can be found every twenty yards.

"How long before work begins are the caves reinforced?"

He tells me that it varies, but where the new ground was broken was a slow build.

"They had time between the location being chosen and the festival taking place. In fact, they finished the supports about two years ago. I remember because they had an accident also. There was a minor cave-in that took the lives of two of the workers. Inspectors couldn't determine the cause and after a little over a month, work resumed."

Seeing the curiosity on my face, he asks if I think the two incidents are connected. For an answer, I suggest we search the left path. Upon taking the path less traveled, I notice that the slight decline we've been traveling increased dramatically. "Yup, that's why the powers-that-be chose the other area, the ground is fairly level there." The angle of this path is making it difficult to continue setting up lights as we go. A fact that doesn't sit well with me.

The low light and steep decent bring our pace to a crawl, making me feel incredibly exposed. It also makes me wish I'd picked up night-vision goggles, but I had no idea where to get a pair in these parts. Interrupting my thoughts, a chant begins echoing off the walls, once again making it impossible to pinpoint its origin. Making matters worse, the single voice is joined by several more.

"It appears you were right, Gus; sounds like there's more than one." Not hearing a response, I realize that I hadn't heard from him for several minutes while lost in my own musings. "Gus, if you can hear me, make your way out of the cave. There's more than one of these guys, and there's no way we could take them on ourselves."

Good job, James. I'm lost in a cave and sent my only assistance running because the two of us can't survive this. Now you've got to do this solo, in the dark. And all this is assuming that Gus and the others aren't actually responsible and playing me for a sap. Chances are just as good that Gus is dead as they are that he's hiding behind a stalagmite again. I sure as hell wish I had Thaddeus and Elizabeth here with me watching my back, but if they were around I wouldn't even be in this mess.

The chanting has continued uninterrupted, but now I see the dim flickering of fire coming from further down the decline. With the light increasing exponentially, I use it as my guide through the cave. While I'm positive that I'm approaching the source of the chanting, the volume remains the same, further supporting the theory of multiple assailants. Unfortunately, that means I'm currently surrounded.

After less than a minute of careful decent, I find a break in the cave wall that appears to have been carved out ages ago. Cautiously approaching the portal into the lit room, I'm startled by the sudden realization that the chanting has stopped. Peeking into the room, I see a pair of torches ensconced in the frame of the opening.

Armed with my Glock, I slowly work my head around the wall to find two identical stone daises, one of which is occupied by Gus, who is nude and lying motionless. There's a limpness to the arm overhanging the dais that assures me he's dead before I can clearly see his face. The room is otherwise empty, meaning the red-painted attacker and his friends still need to be found.

I approach Gus' body to see what they did to him. The first thing I notice is that he's lost the color in his face much too soon for a recently deceased body. His chest has two bullet wounds, almost exactly where I shot the Indian, and nothing else seems out of place.

On the dais opposite Gus, which I thought was clear, are two spent bullets. Upon further investigation, the slugs are the same caliber and make that I use in Stacy and fired into the Red-Face. This reminds me of an African shaman that was able to transfer wounds and ailments from one body into another, or even to inanimate objects. If Red-Face and his friends are using a similar technique, it would explain how this tribe survived in these caves for so long.

Leaving Gus where he lay, I continue searching the caves. This gives me time to figure out how to stop a tribe of Native American warriors who are able to recover from two shots to the chest.

VI

After what felt like a mile of walking, but in reality was

probably only five hundred feet made worse due to the uneven rocky decline, I reach a valley in the cave. There's a large flat clearing with some rock formations, low hanging pillars, a few small daises with some items I can't quite identify from where I am, and a path on the opposite side. The path looks like an artificially made tunnel on a steeper incline than the decent that brought me here, and is just big enough for someone to crouch in without having to crawl.

The room is lit with four torches built into the walls. Still no sign of Red-Face. I take the time to investigate the objects more closely. Nearest to me is a pile of flat perfectly round rocks, which I can't help but think would be great for skipping on water. There are about two dozen of the stones, and each of them has the same crude carving of a flame with some runes carved around it.

I walk over to the right of the room holding one of the stones, and take a look at a painted hide. While trying to decipher the meaning of the painting, I absentmindedly run my thumb over the carvings of the stones.

Suddenly my musing is disturbed by an intense heat emanating from the stone, but only from the engraved side. The shock of the heat causes me to drop the stone. Landing face down, the heat wave is so powerful that the stone is actually levitated off the ground, until it wobbles enough to flip over entirely. I can see the actual waves shooting upwards to the ceiling. Just as quickly, the heat stops. Cautiously checking the stone with a moistened finger, I find it miraculously cool to the touch, like a soldering gun.

Testing a theory, I rub the engraving with a part of my jacket, and nothing happens. I decide it's safe to put the stone in my pocket without fear of being burned. Placing three more of the stones in various pockets, I resume inspecting the painted hide.

Several skulls and crossbones are inside inverted 'V's that I assume are meant to represent mountains. I interpret this as a warning of death to those who enter the mountains, but it doesn't really explain much as far as reasons go.

"You shouldn't be here."

Turning around, I see Red-Face standing at the mouth of the tunnel holding the damned tomahawk that broke my gun. I hold up the hide and motion towards it with Stacy, "Yeah, I gathered that with all the skull and crossbones." I didn't imagine he'd speak English, and I tell him so.

"There's much you don't know."

"Like how you and your friends learned to speak English, but still paint on dead hides?"

He questions the word 'friend', and expands his arms wide, pointing out the fact that we're alone. "While I do burn with the fires of my fallen brothers, I can assure you we're alone in here." He answers my question of hearing other voices by dismissing it as an acoustic trick of the caves.

I don't completely believe him, but I must admit the plausibility of his claims. Deciding it best to see both entrances in case he's lying, I position myself underneath one of the torches equidistant from each opening. This also gives me more options of escape if things go south.

Keeping pace with me, the Indian circles around, always staying on the opposite end of where I stood. His new position gave him view of the now slightly diminished pile of heating stones, "Souvenirs?"

"Hey in my line of work these could prove useful."

"So this isn't just a one-time thing, you're a professional grave robber?"

After telling him I'm not here for any graves beyond the miners he killed, I explain, "I'm a detective and specialize in the paranormal and supernatural. A friend asked me to look into what happened here, suspecting there was something beyond what the police could handle."

Apparently sensing the truth in my words, he lowers his tomahawk and spear. "I apologize, but I've been tasked by the elder chief to eternally protect my tribe's mountain burial crypt, and have done so for hundreds of years before your people came to this land."

Understanding the dedication someone could have to their duty, I think it's best to leave him alone in the caves. Besides, I wouldn't know what to report to the authorities. I tell him that I'll leave him to his sacred watch, and not attract any more attention to him, then turn to leave.

Instantly my view is obstructed by a spear embedded into the cave wall mere inches from my face. "I am the Red Soldier, sworn to protect the secrets of my people. I cannot threaten my tribe's safety on your word alone. You are not permitted to live."

Despite the realization that I'm in for another fight for my life, I wonder where he learned to speak such proper English.

"Just one of those stones in your pockets at the entrance

would set off a chain reaction creating a path to the entrance of our burial crypt."

Still trying to avoid a confrontation, I tell him that I'll leave the stones I took, and will never return.

"After experiencing your people's penchant for taking that which isn't theirs, I can't trust you."

With that, he whips his tomahawk right at my head. Ripping the spear from the wall I use it to deflect the flying ax, splitting the handle of the spear in two. The tomahawk curves through the air and gently returns to Red Soldier's hand.

Using rocks growing from the ground for footing, the Red Soldier launches himself in the air before sending the ax once again towards my head. This time I take the torch from the wall above and use the metal handle to protect myself, but before the ax reaches me it wavers and hits the ground by my feet. Red Soldier lets out a scream of pain that is echoed by a second voice seemingly coming from the flame as the fire dies out.

As the tomahawk magically returns to his hand from the floor, Red Soldier commands from one knee: "Unhand that, you are not worthy to touch him."

Not letting the fact he said 'him' hinder me, I aim Stacy and shoot Red Soldier in his throwing arm. Little did I know this Indian happens to be ambidextrous. He takes the tomahawk in his left hand and once again throws it. Diving behind more rocks, I see the ax hover in the air, still spinning, and then fly at an angle once again towards me. Without enough time to aim and fire, I run towards Red Soldier, who is just now getting to his feet, and tackle him with all my weight. Positioning him on top of me, my hopes of the tomahawk hitting him end when it simply returns to his grasp.

With inhuman speed he swings the ax at me again, but I already have Stacy drawn at his midsection and unload the remaining five shots, stopping him mid-swing. Still alive but clearly in pain, I roll him off of me and make a mad dash towards the nearest torch.

Tearing it from its frame, I elicit two more screams of agony, while simultaneously diminishing the remaining light in the room. Like Gus mentioned when we first reentered the cave, Red Soldier has superior vision, even in little to no light.

Taking the long way around to the next torch trying to avoid Red Soldier, I turn on three flashlights, pointing them in various areas of the room. Red Soldier grunts the same grunt from his previous two tomahawk throws. Either he sees me, or his magic ax can hit me regardless. I'm too far to reach either of the remaining torches, so instead I activate one of the heating stones from my pocket and aim it at the torch. In mere seconds a wave of heat blows the flame out and dislodges the torch. Immediately after, I hear the tomahawk clang to the ground by my feet.

Blindly searching for it before it can return to Red Soldier's hand, I grip the handle and feel it quickly tug against my hold before relenting and resting easy. Still not sure if he threw the ax at me because he saw me or because he could hit me either way, I opt to hold on to the tomahawk until I have an unobstructed view of the remaining torch.

Literally crawling on my hands and knees, with Stacy in one hand and the tomahawk in the other, I crawl right into Red Soldier's legs. Before I can shoot or cut him, he delivers a swift knee to my cheek, flipping me over. I lose Stacy, but I make sure to keep the tomahawk in hand. Seeing the glow of the remaining torch behind a pillar, I throw with all the strength I can muster from my back, hoping whatever mojo that caused the ax to fly around like a bat was still active and worked for me. Before I can find out if the tomahawk still works, Red Soldier kicks me in the ribs hard enough to cause me to slide several feet. Coughing the remaining air in my lungs from my body, I know he cracked some ribs. As he stands above me with a foot raised above my head, the tomahawk finally hits the torch, extinguishing the flame and dropping Red Soldier to the ground next to me, unconscious. The tomahawk returns to my hand and cradles in my palm seamlessly. I raise the ax overhead, planning on striking Red Soldier in the head to ensure his death, but I respect his mission too much, even if I don't understand it. I can't muster the fortitude to kill him, especially with his own weapon.

VII

Taking time to regain my breath, I collect Stacy, more of the heating stones, and the flashlights, all while Red Soldier lay lifeless where he fell. Respecting his mission and the sacrifice he made for his people, I decide to cave in each entrance of the torch room, and the top of the tunnel leading to the hidden stones. Not well versed with explosives, I'm not too sure how much it will take so I likely overdo it and draw a fuse to the entrance of the cave.

Hoping I did everything according to the directions, I flip the switch, and am left with thoughts of Red Soldier and the fact he sacrificed himself for what he believed in, and Gus who died in search of what happened to his friends. This makes me wonder how I could ever question Elizabeth doing otherwise, even more so, how I could ever do any less.

As the explosion erupts and echoes out of the cave, I picture the eternal resting places for the two that fell today and remember the two torches by the dais with Gus. As I tip my hat to the two, I doubt the explosion was enough to put out the flames and even hope the Red Soldier can finally rest.

VIII

For the third time I stand on this stoop, and each time different emotions pulled at my heart. Victoria opens the door with tears staining her cheeks, as though she hasn't stopped crying since the last time I saw her. Unsure of what words would be worthy in this situation, I instead present her with the two halves of the spear that Red Soldier had broken.

Silently, she takes them from my hands and reenters her home. However, this time instead of slamming the door in my face, or even cursing me off, she leaves the door ajar, and walks in.

Liquid Marble
From the Casebook of Detective James S. Peckman
By Alex Azar

My happiest memories are of fishing with my father. Twice a summer, we'd go midnight fishing with tours out of Point Pleasant, NJ. I remember it all so vividly: the sea salt in the air, the gravel beneath my feet as we walked to the boat. My father and I would board the craft and barely speak until one of us caught something. Then, after six hours, we'd head back to shore and I'd watch the calm of the black sea become ravaged by the white waves cascading off the boat. When the liquid marble faded to black, I knew my happiness was over.

These memories are what makes this case one of the more disturbing, and why I chose to begin with this one. At the time, not many people knew the name James S. Peckman or Argus Agency, but after this case the paranormal underground knew I meant business.

I

It's an uncommonly cold summer and a young man by the name of Greg Miller enters my office. On an average day, he would be seen in a fine neat suit, briefcase in hand, working in the city-- that's New York City for those of you not from the Tri-State Area. However, this is no average day for Greg, nor has it been an average week, and he is no longer, 'neat' or 'clean.' The top three buttons of his shirt are undone and his tie is loose enough to fit around his waist. He clearly hasn't shaved for several days. or possibly even showered for that matter. I motion for him to sit down as I put out my cigarette and wave the smoke away. "Hello, I'm Detective James S. Peckman, how can I be of service to you?"

While tapping his foot like a man on speed, he keeps sporadically bobbing his hands, as if he's waiting for the words he's looking for to fall in place before him. I already know, before he says anything, that it's his love that's missing. I've been in this business long enough to know that few things render a man like him speechless like the untimely loss of the love of his life. What I need to know is: what makes this case so special? Why did he come to me and not the police? But you can't rush a man in this situation. It needs to be handled delicately, so I either stay quiet and let him work it out in his mind first, or in a comforting voice reassure him that everything's going to be okay. I don't have a comforting voice, so we wait.

I silently offer him a cigarette with a motion from my pack. He declines. "Thank you but no, I don't smoke." Better for me, since it's my last one, but it got him talking. "Mr. Peckman, it's my fiancée, she...she, my fiancée is missing. Jill's gone, she's just... she's gone."

"Mr. Miller, I understand you're devastated and desperate to find your fiancée, Jill, but I don't understand why you didn't go to the police. They usually deal with missing person cases." Of course he's going to say something like 'she was taken by something inhuman' or 'she wasn't herself anymore.' Ten-to-one it wasn't human.

"This thing wasn't human. We were out for a late night swim during the weekend in Maryland. As we were getting back to shore, this thing, this fucking monster jumped out of the water behind us, and just took her." Reliving these moments are hard for him, so I give him a few minutes before I ask questions. I thought I was supposed to become desensitized to this, but I swear with every case I feel the client's stress and pain more.

After taking a few deep breaths myself, I ask my first question: "Do you mind?" signaling to my last cigarette. He tells me it's okay, so I light up and ask him if he could describe what it looked like. I figure the creature chose a spot that was conveniently 'too dark,' or 'it all happened so fast,' but Mr. Miller proves me wrong.

"I can do better then tell you what it looked like, I can show you." He reaches for his briefcase, and I think to myself that he somehow got a picture of this thing. Instead, he produces a drawing; I take a closer look and discover it is a miraculous painting reminiscent of a Frazetta. It's of a sea creature leaping out of the water with its webbed hands extended in the air, ready to crash down on some unseen prey. "I saw this poster in a bookstore window and knew it was the same monster. It's by some recluse I can't find any information on him but his name's…" I cut him off.

"T.J. Halvorsen." Past regrets are beginning to resurface, and a knot in my stomach grows to the size of a softball. "He went crazy after the loss of his wife. Some big shot, self-absorbed, police detective sent him to me thinking the case was a waste of time and, unfortunately, I was already on a case." I always knew there was something more to T.J.'s case, but at the time I didn't have the manpower to take it on. "Maybe it's time I followed up on him, though." I can see Mr. Miller's hopes slightly raised. He thanks me, and I assure him I'll do all I can. We say goodbye with wishes of luck and, as he's about to close the door behind him, Mr. Miller stops and pokes his head back in.

I raise my head from the poster to ask him if he wants it back but he interjects. "Mr. Peckman, the drawing's a little off. That gem: it's not in the center of its head, it's to the left a little, don't know if that helps at all."

I point at it with a smile, "More than you know." Not really, but he needs to feel helpful in a situation like this.

II

Following a quick call to my web researcher, I was on a train headed to Rhode Island. Sara is one of Argus' three researchers. Kelly and Arnold are our ancient researchers; they go through old texts and scrolls, and right about now they should be knee-deep in papyrus looking for this sea creature. But Sara was able to get what I needed more quickly. She's a net researcher who works from home when she's not acting as secretary, so it's safer for her.

Sara was able to get me Halvorsen's last known address. I just don't understand why he would choose to live on the water, this couldn't be right.

"You see, detective--Beckman was it?"

"Peckman."

"After my wife was taken from me, I moved to Oklahoma,

about as far from any major body of water as I could get, as most people expected." This man in front of me has a beard easily over a foot long and is wearing a tank top with suspenders and the potbelly of a seasoned drinker; nothing like the pictures Sara sent me. "But I began to forget about my wife." I cut him off before he gets on a depressing monologue.

"But Mr. Halvorsen, it's been several years; it's perfectly understandable for you to move on."

"For a detective, you sure don't listen very well. I said I began to 'forget', not move on." Okay, I'll give him that and I acknowledge my fault by motioning for him to continue and assuring him I won't interrupt. "As I was saying, I forgot about my wife and worst of all, that damn beast that took her from me. Something about what happened haunts me through the water, but away from the water my mind began to go blank. That painting you showed me, I wasn't able to paint it until I moved here. I painted it in that room right there." I lean forward in my seat to peek into the room he's pointing at. I see an easel facing a large window overlooking the water, but from this angle that's all I can see. I ask him if he minds if I go in the room. After he says it's ok, I enter and...?

"Mr. Halvorsen?" I can barely get my thoughts together. The walls and floor are covered with original paintings, but they're all the same monster in the same pose. There have to be at least fifty, maybe even seventy of the same paintings as the poster Greg had given me.

"Now I can never forget." he says with a twisted smile.

I agree as I rush towards the door to leave, uncertain of his mental health, and tell him I have to catch my train. With a foot out the door, he asks me why I travel by train. I tell him it's because of convenience. I leave with one last thought; too bad the ruby wasn't centered.

III

"Sara, it's me. I'm on the train back to Newark. The Halvorsen address was right, but now I've got more questions than before. What I need of you is to get me a list of all missing persons from the Maryland coastline. Get as much information as you can about each case and fax it over to the office." She inquires about Halvorsen's wife being kidnapped in Rhode Island. I tell her that we have to take everything from his testimony with a grain of salt because the artist seems a few colors short of a full palette.

She never fails; I step into my office and that see Sara's sent over an encyclopedia's amount of info on the Maryland cases. And, as always, Cereal has gone through the stack hoping there's some work for him. Cereal's a hunter we keep on the payroll in case there's any heavy fighting going on, but for insurance purposes we call him a 'detective'.

I sit down ready to start reading with purpose, when the burly frame of Cereal fills my doorway. "In the past fifty years, there's been a missing person case every five years that fits the same situation profile as the artist and client."

"So, we've got five years to stop this thing."

Instantly Cereal corrects me. "You've got five years, Warrior. Jill may not, but even so, this thing is acting alone. You should be able to handle it." He tosses a pair of diving goggles onto my desk and leaves after saying, "Besides, I don't swim."

IV

"Five messages in less than a day, can you believe that?" As I explain to my partner how surprised I am, that a male client is acting like this, it's inevitable that Mr. Miller would call again. Before I decide to finally answer my phone I tell Rich that Greg must truly believe, in the depths of his heart, that his fiancée is still alive.

Following extremely brief pleasantries, Greg bombards me with questions. "Why haven't you called?" "Do you have any clues?" "Is there any hope?" "You think I'm crazy, don't you?" As he begins to lose his breath, I decide to join him by lighting up a cigarette. Calmly, in between drags, I answer his questions, those that I can remember anyway. "You're not crazy. I have a very solid lead that I'm following up on. I have a train out to Maryland tomorrow." He asks me 'why a train?' A plane would be quicker and he'll pay for the expenses. I remind him our contract already stipulates all expenses will be included in his bill, and then continue to explain that, "Trains make more frequent stops in case there's a change in plans and I need to return or change directions." There's a momentary pause where I can almost hear him rationalizing it in his head.

Soon after, I hang up the phone, and turn in my chair to see Rich standing in my doorway, his tall wiry frame not blocking much of the light coming from the waiting room. Yes, his name is Richard, Rich, Dick. He's a private dick named Dick. The jokes are limitless but after knowing him for six years, you become null to it, like dead bodies after working in a morgue. He waits till I finish my cigarette and put it out till he asks why I didn't tell the client the real reason why I don't take planes. "Why don't you tell him you're afraid of flying?"

"I'm not afraid of flying. I just don't like to." He then chimes in that it's probably best that the clients don't think we're afraid of anything.

V

"Hello, Detective Peckman."

"Hi Manni, you sure you're up for this?"

"Detective Peckman, with what you're paying me I'll find you the Loch Ness Monster if you asked." After joking with him that if I ever get hired to look for Nessie, he'll be coming with me, I explain to the diving instructor I may need his help for more than one day. He assures me I have him for as long as I need and we'll discuss further compensation after we solve the case. After 'we' solve the case? He believes me, no hesitation, no looks of crazed confusion. He actually believes me, almost as if he knows something's wrong. But I think a lot of it is his overzealousness; he's eager to play Cowboys and Indians.

We get in his boat and begin searching some nearby caves, riding the liquid marble. As we come up empty-handed cave after cave, he asks me about my old cases and the "weirdest shit" I've ever seen. I show him Gwen, my tomahawk, and tell him the story about how I received her. The entire time I'm telling my story, he's as wide-eyed as a child meeting Santa Claus for the first time. Now, by the end of the day, after ten hours of diving and searching to only come up empty-handed, I look like a child who was just told Santa wasn't real.

As we head back, we see a pair of lovers on a rock formation. I comment about how unsafe that looks, and Manni's eyes light up again. He tells me of a secluded cove less than ten miles from here that's supposed to be off limits because of the dangerous tides.

However, because of its seclusion, it's often a lover's hot spot. I joke, "Why, Mrs. Robinson, are you trying to seduce me?" Following a brief chuckle, Manni says the cove may have some underwater caves. After agreeing it's the best lead we have, he suggests we wait till the morning so we can refill our air tanks and wait until the tide drops. He offers me a couch to sleep on for the night, but with him being a nonsmoker I stick to my plans of staying at a local motel.

Six am the following morning, he begins knocking on my door to wake me up. Little does he know I'm already on my third cup of coffee and fifth cigarette. A bad idea, Manni tells me. I shrug my shoulders and tell him, "Too late now, let's go fishing."

VI

"You see, Peckman, this is Assawoman Bay and just north of here is where we're going."

"Assawoman?"

"Hey what can I say? The locals call the cove we're headed to 'The Glory Hole.'" And before I could reply, Manni stops the car and informs me: 'We're here.' We get the boat to the water and triple check our gear before setting out. Unfortunately, we don't find any caves. Just as I'm about to tell Mani to head back, he notices an odd current affecting the boat.

"Why is the current odd?" To me waves are waves, the beautiful liquid marble I watched as a kid.

"The current feels like it's coming from the cove wall. There must be an underwater path leading to the other side, out to sea. There may be some caves down there." I need no more convincing. We get the tanks on and jump in. What feels like hours searching in the dark waters turns out to be all of five minutes. But we luck out and find a large cave. After climbing out of the water, I motion for Manni to stay by its edge, while Gwen and I check things out. A few feet in and I can barely see Manni or the boat through the fading light seeping through the cracks, casting ominous shadows in every direction. But after walking a little further, I hear some whimpering behind a stalagmite. I never was able to remember which was which, but spending the better part of a case in a mining cave fixed that. That's irrelevant now, though; she's here and still alive with no sign of T.J.'s creature. Jill sees me as I round the rock formation and step into a beam of light, but she doesn't run to me, she doesn't even stand up. That's when I notice her legs, they're both broken below the knees. There's blood everywhere, but there seems to be no other injuries on her. I call for Manni to help me get her out of here, when I realize she hasn't said a word yet.

"Jill, my name is James S. Peckman. I'm a detective and Greg hired me to find you." She nods. "It was a creature that took you, correct?" Her body begins shaking, but she nods again. "Where is it now?" She rolls on her back, clearly in pain, and points straight up. I look up just in time to be bombarded by this behemoth, easily seven feet in height, made more menacing by the dark surroundings. Manni runs for Jill, trying to avoid the creature, but it has a massive wingspan that effortlessly clobbers him. Manni must have hit his head because he's out cold, but luckily his harpoon landed by me. As the beast moves in on Manni, I grab the harpoon and call out. The distraction works; it turns for me and lets out a guttural growl that ends in more of a gurgled squawk. It then takes a deep breath through gills on its neck, and it spits out this black ink, like a squid, all over my face.

I can't see anything, but I'll be damned if I let that stop me. I have to clear my head, listen to its footsteps. Crouch down James; make it come to you, Wait for it... listen to the wet webbed feet slap on the rocks...wait James... locate the labored breath of surface air from the creature... Now! It shrieks letting me know I connected. I take this time to clear my eyes and see the monster leaning against the wall bleeding from the shoulder. It's bleeding red?

I don't know what I was expecting but definitely not red. It looks at me... and it smiles? I really think that was a smile and without taking its eyes off of me, it reaches for its head and, "Aw no. What are you doing? Don't do that." It rips out the gem from its forehead and tosses it to my feet.

It's hard for me to see the gem, but when I pick it up: "What the hell am I supposed to do with this? Don't walk away from me; I'm not done with you." Of course it doesn't listen to me. It gets to the water and turns around, only to let me see it rip the harpoon out of its shoulder before diving into the water. "Manni! You better be awake!" He moans in pain to let me know he'll be ok.

"Is... is it... it gone?"

"Jill, you'll be okay. Manni and I will get you out of here and straight to Greg."

152

VII

I get back to Argus on Friday at around three in the afternoon and nobody's here except Cereal. "Hey, Cereal, you know where Sarah is?"

He chuckles before even looking at me to reply, "Yeah, Warrior, her and Dick went someplace called The Glory Hole for the weekend."

I panic before I realize he's joking. "Really? You're missing out. They've got this great sea creature you'd love to get your hands on."

He then lets me know she's out getting lunch. "Oh, and Dick is hunting Bigfoot."

"You've got to be kidding me; someone hired us to hunt down Bigfoot again?" He says the name 'Bigfoot' was never officially said, but it sounds a lot like it. With Sarah out, I take it upon myself to call the old man. It takes me a while to find his number in the Rolodex because I can never remember his real name. Cereal lets me know that it is George Gidious. Sounds like a reject from a hero convention; acts like it too.

"Ah, Ancient Warrior, how good to hear from you directly. Did Sarah finally find a better use of her secretarial skills?"

"Listen, old man, I don't have time for your jokes. I've got to bring you a gem…"

"There better be a platinum ring attached to that diamond."

"You senile psychotic bastard, I'm serious. I just fought this water creature. It ripped off a ruby from its forehead and tossed it to me before it swam away." After he tells me it's okay to bring it over, I hop in my car. Despite the fact I haven't slept in over 30 hours, I feel more invigorated now than when I first signed on for the case.

I make it to the old man's house in record time, if not for breaking a few laws. I walk into his antique-looking Saddle River mansion, in awe, as always, of the sheer amount of history within these walls. I meet him in his study and he's ready with his glass of Amaretto and pipe filled with his favorite ancient Tibetan herbs. I take my usual seat across from the old gypsy psychometrist. After sliding him the ruby, he tells me the gem doesn't seem too special.

"I don't care much about the gem, but tell me if you can get anything about the creature from it."

He nods, and without another word places his hands around the gem without touching it. He starts feeling and seeing the gem's past. He starts telling me about the miner who was slain by his master for trying to keep the rock. I tell the old man to skip to when the creature gets involved.

"The ruby was forged onto the bottom of a sword for a Viking chieftain in the early 1300's after a victorious battle. Following a string of upsetting defeats, the Viking blames the tribe's seer. The tribe decided to travel to the New World in hopes of a change of luck, and the chieftain warns the seer that another tragedy will result in the seer's execution."

I couldn't take any more of his babbling; his scratchy voice is enough to make babies weep and grown men sick to their stomachs after a few syllables. Unfortunately, I've grown somewhat used to this, but still... "Enough, old man, stop with the Viking history and tell me how this pertains to the sea creature."

"Patience, Ancient Warrior..."

"Stop that crap; we're not getting into this again." He knows how to get under my skin.

"Okay Detective James S. Peckman." He says it with a wobble in his neck like it's too much to ask to be referred to by my own name. "I'm getting there. As I was saying, during their journey several of the tribesmen fell to the scurvy, including the leader's second in-command, his own son. The leader saw this as the final tragedy and the seer's fault. Before tossing him overboard, the leader knocked the seer unconscious with a hit from the butt of his sword, embedding the ruby into the seer's head."

"Unconscious, the magics within him were uncontrolled and adapted him to his new environment. He became the perfect creature of the sea. He spent his days continuing the journey he was on. Hundreds of years later, he arrives at the 'New World' to discover his brethren have long since perished. Now, with no chance of redemption or revenge, he simply wants to die."

I just don't get it. "So he does this by kidnapping defenseless women on vacation?"

The old man looks at me like the answer should been obvious. "He's still a Viking at heart; he needs to go to Valhalla. So..."

And then the answer is obvious. "So...he kidnaps the women, thinking like the days of old, their husbands, or boyfriends, would hunt the creature down and kill it in battle. Only thing is, none of these men ever found their wives and I was his only challenge…"

VII

"…so I have to go back to that cave and kill it in battle, or this creature will kidnap another girl every five years until someone else does. That's why Greg Miller kept calling me, obsessed with the creature rather than finding his wife, and that's why Halvorsen went crazy painting the monster nonstop."

As I pack my weapons, I can tell Cereal is confused about something. "Why five years? Why not every year? Or even every day, if it wants to get maximum attention?"

Trying to hurry out, I rush my answer. "I don't know; maybe because it wants to give the guys time for the hunt, or maybe just because it's not really evil. I don't know, but if you want to find out so badly you can go." Holding my bag out to him.

And Cereal, as always, replies in his calm deep voice. "Don't get mad at *me* because you haven't slept in two days and now you have to go fight a Viking zombie sea monster." He adds, with a jovial tone in his voice that implies humor, "Besides, I told you, I don't swim." Too frenzied to laugh, we exchange goodbyes with respective head nods and as I'm about to exit, he lets me know that he'll be leaving to help Richard out on the Bigfoot case tomorrow. He offers to wait until I return and we can go together. I nod again and slam the door behind me.

IX

"Manni!" I bang on the front door frantically until the groggy diving instructor answers the door in a free flowing robe revealing his too-tight tighty whities. Confused to see me, he asks what I'm doing here. I tell him he has "to take me back to that cave so I can kill that creature and save the next girl."

"Next girl?" I begin to explain, but he cuts me off, yawning his words. "James, James it's two in the morning. Even if we found the cave again, you won't be able to see shit in there. Wait till tomorrow and I'll get some spotlights, a couple of friends to help kill…"

"No!" I cut him off with more anger in my voice than I

intended. I explain to him that I have to be the one to kill it because it challenged me, and it needs to go to heaven, and it's waiting to die honorably. I don't think anything I said made a lick of sense, and the look on Manni's face confirms my suspicion. "Look, I'll explain in the morning, but you're right. Let's get some rest."

X

"So, what you think is that the thing we fought is some kind of zombie Viking beast wizard that's sick of its life and just wants to go to Van Halen."

"Valhalla, yes."

"Because suicide isn't honorable. I won't pretend to understand any of that, but fuck it let's go kill us the Creature from the Black Lagoon." Saying that, Manni gulps the rest of his coffee, and with a face of disgust claps his hands together and lets out a "woo" of enthusiasm.

We spend the next two hours gathering the various equipment we anticipate needing and a few 'just in case' items like barbed wire and gasoline. After picking up some very expensive self-generating waterproof spotlights, Manni spends half an hour arguing with his scheduled appointment. I hear all I wanted and decide to step forward to show the prospective diver Stacy and tell him, "You're welcome to join us if you'd like." I guess the sight of a Glock 9mm was enough, because he was running away before I finished my sentence. Manni makes some remark about having to explain that at their next lesson.

After we set off, I begin placing all the non-waterproof items in a protective bag. I finally put Stacy gently on top before sealing it. I keep Gwen on me, knowing she's not afraid of the water. It takes us a little longer than I would have liked to find the cave opening and even longer to unload the boat. But after making sure the cave is empty, we begin setting everything up and wait for the creature.

XI

"So that's why the old man calls me Ancient Warrior."

"Really? Because…" Manni is interrupted by a familiar growling squawk. I toss Manni the bag of weapons after arming myself with Gwen and Stacy, and tell him to begin circling round the back of the creature and wait by the water.

I reach into my scuba suit and toss the creature the ruby. "This isn't enough; I want your whole deformed Viking head." Not surprisingly, the creature welcomes the challenge by charging me. The moment it's about four feet from me, I throw a switch to turn the spotlights on, blinding the creature. I dive to the side, dodging the blinded creature, only to find out it isn't blind. I was hoping it was accustomed to the dark of the depths, but clearly not. It turns to me and spits out its ink. I dodge again and fire two rounds from Stacy. They both hit, but don't even slow the creature down. In retaliation, it fires several of these quill-like darts from the center of its chest, and one hits me right in the gut. Fearing it's poisoned, I pull it out immediately. Then, out of anger, I unload the rest of Stacy into it with hit after hit. The creature didn't fall until the entire magazine was emptied of all seventeen bullets. But fall it did, and before I got to use Gwen. Manni seems disappointed. I keep the gun handy as I double-check to see if this thing really is dead, but I wasn't even sure if it had a heartbeat. It wasn't moving, and that was good enough for me. I check my quill wound, and this creeping black ink is growing from where I was hit. There wasn't any pain, but that didn't stop me from damn near shitting my pants.

After loading up the boat, we tie the creature to the back and tug it ashore, where the police, media and Manni's student, who was frantically pointing at me, greet us. Before pulling the creature completely out of the water, the police tell me to raise my hands and let my prisoner go.

Manni tries to interject, but the police stop him, and tell Manni that he's in shock. As he steps forward towards the police, the ropes securing the creature rip from our hands. The creature shoots from the water, grabbing both Manni and myself by the throats.

An officer fires and misses, then the man obviously in charge tells him to hold his fire for fear of hitting one of us. I kick free and pull my tomahawk Gwen out and throw her, aiming for the creature's neck. In a single step, the creature tosses Manni to the side, dodges Gwen, and grabs me by the throat again, all faster than I thought possible. It pulls me close to its face and, with acrid breath, laughs right at me, its vile fumes traveling down my throat and up my nostrils. I place my hand against its throat and whisper to where its ear would be, "Game Over."

At that moment Gwen returns to my hand, as she's enchanted

to do, and cuts the creature's head clean off. Landing on my feet, I wipe the creature's blood from my face. I take a look at the quill wound. Whatever that black ink was, it begins to recede and feeling is coming back to my midsection. I look up to see the crowd's faces. From spectator, to officer, to media, all jaws hung, either in horror or awe. They're clearly waiting for some kind of explanation from me and all I can think of saying is, "See Manni, I told you, no matter where I throw Gwen, she'll hit my intended target, then return to my hand."

Manni doesn't react; I guess all this supernatural stuff just caught up to him. He's handled it so well for so long, he deserves a break. The head officer comes over to me, presumably to ask about the whole situation, but I see this as an opportunity for free advertising. I walk the officer over to the multiple news cameras and say, "Hello, Officer, I am paranormal Detective James S. Peckman of Argus Agency out of Newark, New Jersey." Pointing to the beheaded creature with Gwen, "And that, is how we get things done."

Full Circle
From the Casebook of Detective James S. Peckman
By Alex Azar

Trust, like women, is a fickle thing. Again, like women, it's hard to gain and all too easy to lose. Take my first partnership after I left the police, with Thaddeus Coleman. After I left the service, an old acquaintance suggested I look up Thaddeus, who had set up shop as a PI after retiring from the force himself. At the time, I was all but ready to cut every connection to anyone who ever *thought* of being a cop, so it took me a few months to swing by his office. However, when I finally did, we got to talking over some drinks and it turned out we had similar sob stories that drove us from behind the badge.

His wife of 23 years, an EMT, was caught in a fire that had no probable cause and was contained to her immediate vicinity; she died two hours later at a hospital in his arms, burnt beyond all recognition. I told him about how my wife and daughter died in a car accident at 10 mph, crashing into a guardrail. The car looked like it was crushed by two eighteen-wheelers, but traffic surveillance cameras show my wife driving below the speed limit, then inexplicably swerving off road into a ditch, hitting the rail.

We discussed the absurdity of the 'facts' about both incidents and formed a friendship over pain. It was nearly five years later when we went into business together with another PI. Unfortunately, Thaddeus and I had a falling out over a particular case, but this story is about how trust can sometimes come full circle.

I

I'm just about to step out of the office for lunch and enjoy the spring day, when my next case walks in. Seeing the tears and eyeliner running down her cheeks, I figure lunch could wait. She stands there with silent sobs and even the ruined makeup can't hide her attractive features, capped by piercing blue eyes that have surely bent men around her little finger. After a few moments of shared silence, I figure she's ready, so I start the way most of these conversations do. "Hello, I'm Detective James S. Peckman, how can I be of service to you?"

"My name is Madison LaSalle. I came here because you deal with… uh…" I want to say 'weird shit' but I fight the urge. I figure I should be more professional. "Well, because you deal with, I'm sorry but I don't know any other way to put it, but weird things."

I have to let out a little chortle and tell her that I couldn't have said it better. I continue and ask her what's so weird that she has to come to Argus. She thanks me for being understanding and not looking at her like she's crazy, a look I'm sure she's gotten every other time she's told her story. "My husband and I were walking back to our car after a movie when this car almost hit us in the parking lot. Stan, my husband, began yelling at the car, which slammed on its brakes and stopped in front of us. The driver rolled down his window and killed my husband with his fingers."

I shoot her the crooked look that I'm sure she's gotten before. Before she thinks I don't believe her, I jump in. "I just want to make sure I understand you. This man killed your husband with his fingers?"

"Yes, but he wasn't a man. His skin was yellow, not Asian yellow, but yellow like a dirty taxi." I ask her if she means he choked her husband or something of the sort, but she tells me this guy's fingers grew out like pool cues and stabbed her husband four times in the chest. I'm inclined to ask her what the police said, but she doesn't give me the chance. "The parking lot had a surveillance camera that caught the whole thing on video. After the police viewed it they thought I was even crazier, so they showed it to me. It shows Stan and I walking into the parking lot, the car almost hitting us and Stan yelling, but when the window rolls down there's a normal guy sitting in the driver's seat and instead of his fingers stabbing Stan, he has a gun and shoots him four times."

I tell her she's very brave and that most people wouldn't be able to talk about something so tragic so soon. More importantly, I tell her I believe her, which I do, and no, she's not some supermodel bombshell that I'd follow into hell, she's just an average woman who I know is telling the truth. Call it the fear in her words or the truth in her eyes, but I know she is. I've seen too many frauds and psychos to not know the difference. A fraud wouldn't admit to the existence of a tape disproving them, and a psycho wouldn't believe that I believe them and would have walked out, cursing me already. There's just something in her eyes that tell me she's telling the truth.

Already believing her, I find no choice but to take the case. I let her know I'll look into it, but I can't make any guarantees. Any clues left in the parking lot would have been swept away in the past three days, and all I have to go by is a video tape I may not even be able to get my hands on. Although, I still have enough connections in the department that getting the tape shouldn't be a problem. Madison thanks me with a huge hug and by wiping her mascara on the shoulder of my light blue shirt.

Now comes the difficult part. I've been doing this long enough, but I never quite got the hang of the subtlety of asking for payment. I still feel awkward asking for money from a person who's already at their most vulnerable. "Ms. LaSalle, before we continue there is the matter of… and I'm sorry to have to do this now but…" She cuts me off by gently raising her hand. She tells me that Stan was very successful and payment won't be an issue. She says she's willing to dedicate all of Stan's fortune to finding his killer. I tell her that's a good thing, but it's my job to wrap this up as soon as possible, which usually means less expenses. She thanks me again with a hug and staining the other shoulder of my shirt. After assuring her that I'll begin right away, I ask her to return tomorrow so she can sign the contract I'll have my secretary type up. As she walks out, she wishes me luck, and I ask her to keep faith.

II

"Lou, I need to see this video. You've always been able to get me evidence before; what's going on?"

Lou Triano, one of the few men I still trust on the force, has always been my key to the evidence room. He's never failed, but now he says I can't get this one tape, a tape we both know will never be looked at again. He tells me they have a new mandate for evidence linked to 'questionable' cases. Apparently, Madison convinced at least one other person that she wasn't crazy. After practically begging Lou, he tells me I can't take it but he can set it up for me to view it in the evidence room. At this point I'll take anything I can, so I agree.

Okay, there's Madison, and that obviously must be Stan. There's the car that nearly hits them. Wow, she wasn't kidding, he was less than a foot from them. Stan starts yelling, the window is rolling down and... well that's a disappointment. I was hoping to see this yellow monster, but it's an average looking guy. There's the gun and the four shots. He drives off, nothing. Damn it. One more time; there has to be something I'm missing. Near hit, yelling, window, shooting, drives away. I can't let the case end here, let's watch it again. Two of them walking, car almost hits them, the window rolls down, draws the gun and shoots, then... what was that? Rewind, slow it down, hmm seems like he's looking right at the camera before he drives off. Freeze-frame it, he is! He is looking at the camera, directly at it, even if just for a second.

"Lou! Lou, get in here." After berating me for yelling when I shouldn't even be here, I ask him if anyone noticed that the driver looks directly at the camera as he's driving off. He tells me no, and that it doesn't seem to be any kind of break; they ran his picture and didn't come up with any matches in any of the local precincts or any in the City. "Hmm, what about the plates? They're too blurry for me to see but I'm sure the tech department was able to clean up the image enough to pick up the plates."

"Yeah, we ran the plates, report came back from South Jersey, car was reported stolen over a month ago by a family man. And before you ask, we checked his record. He's clean, his wife's clean, his whole family is clean." Damn it, what am I missing? I watch the tape again, not thinking I'm going to find anything new, but I've been wrong before. Two of them walking, near hit, yelling, car stops, window lowers, hand draws gun.

"Lou, it's a long shot but can you crop in on the hand?" He tells me they saw the ring before and couldn't find any significant matches, but I have to see it any way. He shows me a print out of the freeze frame. No way! "Holy shit! Nothing significant? That circle triangle is the symbol of Ibn'Roth. He claims to be the son of Roth, a millennia-old god." I grab my coat and prepare to run out, but ask for the sake of due diligence: "What's the number on that license plate?"

"Tango, Charlie, 2, Juliet, Sierra, Papa"

"Lou, how did you miss this?" I can't believe Lou, of all people, doesn't see it. Gotta call Sid, let him know what's going on. Sid's another detective at Argus; he's a good man in a bad situation. I don't know of many black PI's, but he's the most trustworthy one I do know of--detective that is, not black guy. On what turned out to be his final case with the police, he and his two partners were caught in a shootout between two rival gangs. His partners were killed and he was shot in the head. Somehow, he survived, but ever since his partners have haunted him. Luckily, they act as aides as opposed to hindrances. They're more like extra eyes behind his back and they also act as a link to the afterlife. But of course, they can't tell him to answer his damn phone when I need to talk to him. I hate cell phones; I swear I'm getting rid of this thing. They never work when you need them, and when they do they act as a leash for people you don't want to talk to.

"Sara, I can't get hold of Sid. If you can reach him, let him know to call me ASAP." Damn, this can't be happening. Did he find something new after all these years?

III

Damn it! Is this really happening? If Ibn'Roth is really back, that means he's gotta be involved; Thaddeus gave me the sign, didn't he? I can't believe how quickly this one has dovetailed, but none of this explains how Stan and Madison are involved. Are they even a part of this, or were they just pawns to draw me in? Sid finally calls back. "Where the hell you been? Ibn'Roth is back, I'm on a train to Chicago right now, I need you to meet me there 'cause I think..."

"James, I'm sorry, but I'm in Argentina following a lead for a case I'm on. This is going to take at least another month, but if you still need me then I'll fly straight there." I tell him if this isn't wrapped up in a month I'll probably be dead, then I wish him luck before I hang up.

Okay, let's think this through. I'm on a train to Chicago, a city I've avoided the best I can for the better part of four years, following the slimmest clue I've ever had. That ring means the driver was a Privileged of Ibn'Roth, but the license plate looks like it's a clue sent by Thaddeus, after all these years, and I'm talking to myself. Whatever is going on, it's not good and I'm probably in way over my head, *again*. Damn it, nineteen hours on a train after a three day hiatus before even getting wind of this? I really should learn to take the damn plane. I wish Sid was here with me, shit I wish Liz was still around to help me out on this one. Without another thought, I reach into my jacket and pull out my rosary beads. "Liz, I've seen too much shit to think you're not listening to me from somewhere, so I want you to know I'm heading back, and it looks like I can finally right the wrong of your tragic death. I'm sorry it's taken me this long, but fate has played its hand. I hope you can forgive me and rest easy after this is all done; Lord knows you deserve it." Well that wasn't fun.

I'm finally in Chicago; the station is only a little further. Time for the last luggage check; Stacy, my Glock 9mm, in my side holster, and Gwen, my magically enchanted tomahawk tucked into my pants. In my bag, I've got a mix of magic items I inherited from the time I used to work with Thaddeus. That should be all I need, but I brought along clothes in case this takes longer than I think. Of course, it'll have to take the end of the world to force me to stay in this cursed city.

There it is: The Brood, a bar that's a front for all things paranormal. Supposedly it's named after the children of the gods that came before us. Ibn'Roth is reported to be one of these Brood. Just as I place my hand on the door to pull it open...

"You really need to learn to fly. I've been in town for half a day waiting for you," a voice says from behind me, and I see the face it belongs to in my head before I turn around. The voice belongs to a tall lanky black man with a shaved head, shaved for no other reason than the fact he's embarrassed of his growing bald spots. I turn and lock eyes with Thaddeus Coleman, but refuse to draw Stacy in such a public place. Smart move; Thaddeus was empty-handed, but I know he has Bruce and Dick on him. He's the only person I know who named his weapons after male characters, it's weird even for a Batman fan.

"Thaddeus, I wish I could say it's good to see you."

"Jimmy Peck, I wish I could say it's been too long. I assume you got the same message."

"It's James to you, and yes I got 'your' message loud and clear." He chuckles and says he should have known I'd blame him for all this, but he knew I wouldn't send any kind of message, even for revenge. So he knew it was a legit calling of Ibn'Roth.

"James, I know you don't want to be here, and even less to

work with me, but someone wants us both here. I got the same message as you, but I'm sure the license plates were opposite." He tells me of everything leading up to the plates, including Madison LaSalle, a yellow guy with magic fingers killing her husband.

He builds the case exactly as I experienced until he gets to the damned license plate. I tell him he was right about them being flipped in the video. "My plates were TC2JSP, not JSP2TC. Small difference, but clearly done for one purpose."

"Naturally. Whoever set this elaborate trap wanted each of us to think the other was sending the message." He tells me he rented a motel room up the street and suggests that we go there to come up with a game plan. Even watching his mouth form words drives an urge for me to break his nose with the butt of my gun. And of course, in his typical smug manner, he acknowledges the fact I have every right to want to rearrange his face, but also points out neither one of us can handle what's going on alone. Reluctantly, I motion with a hand for him to lead the way.

IV

As we walk up the outdoors flight of stairs to the second story of the motel a thought occurs, what if this is all Thaddeus' doing and he's just luring me into a trap. While still following him, I draw Stacy and hide her in the sleeve of my pea coat. He knows fear of Ibn'Roth returning would cloud my judgment, but he's not a villain, even after what he did. He just made a bad decision; a tragic decision, but a decision nonetheless. Suddenly, he stops at the top of the stairs. "You know, James, I know you don't trust me, but you could at least respect me enough to not think I wouldn't notice you arming yourself. This is the room, here." He pushes the door with an exaggerated swing to let the door swing open on its own, showing me our less than bearable accommodations.

I hesitate to enter, looking in from the doorway, with him waiting behind me. He concedes to my anxiety and offers to discuss matters at the diner across the street, but adds that we may not want anything we have to say to fall on civilian ears, or that it may not be civilian ears at all around us. Again, seeing no other option, I walk blindly into the unknown: first, coming to Chicago following a ring and a tape, and now into the confines of Thaddeus Coleman. I take my jacket off, holding on to Stacy the whole time, then sit on a chair next to the window. I'm at an angle where he can see Gwen in my waistband.

He sees the blatant show, and chuckles before he takes his jacket off. He flops it on the bed and holds his arms out wide, showing his dual holsters, both empty. Not to mention his pouch of goodies isn't attached to his belt like normal, nor can I see the butt of his dagger from behind him. Seeing my look of confusion, he says, "You lost trust in me, not vice versa. It's almost been four years and you're still the same man I trusted my life with time and again."

I say he's right, it has been four years, but how does he know I haven't changed?

"You saw the same clues I did, you still came here by train, and you still have London's eye in your wallet."

He's right on every account, especially that I still have the eye of London, my daughter's teddy bear, which goes to show the people who know you the most are the ones that can push your buttons the easiest. "True, I still have her teddy's eye but I know you still have your wife's EMT card in your wallet even though the picture was burned off." He tips his imaginary hat in a symbol of touché.

It's beginning to feel too much like old times; I have to change the subject. "So, do you think it's really Ibn'Roth trying to come back, again?"

"Of course I do, and so do you or you wouldn't be here."

Letting my frustration get the better of me I snap back, "Whether you're right or not, please stop talking like you know me and everything is still kosher between us." I hang my head and apologize, tell him I want to hate him for what he did but this does feel like old times. He pulls a bottle of Walker out of his bag, and I ask if we're just going to rush into the Brood with guns blazing. We weigh our options but we skirt around the fact, that it took four of us to stop him last time and one of us didn't make it. "And this time he's got help from some demon that apparently can be in two places at once and manipulate video records, oh and not to mention shapeshift, making it all the more difficult to track him… her, or whatever it is."

We cheers our drinks for a temporary leave of this insanity, he then breaks the ensuing silence. "I see you've never replaced the gun you lost in those caves, huh?" He pauses to elicit a response, but when he doesn't get one, he points out, as he often used to, "You know it was bad luck going on a mission with an unnamed weapon."

"So with Elizabeth, it's my bad luck that got..."

"No! Not what I was saying, James. I made that decision. I just meant in the cave... never mind." He must realize the memories brought up just by being with him carry bad feelings. He shuts up, for now at least.

About to fall asleep on the chair, he has to disturb the silence again. "What were you planning on doing, walking in there by yourself? Ask the bartender to point the way to the sneaky yellow guy?" I chortle and tell him it's still the best idea we've come up with. He agrees and shuts the light off.

V

"Okay so we're going in, ordering two drinks, and waiting till we find our mark." Sounds good to me; I nod. We round the corner and enter the bar. I hold up two fingers and tell the bartender two Walker and Rocks. The one thing to remember when ordering at the Brood is that the bar is dedicated to a race of ancient alien gods; with that in mind, never order anything 'on tap'. Trust me, it's not what you think. I get our drinks and take my seat next to Thaddeus.

Now we wait. In the subsequent half hour, two people enter and they both order something on tap. Thaddeus nudges me with his elbow, motioning with his eyes to someone sitting behind me who's been here longer than we have. He says this guy has been watching us from the moment we walked in. I let him know almost everyone in here has been watching us like hawks. "We don't belong here, and you know full well that the same thing happened last time we were here." He concurs, but insists that the man behind me is the yellow shapeshifter. When I ask him what proof he has, he reminds me of the ring the guy in the video was wearing. At its mention I'm inclined to turn around, but I know that would be a bad move. Thaddeus continues, by saying that he hasn't seen the ring, but this guy has been hiding his hand. With that, I give him a look that he knows means 'give it up.' He admits defeat by taking a large drink from his beverage. Another person walks in the door and...it's Madison. Thaddeus sees her also; we both slouch down in our seats. Looking at her from the shadows, seeing her all made up, with no tears and no red eyes, she looks like a classical actress, like a Katharine Hepburn. But that doesn't explain what she's doing here, unless..? And sure enough. as she orders a drink on tap. she turns into the yellow monster she herself described in both Thaddeus' offices and mine.

Before getting his drink, the monster walks into a door leading to a room next to the bar. The bartender follows, as do several of the 'patrons': some sporting tails, others horns, and even more with both. The surly bartender, with fangs extending far beyond his now deformed maw, peeks his head back through the doorway. "Ya'll fucks kna what ta do; if not get the fuck outta here!" He then disappears back into the abysmally dark room with the others. That's when we find our target.

Without a word to one another, Thaddeus and I move in on a nervous figure sitting at the bar looking right and left, left and right, clearly not knowing what he's actually looking for. We approach the mousy-looking patsy from opposite sides and each press a gun into his side. "So, what brings you here, stranger?"

Knowing he has no way of telling whether we belong here or not, we press our advantage. "You heard Donovan, 'if you don't know what to do you should probably leave.'" I see that Thaddeus is glad I took the role of the aggressor, because his strengths weren't his investigation skills, and he was particularly bad with names.

Then the stammering and stuttering begins. "Wuh wel ...well, I...I...I was told iiif if I if I wanted to huh helpp th the mmmulti ffaccc faced god a and nd be apuh...part of th th the res re resurrection, I I I shu should coh come hu here an and wuh wait."

With the patience and tact of a rapid bull in a china shop, Thaddeus interrupts, slapping the poor guy in the side of his head. "What the hell is wrong with you? Are you scared, cold, or just dropped on your head as a kid?"

"Fuh fuck you!"... he pauses as if to think. "All three" which he's able to say clearly. Thaddeus asks whose resurrection he was talking about, and this guy has enough fortitude to give Thaddeus a crooked look, and I saw that I had to cut in.

"We only ask because there is more than one resurrection reaching fruition soon." It's fun trying to talk like a cultist every once in a while. After weighing the conversation in his head, the mousy guy feels comfortable enough to answer without any trouble: "Ibn'Roth."

The name hits my stomach like a gallon of rancid milk and lemon juice. Thaddeus sees how disturbed I've become and decides to continue for me. "What the fuck do we need a stuttering fool like you for? What can you do for the powerful Ibn'Roth?"

Obviously frustrated at our lack of faith in his worth, he painfully tells us that now that the anchor has been found again, he's to use his abilities of aural-psychometry to make sure all things are ready at the sacrificial altar. After he finally finishes his stuttering, Thaddeus and I both know what he means by 'the anchor', so Thaddeus pulls the stranger close and whispers something into his ear. The guy instantly disappears from his seat, running behind the empty bar area, and before I can ask Thaddeus what he told him, he returns at a much slower pace. He pauses to look us over, then sprints again, this time towards the exit. He turns back to address us: "You tuh tuh two are fuh fu fucking cr crazy."

Thaddeus wonders how a punk like that could have received such a powerful ability. Not knowing how to answer, I suggest we finish our drinks and leave.

I ask him what he said to make the stutterer run off like that. He says, "I told him to check out this bar before their last attempt to resurrect Ibn'Roth." Clearly the discovery that we're two of the people who helped thwart them before, or 'the hated ones' as we're known in their little circle, was enough to frighten him.

As we walk out the bar, I can't help but wonder who this multi-faced guy he was talking about actually is. Before my musing can take me too far into thought, we see our little stutterer talking to two men that my instincts say are more than men. Thaddeus must notice it as well, because he's power walking away like he's on speed, and I follow suit. "Th tha th that's ss theh them!" he calls from behind.

Knowing we've been spotted, we turn into the first alley we see. Thaddeus runs into the wall at the end, while I climb the fire escape just above where he is. The two 'men' rush in and laugh at Thaddeus' apparent predicament, having clearly forgotten about me already. They close in on Thaddeus. Relaxing, they shift out of their human forms, to reveal they are 'Privileged' demons. *Privileged* is the title of humans and demons alike that are sworn followers of a Brood god, in this case Ibn'Roth. They are distinguished as such by having the mark of Ibn'Roth on the left side of their face, with the circle around their eye, and the triangle covering the corresponding cheek. Most of the Brood allow their Privileged to choose where the mark goes. This isn't the case for Ibn'Roth, who doesn't want his followers to hide who they are to the rest of the world.

Waiting for Thaddeus to give me the signal, I climb to the outside of the escape ladder, readying myself in position. Still not turning around, he steps back from the wall and places his hands on the top of his head as if to surrender. That's my cue; I drop down and kill the Privileged to the left with a tomahawk chop to the side of his throat, with my other hand covering his mouth to muffle any screams. Shocked, the other Privileged turns to me, allowing Thaddeus to turn and place a gun to the bottom of his jaw. He also covered his Privileged's mouth, slamming the creature's head against the opposite brick wall. I look at Thaddeus and can't help but smirk; couldn't say how many times moves like that saved our lives.

"I have two questions, and you're going to answer them quietly after he removes his hand from your mouth. If I don't like your answers or if you're too loud, you'll need the strength of Ibn'Roth himself to keep from crying after I'm done with you." The moment Thaddeus removes his hand from his mouth, I move my Glock in front of his face so he knows I'm not joking. "Where and when?"

"*Cron einnod ayasor...*" Thaddeus gives him a stiff hook to the gut and whispers at him to speak in English; the calmness of his voice has all the intimidation of looking down the barrel of a loaded gun. After coughing for several moments, the Privileged continues. "You're too late; you can't stop the coming of Ibn'Roth. Tomorrow night he returns, with or without me." I ask him again: where? He starts to laugh, and tells us we already know where, and his laughing increases. He continues his laughing while talking in an alien tongue again: "*Cron einnod ayasor toyap senoni dech.*"

Thaddeus and I look at each other, not knowing what's going on, so Thad instinctively hits him again. When he picks his head back up, I shove my gun in his mouth and ask what's so funny. Still no response, so I cock the hammer and, instead of stopping, he continues while he uses my finger to pull the trigger, blowing his head wide open, and sending his brains all over the brick wall behind him.

Covered with bits of blood and brains and other juices, Thaddeus and I look at each other, again not knowing what to think until…

"He was calling me in our tongue." We turn, and I see the yellow guy from the surveillance video standing behind us. Next to the yellow guy is the yellow guy, and another yellow guy next to him, and about fifteen more of the same yellow guy. "And he was laughing because his and his friend's sacrifices have been fulfilled." I see the twenty or so mouths move in unison, but I only hear one voice coming from the yellow guy in front. Are the rest merely illusions or...? Wait, did he say that those Privileged sacrifices have been fulfilled? What did it have to do with us? Before I'm able to think too much about what Thaddeus and I have walked into, the two copies at either end move toward us and tell us to drop our weapons and raise our hands.

Now I know they aren't illusions. Each one has a voice and is tangible, which makes each one a threat, and the bad news keeps coming. "I am Xordam, the lord of deception, the multi-faced god, and you two will be sacrificed along with a third tomorrow night." Apparently the Privileged's sacrifice was to draw the two of us out. But who's the third…

VI

…The ache on the back of my head and blurry vision tell me all I need to know. I was knocked out, probably from a single blow, and a good one at that, I don't remember even preparing to defend myself. "About time you came to, James, you're the young one here and I've been up for what feels like two hours." I tell Thaddeus he's old and senile; it was probably only ten minutes. After a quick chuckle, I scan our surroundings. I see a green-painted wooden bench secured in a cement ditch that looks like it's been on the wrong side of Chicago weather for decades upon decades. We're in the dugout of a Little League baseball field. If history is any indication, I know exactly which field we're at.

Thaddeus hands me what looks like a brown mucus-covered maggot, but after all the years I worked with him I know precisely what it is, and will never be able to forget. The thing that makes Thaddeus such a great P.I. isn't really his investigation skills or, as we learned, his interrogation abilities, but the gadgets that he has. When he first stepped into the world of a paranormal investigator, Thaddeus had the fortuitous notion to substitute monetary payments for items of the supernatural variety when possible. This has proven crucial to his longevity in the lifestyle.

I place the tele-maggot in my ear with the hand that isn't

cuffed to his and to the chain link fence that creates the fourth wall of the dugout facing the field. After the maggot burrows into my ear canal to the drum, Thaddeus and I become mentally linked. Basically, if I want to talk to him all I have to do is think it and he can hear it in his head and vice versa. The major drawback is if there's anything I don't want him to know, I can't think about it--and as everyone knows, the less you want to think about something, the harder it is to think about anything else. I ask him what other tools he has and all he tells me is that he came as prepared as he could under such short notice.

He tells me something I was already able to figure out myself: they didn't search us for other weapons. Either they're careless and thought that the guns they made us drop in the alley were all we had, or Thaddeus was able to activate his cufflinks before they knocked him out. His cufflinks are enchanted to hide any weapons on him from anyone doing a search. Me being handcuffed to him might have put me within the proximity of the cufflinks' range. He doesn't dress this way to impress the ladies, that's for sure. Unfortunately, a third option occurs to me; they may be confident that no matter what we brought to the party, it won't be able to stop them. That in itself is a scary thought, even if it's not true, but it drills into your mind… *What if we fail?*

They have us handcuffed with our backs to the fence, facing the gray wall where someone with the colorful name of C-Money shamed the English language to let everyone know that he "wuz here". I try to look behind me to see if I can figure anything out, but the position my arm is in makes turning around extremely painful. I give up trying to see behind me, deciding whatever is there, I probably don't want to see.

Unfortunately, my mind doesn't give up. I think back to the last time I was here in Chicago, and catalogue everything I know about where we are. We're in the visitors' dugout for Hamlin Park, a baseball field just inside city limits. The park was closed down after the paranormal forces began using Chicago as a traveling hub between different planes. There's something about the evil in the city that attracts them. I know what you're thinking, 'What about New York City?' Let me tell you, New York may be a scary, impersonal city, but Chicago has been evil long before New York became the center of attention. Besides, many of these creatures and demons may belong in hell, but they love the cold.

They used the pitcher's mound as a honing focus for the energies resurrecting Ibn'Roth last time, this is exactly where Elizabeth died and this is exactly why I've avoided this damn city.

Hey James, snap out of it. Thaddeus' voice, or more accurately his thoughts, booms between my ears.

It's been so long that it's easy for me to get lost in my own thoughts, "I forgot we were linked."

Listen you're right, this is where Elizabeth died; yes this is why you hate me but now is not the time to bring yourself down. I hate it when he's right, especially when it comes to anything to do with Elizabeth. We need to figure out how they plan on bringing Ibn'Roth back, and why they brought us here.

"And who's the third person that they mentioned in the alley Thaddeus? Sid was with us last time we were here, but I just spoke to him; he's in South America."

And Liz was the only other one with us, so it has to be someone new entirely.

"Maybe not, Thaddeus. Elizabeth died violently in the midst of a lot of energy; we've both encountered instances where spirits become anchored to their place of death. Maybe that's why they brought us back to the field."

We made sure they can't use the same method of resurrecting Ibn'Roth, so it'd have to be a different reason they brought us back here. You may be right James, but that doesn't explain what we're doing here if the resurrection isn't until tomorrow night. Or even what we have to do with all this.

"What else do you think? They always need sacrifices. And who better to foot the bill than the same two that screwed them over last time?"

Enough with the good news James, it's awfully quiet around here. I don't like it; I can't take this for a whole night.

Maybe, they left us here to drain us mentally and physically. Make it less likely we'll be able to resist tomorrow night. They may just want us to mentally defeat ourselves by thinking of the worst possible shit that could happen; yet none of it actually comes to pass. I resume my futile attempt to see behind me, but the lack of voices, or noises in general, ease my mind somewhat.

I think you're right about draining us mentally, but not about things not coming to pass. Like you said, they didn't bring us out here just for the fun of it. We're probably here to be sacrificed after they torture us.

Pulling Stacy out of her holster, I let Thaddeus know that I don't intend to wait around all night to figure out. I point her at the cuffs before Thaddeus slaps the gun away.

You may be a good shot James, but I don't trust the ricochet.

We can't stay cuffed; whatever it is they've got planned will be that much harder if we have both our hands free. He shuts me up by pulling what looks to be an ordinary piece of tape out of his jacket, but again I know better. He places the tape around the chain of the cuffs then spits on it. With his saliva wetting the tape, he says the Gaelic word to activate the spell and the tape begins to melt away in a bubbling dance of blues and greens that takes the chain with it. We both know enough to not let any of it to touch us as it falls and hits the cement floor of the dugout. Instantaneously the kicked up dirt evaporates under the boiling mass, and the cement follows suit, and it doesn't stop until long after it's gone from our sight. Ten seconds after the spell is cast, the magic properties that were activated with the saliva fade to nothingness. Like I said, it's not his detective skills but his little gadgets which seem to get him out of any trouble he finds himself in.

I struggle to avoid slipping into thoughts of our old cases together.

"Those were good times, huh?" But I guess it doesn't work. As difficult as it is to stop thoughts from crossing my mind is to remember to listen to every thought in his mind, not just those directed to me.

Exactly James, so we shouldn't have to go over any more plans, right?

Without a word, or thought, I jump up, holding Stacy out, hoping something catches my eye. Now, more than ever, I feel like I need to shoot something. Thaddeus rises slowly drawing his remaining gun and something else from his coat's inside pocket. We walk out of the dugout back to back and step onto the field. I can't help but think this is what they wanted and Thaddeus confirms the thought with one of his own. Nevertheless, we end up on what used to be the pitcher's mound, the exact spot where Elizabeth died. We make a few circles until we're both absolutely certain that there is no ambush waiting for us.

I take a knee and seem to automatically begin praying to Elizabeth. I pull out my rosary beads, finding myself especially glad they didn't search us. This would have sent them into a frenzy, possibly killing me before they could drag me here. Not that they have anything against religion itself, just any religion that doesn't acknowledge their own gods, like Ibn'Roth.

Thaddeus asks me what he always asks me when he sees the beads. *How can you believe in God after seeing all that we've seen?*

I let him know what I always do when he asks that. It's all that we've seen that reinforces my faith in God. And it's true, after seeing all the evil shit that this world digs up and attracts from other worlds, I have to believe there is some force of good out there protecting us from the evil we don't even get to see. With that thought running through my head I place the beads on the mound, telling Elizabeth that I'll pick these up when she's safe again.

And right on cue, two guards of the ceremony come running towards us. As they get closer I can see that they're more Privileged, this time human. But I still can't understand them because they're speaking that alien gibberish that we heard in the alley. Knowing what that gibberish brought last time, I don't even look at Thaddeus for confirmation; I just begin shooting at them. What Thaddeus said earlier about his trust in my aim was founded on years of first-hand experience. The first bullet hits the closer of the two square in the chest. My second shot is a glancing blow to the other's shoulder that spins him out of the way of the third bullet, which embeds itself in the back wall of the home team's dugout. No longer moving, the Privileged welcomes the fourth bullet with his throat. Thaddeus suggests we get out of there before any more Privileged, human or not, show up.

VII

Hiding our newly acquired matching metal bracelets, we hail a cab. And let me tell you, if you think it's a pain to find a taxi in New York, try finding one without a call in any other city. But eventually we get one, and the driver laughs this high-pitched, almost girly laugh that contradicts his burly frame and woodsman beard. He makes some comment about us being crazy walking out here with the storm approaching. Realizing we don't know what he's talking about, he tells us that a storm just sort of appeared a couple of hundred miles north of us and is traveling here quickly; should be here by tonight. Like I said, they love the cold. The driver says he wasn't planning on picking up any more fares, but he saw us walking and took pity. We thank him for his generosity, and ask him to take us to The Brood. Again he laughs his girly laugh and calls us crazy for wanting to drink instead of calling it a night.

Thaddeus tells him; "There's no better way to prepare for a storm than by getting drunk."

The driver laughs again and pauses before agreeing. "You two seem like a couple of good guys and I was just planning on calling it a night, how 'bout this? Fare's on me, if the first round is on you."

Good job, Thaddeus, now you've got a civilian involved in this. It's up to you to fix this; I'm not having this man's life on my conscience.

If that's how you feel, James. With that thought, Thaddeus grabs my hand lifting it up and caresses my face with the other. "Sorry, honey, this is a party of two--but give me your number. Maybe we could do it another time." It's seriously scary how quickly he flipped that switch in his head. What's more scary however, is how disgusted the driver looks at us. He forces us out and we walk the rest of the way. To think with everything this world has gone through, people could be so ignorant of the reality around them.

VIII

After a long, cold, silent walk we pass our quaint little motel, which looks more appealing than ever. Let me correct myself; for the first time, it actually looks appealing, inviting even, but a quick glance is all we can afford. We know Xordam will continue with his plans tomorrow night with or without us for sacrifices. As we learned in the alley yesterday, there are more than enough people willing to sacrifice themselves for the resurrection of Ibn'Roth. Another minute or so and we're outside the door of The Brood, with no plan and, even worse, no idea of what to expect.

Knowing that Xordam can alter his looks and create duplicates of himself, we have to handle this carefully. Then a thought occurs; actually it's Thaddeus' thought in my head.

Let's check the alley and see if my gun and knife are still there. They were sloppy enough not to search us; they may have left them on the ground. Worth a shot.

We check the alley for the weapons, but no luck with that.

"Listen to that, Thaddeus. I can hear some voices from the vent, but I can barely make them out."

If you concentrate you'd have learned that they have the 'spirit' and all should be in order, but they haven't heard from the two guards at the field. They're concerned because Xordam hasn't returned yet.

The spirit has to be Elizabeth; we have to get in there.

Listen James, I want Elizabeth back as much as you do, but we don't know what's in there. We should think this over.

Screw that; we know Elizabeth is in there, and we know Xordam's not. The situation isn't going to get any better thinking it over.

Not being able to argue with my rationale, Thaddeus motions his hand, letting me lead the way. With all this running through my head, it's almost possible to forget how cold it is, but the tingling in my feet that turns to stinging reminds me this is Chicago in the center of an unnatural storm blowing off the Great Lakes. They sure do love the cold. After another quick inventory check, we realize if we're going to save Elizabeth and stop Ibn'Roth's return, we have to do it quick.

IX

I check the stained-glass window at the front of the bar and see that they closed early. No civilians are present; only the bartender and four people with the marks of Ibn'Roth. I don't know what would convince a human to forfeit his mortal life for a slim chance at marginal powers if Ibn'Roth is ever successfully resurrected. But every time I deal with this, there's more and more of them, and they always seem to be in groups of two, as though they have a buy two-for-one deal on human souls. These Privileged give up their humanity, or 'demonity' as the case may be, and the only thing that is guaranteed in return is a magical tattoo and death, usually a bloody one.

During my observations and musing, Thaddeus lets me know that I should move away from the window. Before I can even figure out what his thoughts mean, he tosses two pellets at the window. Seeing them in the air, I dive out of the way knowing what's to follow. Before I even hit the floor, the wall explodes into the bar, killing three of the Privileged. While the fourth is still confused I throw Gwen at him, and as she's enchanted to do, she hits the mark, killing him. I give Thaddeus a dirty look, letting him know, "So much for subtlety." Gwen returns to my hand like she always does.

Hey James, you were the one who wanted to get in and save Elizabeth.

Without further argument we step into the bar, or more precisely onto the bar, looking for the bartender, whom we can't see amidst the rubble.

I try telling Thaddeus to keep his eye on the back door, knowing someone will come rushing out, but before I can think it the bartender jumps out from behind the bar--go figure--and there's a psychic backlash. The wave of mental energy is so powerful it fries the tele-maggots in our ears, rendering them useless. This has only happened to us once before, and it was dealing with a psychic of incredible power. The bartender doesn't seem to be as powerful, 'cause he's writhing in more pain then either of us, holding his head. Thaddeus doesn't miss a beat and puts two bullets in his chest, dropping him dead, not to mention the other four that shatter a few of the remaining liquor bottles.

Curious as to why that back door hasn't opened yet, I motion for Thaddeus to check it out while I search the bartender. Bending behind the bar, trying to avoid the glass of the various bottles and shards from the mirror, which is mostly fallen and strewn about the floor. The remainder of the mirror is cracked and still hanging, reflecting dozens of distorted images of Thaddeus. Slipping on some broken bricks, I do exactly what I was trying to avoid and cut my hand on a broken bottle, dropping Gwen. Luckily, the slip puts me right on top of the bartender and I can immediately see the two bullets worked.

Meanwhile, Thaddeus notices that Xordam must have entered through some secret entrance. He 'notices' by way of a supernaturally powerful punch to the chest, sending him halfway across the destructed bar onto a pile of bricks. Xordam fully emerges from the back room, holding a woman by the hair. She must be who they anchored Elizabeth in, and plan on sacrificing along with us tomorrow night. I'm so sleep-deprived I'm not sure if it's tomorrow night or tonight.

She's kicking and struggling as would be expected, but for an instant I get a clear look at her face, and she looks like Madison LaSalle. It seems as though Xordam used her appearance when fooling Thaddeus and myself. Thaddeus, getting back to his feet, gives me a look suggesting he knows what I'm thinking, and he disagrees. "He's a multiplier," is all that Thaddeus says, and it explains his thoughts. Thaddeus believes they are both Xordam trying to fool us into saving 'Madison', leaving him available for another attack or an escape.

Before we can discuss it, Xordam begins multiplying, as does the girl in his arms, and before I fully understand what's happening, there are dozens of couples over what's left of the bar. Then another thought occurs: what if we're both right? What if Xordam anchored Elizabeth into one of his doubles? I shout to Thaddeus that if we kill Elizabeth's host body her spirit will die along with it; she needs to be released, not killed.

During this debate Xordam holding Madison, and Xordam holding Madison, and again Xordam holding Madison keep circling us, making it impossible to tell which is the original couple. Not having those damn maggots is making it difficult to form a plan with Thaddeus, who's halfway across The Brood. Not even sure if killing the original Xordam will erase the rest or have no effect outside of the single death, I shout to Thaddeus: "There can be only one!" Hoping my guess is right.

The same time that Thaddeus and I raise our guns, aiming from one Xordam to another, every Xordam raises a hand with an extended finger growing like Madison described back in Jersey, as countless pairs of captivating blue eyes that warned of trouble in my office mere days ago plead for us to help. Xordam, clearly frustrated at this standoff, begins yelling, initially in his alien tongue, and then so we can understand, "You will not hinder the return of Ibn'Roth a second time. I don't need you two, only her." Shaking the Madisons with a single arm, or Madison with his free arms? "I simply thought it poetic to sacrifice Ibn'Roth's two previous thwarters." I wonder again why Sid is exempt from this fiasco, but thankful that he won't have to see Elizabeth die twice. "Your sacrifices aren't necessary, and I will not allow you to interfere with me any longer." Searching the room, I see the one thing I need to end this. I squeeze Stacy more confidently than I ever have before, and as perfectly as ever she hits her target square in the forehead, killing a Xordam in the far back closer to Thaddeus.

Thaddeus, who must have seen what I saw, fired at the same time, and hit the same target almost as perfectly as I had. Slowly all the remaining Xordams and Madisons, begin to boil and evaporate into nothingness. All save for the single Madison that the original Xordam was holding hostage. After the rest are completely gone, the remaining Madison begins to shake, then suddenly drops to the floor, and in the wake is a familiar face, if only an apparition of our departed friend, Elizabeth Gomez.

X

Elizabeth floats over to Thaddeus and me, who have walked next to each other to congratulate ourselves on a job well done. Putting an intangible hand on each of us: "I'm glad you two were finally able to notice all the copies had the wrong color eyes."

Thaddeus and I look at each other confused. "You have green eyes?" I wonder aloud.

Thaddeus agrees by saying he thought hers were brown. He clarifies how he knew which Xordam to shoot. "Even though all of the mouths were moving, only the one had breath coming out of it."

"Breath?" I again wonder, confused. "His was the only reflection that could be seen in the mirror." After a quick chuckle together, I notice that Elizabeth is beginning to float away, in a very Hollywood way. She's looking down at us, as Thaddeus joins me in watching her leave.

None of us can seem to find the words to say at a moment like this. Eventually, just before she reaches the ceiling, Elizabeth tells us that she's finally free. "I've been dead for too long to not know Heaven's embrace. I thank you both for bringing me. Jimmy Peck and Thaddeus working together again, guess everything is in a constant cycle. If that's true, I'll see you again. I love you both."

With that Elizabeth begins to ascend closer to the ceiling, and my mind is screaming to say something to her—anything--but the words can't form. Thaddeus, even without the aid of the tele-maggots, knows me well enough to help me to start talking. He gives me a slight nudge with his elbow.

"Elizabeth, wait! Liz, there's so much I want to say, so much I need to say…" A ball forms in my throat the size of a grapefruit, and it blocks all sounds coming from me save the sobs that ensue. Liz, for all her will, can't stop her ascent or even slow it; she just looks down to me with sorrowful eyes and tells me she knows, just before her head penetrates the ceiling, with her body following through. This Hollywood moment, which seems to last forever, is abruptly cut off by the sound of bricks crashing to the floor from the decimated wall, snapping me out of my private musings. Thaddeus places a hand on my shoulder, and again no words are needed between the two of us. All that's needed is an understanding that, for the second time, Liz has been ripped from our lives, but this time I don't think my nights will be plagued with images of her death.

XI

Standing in the open-walled hallway outside of our motel room, Thaddeus and I independently meditate on the events of the past forty eight hours; him, concentrating on his knife as he turns it over in his hand, and me working my rosary beads through my fingers. Finally, I break the silence. "Well, Thaddeus, maybe you were right all those years ago."

Shrugging his shoulders, he says it doesn't matter who was right any more; things have finally been rectified.

I ask him if he'd consider returning to New Jersey with me, and working with Argus.

"No thanks. It was like the good old days, but you created your own niche in Jersey, and I've become too accustomed to life in L.A. But, I'm sure we'll work together again."

Something tells me he's right. As I look at the wreckage that was once the Brood, I can't help but think of Elizabeth's words, about everything being a cycle. If she's right, everything that once was shall come back to bite us in the ass, and that probably means the power of Ibn'Roth will come back full circle as well.

Dead, Book of the Dead
From the Casebook of Detective James S. Peckman
By Alex Azar

I hate reading modern detective stories that relate everything that happens to the movies. Rarely does this crap ever mimic the atrocities that some call cinematic experiences; more like celluloid extortion. Vampires don't look like models or teen heartthrobs, Frankenstein's creation, who isn't called Frankenstein, is not a brainless oaf but more articulate than most Ivy League graduates, and zombies don't eat brains, they feed on the souls of the newly dead to delay their own decay. But damn it, once in a while Hollywood gets it right; werewolves killed by silver, check. And that damned Book of the dead, yeah it's real, too.

I

It's the end of November and the air conditioners are on high. It hasn't been an Indian summer by any means, but this week is especially hot. The air conditioner humming, ceiling fan rattling, and the energy-draining heat is a perfect combination to put anyone to sleep. Couple that with a lack of work, and I'm perfectly content dozing the day away, but that always seems to be against the Fates. Just as my eyelids are getting too heavy to hold open, I hear my intercom's buzzer, followed by Sarah announcing a potential client. "James, there's a man here to see you: Samuel Campbell." I don't even have time to reply before she says she's sending him in.

I light a cigarette in a vain attempt to wake up, or at least to look awake. Mr. Campbell walks, in holding a large satchel, around the same time the first puff of smoke leaves my mouth. Before any pleasantries are exchanged, I ask him if he minds, indicating the cigarette between my index and middle fingers. He shakes his head no. I take another drag and offer one to him before I exhale. Accepting with a steady hand, he shows me he's not as worried as most people are who come to see me. Every movement of his is deliberate: he knows what he's going to do and how he's going to do it.

I could tell he was measuring me up, just as I was him. Satisfied that he had justifiable cause to be here, I extended my hand. "Hello, I'm Detective James S. Peckman, how can I can I be of service to you?"

Cutting the pleasantries short, Mr. Campbell lays it out there. "Detective, have you ever heard of the Book of the Dead?"

"You mean the Necronomicon Ex Mortis?"

"No. Yes, but it's just Necronomicon. 'Necronomicon' means Book of the Dead. Ex Mortis means dead; adding those words to the end of Necronomicon was from a movie with reverse dendrophilia, by a director messing with the minds of his audience. Necronomicon Ex Mortis is redundant; the Necronomicon, however, is the Book of the Dead as translated by Alhazred."

Interrupting him, I ask if he doesn't mean H.P. Lovecraft. I mean, sure I've dealt with the Brood, and their immortal god parents, but none of my dealings with Ibn'Roth or any of the others has indicated that Cthulhu, Yog-Sothoth, and Nyarlathotep were real. Just because I don't believe in it, though, doesn't mean I haven't read up on the mythos.

Mr. Campbell, who prefers to be called Sam, explains that the accuracies of the beings may differ, but he has every faith that Xordam, Arora, and the other Prime Gods and Brood are the same as those from the "Cthulhu Mythos." His explanation-less explanation oddly has me convinced. I mean, each of these gods go by so many names, none of which are English, who says they can't be one and the same, or maybe closely correlated like Zeus and Jupiter? I don't know but there's something about this guys' calmness that's throwing me off.

He recites a quote he claims is from the Necronomicon, scrawled on what looks to be toilet paper, but I'm going to assume is actually tissue paper. "This passage actually recounts the persuasion of H.P. Lovecraft in much a similar fashion as Alhazred." Apparently, Lovecraft was supposed to be a major player, or a pawn as Mr. Campbell interprets it, in the coming events.

His continued recounting of the Necronomicon is just like reciting bedtime stories for him. And through it all, I can't figure out why he's here. He hasn't once looked over his shoulder in a nervous twitch, nor is he constantly rubbing his hands together or tapping his feet. Not a single trait of one who's in paranormal, occult or otherwise unnatural danger. All he's showing is a vast knowledge of what he believes to be the actual Book of the Dead. Before he can finish his theory of the Necronomicon not being associated to a specific pantheon of gods, demons, monsters, or other nasties, I ask him why he's here.

"You clearly have a far greater understanding of this book than I, so what do you need me for?"

He tells me the book will try to kill him in three nights. "The book is cursed and it passes that curse onto whoever reads even a single passage from it."

"So, if you're so sure you're going to die, why are you so calm? I mean; if I knew I was going to die in a few days, I wouldn't be so blasé about it"

He tells me that his 666 days are almost up but there is a way out, which he hopes I can help with. Apparently, anyone who reads from the book will have six hundred and sixty-six days to live, at the end of which, a demon, or a hunter, or some other hellish being will arrive to usher your sorry ass to hell. That is, unless you write a unique passage in the blood of an innocent infant.

Sam had learned all this by reading the book and has been resigned to his fate, never daring to harm a child, until recently. He claims to have uncovered a great happening that will dawn a new age for the Prime Gods. He also claims that through the book he has acquired knowledge and skills to ward off this coming catastrophe.

Sam has to know what I'm going to ask next: "Well, where is it?" He simply lowers his head and slowly shakes it back and forth, disappointed, like a father being told his son is no good at sports.

"This is why I did not bring it; the temptation would be too great for even you to resist its allure." Should have figured he wouldn't have brought it, but then what's in the satchel? I wonder.

"I couldn't bring it with me, but in three nights' time, whatever the plan may be, I will have it with me and whether I live or die, you may have it. I trust after what happens, you will no longer desire to read from it, but will keep it safe." He further informs me that beyond the book there will be a large cash payment for all services rendered, which I must say I like the sound of.

With that, Sam places the satchel on my desk, opening it to reveal a staggering mound of cash, totaling seventy five hundred dollars. Even before the money, I was convinced to take the case, but for the life of me I can't figure out why I trust this guy. I'm taking everything that's been said on nothing more than his word.

Sam must have seen the struggle on my face, because he answers my unasked questions. "I'm sorry it had to happen like this, but one thing I have gained from the book, and put to use quite liberally, is oral persuasion." Put simply, the inclination for others to believe what he says. And there is no way for me to refute the notion; I simply believe.

He continues to prattle on, and I decide if I don't listen to him, he can't persuade me. Shortly, I notice he stopped talking about himself and the book in general terms, but is actually asking me what I plan on doing about his situation, and avoid having to kill an infant.

I tell him it's hard to plan anything when I don't know what I'm going up against. He agrees, and tells me he's been searching the book for the past several months, trying to find some clue as to the actual executioner for the book. We decide to do our own investigations separately.

We agree he will return to the office in two days to compare notes, and welcome whatever may be coming prepared. He leaves to go search the book for clues of ways out of the infant sacrifice, or the identity of his death. I deposit the cash into the bank.

II

Returning to the office, I call one of two ancient researchers that I've worked with for years--Karen. Normally, I'd reach out to Arnold first, but he's been feeling under the weather. I sometimes forget just how old he is; guess I may be working him too hard. Karen has been training under Arnold for as long as I can remember, and thankfully she hasn't allowed that to smother her sunny disposition or her zeal for the work. On the other hand, I do wish she'd stop chewing gum while talking, but I'll take the tradeoff.

Karen has learned much working with Arnold, and has repeatedly proven invaluable to the team, even after our secretary and her lover, Carl, was murdered. She took it hard, as expected, but doubled down in her work, swearing to find a way to avenge his death.

"Karen, listen up, we got a job I'm going to need your help on."

She asks if I want her to bring Arnold into this, but I assure her that I trust she'll be able to handle this. Somehow, I hear her happiness in the pop of her gum. Once I'm sure she knows what she's looking for, I let her get to it.

I, on the other hand, decide to do a little research of my own and grab a book from my own collection: a biography of H.P. Lovecraft. I remember reading it for kicks while I was still on the police force, and then reading it again after my wife and daughter died; when I was introduced to the world of the macabre. Never before has a single book rendered so many different emotions from two separate readings. I consider myself fairly well read, and I decided to first read this book to get into the mind of such a tortured soul. I often compare H.P.'s life with that of Robert E. Howard.

The second time I read the book was for different reasons, but no less insightful. Having been brought to light on the seedy underworld we live above, I felt an affinity towards the things H.P. saw in his mind, even if they weren't real.

This time, however, I'm looking to see if anything I've encountered in my time bears any resemblance to his "imagination."

During my third read-through, I was continuously brought back to his death, which, surprisingly enough, isn't the end of the book. I read how after returning to his childhood town, he had a boom in creative properties, but it all soon faded after the suicide of his friend Robert E. Howard. Reading that makes me wonder if I associated the two authors on my own, or only after reading this the first time and hearing of the "Lovecraft Circle." After Robert's suicide, H.P. quickly spiraled downward, losing all the momentum he had garnered during his latest writing spree, and he was diagnosed with intestinal cancer.

All of this got me thinking about what Sam had said about Lovecraft being a "pawn" of the Necronomicon and the creatures behind it. Furthermore, it got me thinking about his close relation with Robert E. Howard, who killed himself after his mother slipped into an irreversible coma. Throughout most of his life Howard made comments of depression, and a vague "unreality" to his life, and I can't shake the feeling that there's more to these two authors than their friendship dictates, and maybe it all comes back to the damned Book of the Dead.

III

I finish the autobiography around midnight the next day at home, and can't help but feel that I've wasted too much time and made no headway. Deciding to check my email to see if there's anything from Karen, and… "Ah bingo, come on Karen, earn that paycheck." Sifting through all the information she sent, she keeps coming back to the defense that there is so much clutter about the Necronomicon it's impossible for her to sort through what's fake and what's real (if anything), not something Arnold would have had trouble with.

She does mention that the most common enforcers for Hell are hellhounds, and that we should have wolfsbane in the storage room. Reading it over, it's too easy, too clean. Not to belittle her work, but there's no way that the damned Book of the Dead is protected by a poodle.

Seemingly sensing my apprehension about her research, she adds a footnote to her report:

This seems like a long shot, but something feels wrong about it. In an ancient Sumerian text there's mention of a creature Sakan Dubaba, but the rest of it was badly burned. I researched the name and it roughly translates to Ash Fly. Working from there I found, in a pre-Christian Gaelic ritual for the dead, a creature made of flying ash that for a period of 48 years showed roughly every two years to take their village shaman to the afterlife. All this was reported to be derived from an unknown holy text that arrived with a traveler, and disappeared several decades later. After which the village was completely erased from history.

Sumerian and Gaelic? Is she just pulling at straws to please me, or did she actually find some historical evidence of the Necronomicon? It sounds plausible, even if a little farfetched. If she were right about this Sakan Dubaba character, why would the Gaelic shamans willingly submit to his death? For almost fifty years shamans would ritually sacrifice themselves until the book went missing and the village was wiped off the face of the earth. This is too much to take in at one thirty in the morning.

IV

Pulling up to the office, I know I'm late, made only more evident by seeing everyone's car already here, including Mr. Campbell's. The entire night I was plagued with visions of this ash creature. I hope Karen's right about this.

Putting down the copy of *Sports Drawn* magazine in the pile of other magazines you'd more likely find in a doctor's office, like *Mothers Today*, and *House & Garden*, Mr. Campbell gets up looking very defeated. "Detective Peckman, I hope you had better luck than I did. I was unable to determine the enforcer of the book or a way out of the infant sacrifice."

Looking at Karen: "I think we've found something that could help us out, but I want to go over the details once more." We enter my office, and I invite Karen to join us.

He begins by telling me of the passage detailing the coming death.

The text you hold in your hands is both a blessing and a curse. Within its passages you will find cures to mankind's plagues, and horrors unthought of by man. All of which will be at your command if your will is strong and your mind distant. Having read thus far, your fate is sealed. In days' time equal to the number of the Beast, you will be summoned by the book to join its immortal army. There is no defense. Prepare yourself wisely for the end of days; you have been chosen.

Karen and I are unable to speak following that, until she can muster the strength to ask him if we're now doomed because that was recited to us. I have to admit the only thought going through my mind was why it sounded like the book was talking to the reader, like there's an essence within the book. Mr. Campbell tells us that we are unaffected by hearing the passage; that it only effects those who read it, and that he does believe there's a being or soul within the book.

"Through Karen's research she was able to find repeated mention of hellhounds being the enforcers of Hell, but nothing that ties them specifically to the Necronomicon. We've dealt with hellhounds before and have a defense against them that will protect you without a problem, if they're what's coming tonight." He tells me that there are several references to beings that resemble hellhounds in the book, but he does not believe them to be his executioners. "I agree. Karen has also come across a creature called Sakan Dubaba, which translates to ash fly. We don't know what it means, but we can tie numerous Gaelic deaths to a holy book and ash. We think it's our best shot."

Arnold, who's been listening from the doorway, says he disagrees. "If you hear hoof beats look for a horse, not a zebra. If everything you've uncovered points towards hellhounds, don't look for ashes; not when someone's life is on the line."

I can tell by the look on Karen's face that she wants to argue, but is too scared, either of Arnold, or of being wrong. "Arnold, you know I love you like an uncle, but I think Karen is right about this one. No matter how disparate the connections are, they are there. But before you get upset, I'll keep some wolfsbane with me in case it is a hellhound; simple enough solution." Arnold simply nods, then walks out of the room without another word. I couldn't tell if Arnold was offended or not, but I don't have time to worry about that. Like he said, someone's life is on the line.

V

Usually when I'm working a case I can't quite get my head around, I like to get Richard involved, but he's off to hunt a monster harassing a family in Spokane and he's taken Cereal with him. I'm left with three researchers, my persuasive client, and Sid. Sid's former police partners who died and now haunt him (in a good way) may prove useful in getting an advance warning on whatever is coming for Sam. I send Arnold and Sara home at 4 o'clock, long before the sun sets. I decided to keep Karen for another hour or so, in hopes she could find some last minute information. Arnold's not too happy about this.

We spend the remainder of the evening preparing as best we can before night settles in. Karen decides she's not leaving; she says she needs to see if she's right about this thing or not, first hand. I'm ensuring that all windows, doors, and vents are properly barricaded and reinforced with a healthy layer of wolfsbane, just in case. Sid is checking all of our weapons and ammo, making sure there are plenty of refills strategically placed throughout the office. Tyson, the male ghost that haunts Sid, is doing recon around the office and reporting back to Sid every 5 minutes. Annabel, the female that haunts Sid, is searching through Sam's thoughts to see if there is anything he isn't noticing, kind of a 'too close to the canvas to see the picture' deal. We didn't tell Sam she's doing this. Sid's not sure why they haven't crossed over, or why they're haunting him, but they've saved him from countless situations, warning him not to enter a certain room, or helping gather information about a new kind of nasty and how to defeat it, which is what we're hoping will happen here.

I've seen pictures of Annabel from when she was alive and, not to sound twisted, but I wouldn't mind having such an attractive apparition watching me at night... "Wait, Sid, is Annabel by me?"

He tells me no. "But don't worry, she already knows you're attracted to her, and wants you to know that if she still had her body, you still wouldn't be able to touch her." Ouch, that's fine; when she did have her body I was happily married to Talia, and wouldn't have thought twice about Annabel.

"Sid, it seems like we have everything covered, but I have that feeling that we're missing something." He agrees, but offers no helping in figuring out what we're missing. Sam pulls out the Necronomicon, which at once is both bigger and smaller than I was expecting.

"If I may offer some assistance? I've picked up something that may protect you tonight." He begins chanting in a foreign language, and I don't mean French or Russian, I mean alien foreign: some of the sounds are inhuman, not meant to be uttered by our tongues. I try to ask him what he means by protecting *us*, he implied he won't protect himself, but he holds his index finger up signaling for me to wait until he's done.

Beginning to feel uncomfortable with his chanting, I draw both Gwen and Stacy, taking aim at Mr. Campbell. "Sid, I get the feeling we may be double-crossed by our overly generous, magically enhanced client." I can't believe I didn't see it before; he's not cursed by the Necronomicon, he's using us to get what he wants from it. I take aim at Mr. Campbell's forehead and just as I'm about to pull the trigger, he stops chanting.

"Really, Mr. Peckman, you must learn to trust others as we trust you. I only meant that the protection hex I placed on you three won't be much good for me. It comes from the Necronomicon and I'm sure it has a way around these things for its intended target." I feel like an ass, and tell Sam this; he somehow finds this funny enough to laugh.

In a complete reversal of moods, Sam suddenly looks agitated and worried. Misunderstanding his concerns, I tell him that his faith isn't misplaced; whether it's a hellhound or Sakan Dubaba, I'll do all I can to protect him.

"But what if we missed something? What if it's a different attacker completely, and we're not prepared for it?"

I tell him in my line of work a detective is no good if he can't think on his feet. "Sid and I have dealt with some of the most dangerous things in the world and still survived."

"But no one has survived the Necronomicon; even those evil enough to kill an infant to break the deal still end up dying from the book."

I ask him if he thinks this is because someone who kills an infant continues on the path that led him or her to the Necronomicon in the first place.

"Some people, evil people like you said, live to die. Everything they do accelerates their demise; they were dead before the book found them." He takes little, if any, comfort in my words.

Deciding we need to change topics, I ask who wants the last slice of pizza. "Someone eat this before these bugs get to it." Realizing what I've said, I turn to the flies swarming the garbage pail.

Seeing my concern, Sid puts a hand on my shoulder, "Hey, JSP, what's wrong?" It's late November; no matter how warm it is now, there shouldn't be any flies. Sid draws his weapons and yells to his spectral companion asking for a report. Sam grabs the garbage pail, and in a fit of fear hurls it out the window. Bad move. Not only do the flies that were already in the office stay, the broken window welcomes a flood of new arrivals, bowling Sid and me over.

Apparently it wasn't anything personal, because the flies surround Sam and instantly he begins to cough and gag. Sid dives through the swarm and comes out the other end with Sam in his arms. Suddenly, a shot is fired, and a picture on the far wall of Thaddeus and myself shatters. Sid and I look around the swarm to see Karen shaking holding a gun that was left next to the door.

"Well now we know bullets won't stop a swarm of flies." I

shout for Sid to get Karen and Sam to safety while I try and distract this thing. Sid relays my order to Karen, yelling to me that there's no way I can stop this by myself.

The sound of the swarm is deafening, I can barely hear my own thoughts, let alone what Sid is trying to say to me. I flank the room, and meet up to Sid, shoulder-to-shoulder with our backs to the door out of the office.

"So, what's your plan?"

"Mine? I circled around here to hear what you have planned; you're the one that decided to stay behind."

He tries to chuckle, but is clearly too preoccupied with the situation. When I told Sam that Sid and I have dealt with some of the most dangerous things around, it was only a half-truth. Sid's particular skill set and his 'companions' make him best suited for hauntings, zombies, and the rest of the 'movie' fare, except werewolves: no one should fight a werewolf alone. He's occasionally helped out on some of the big cases, like when Ibn'Roth tried to reenter our dimension, but no one has found more people who were kidnapped by their deceased spouses, or exorcized as many possessions.

We knew that bullets wouldn't do any harm, and I was pretty sure neither would Gwen, my tomahawk, so I grabbed the closest thing to me that might work: a rolled up maternity magazine. Taking a couple of back and forth swings that seemed to do nothing to the swarm, but when I looked at the magazine, it was covered in soot. These flies were turning to ash as I struck them.

This didn't seem to do much damage, but I must have upset the flies, because the swarm changed to a form, and the noise the flies were making started to sound like it was coming from inside a balloon, the way the pitch changed as if it were echoing. Then the flies make the shape of a person, not much taller than an average human. All of a sudden, there stood Sakan Dubaba, who looked like a solid mass of gray ash, and simultaneously like a swarm of flies crawling around a person.

This gives me something solid to work with, and as I was slowly drawing Gwen as to not arouse his anger, Sid must have had the same thought, because he fired two shots in the creature's chest. Unfortunately, what looked like a solid mass was really just more ash flies, which exploded into a cascade of gray fireworks out the back of this hit man for the Necronomicon. The bullets crashed into the opposite wall of the office, probably destroying another picture due to the sound of breaking glass.

Since bullets still weren't working, I forced Sid out of the office and threw Gwen at what would be the creature's neck, hoping it would at least slow this thing down. I knew she would return to my hand after hitting its target. Gwen slices clean through the ash, actually causing it to stagger. Not wanting to let the window of opportunity pass, I rush with both arms out, hoping to tackle the thing to the ground; no such luck. It grabs me by the sides of my head with two hands that feel like vibrating worms in a burlap sack, and tosses me into the wall as if I was a ten-year-old girl.

The good news is that I seem to have its attention now, because it crosses the room towards me without moving its feet, then the flies from his feet and legs disperse in a frenzy, and I see what Sid actually shot. It wasn't a picture frame, but instead my bottle of Johnnie Walker Blue Label, and the spilt liquid gold is affecting the creature's ash composition. Golden indeed.

Grabbing a two-liter bottle of soda, I toss it into the air and shoot it with Stacy. The flying liquid sends the flies scattering. I run as quick as I can towards the door, but I trip and crash into it. I look at the swarm that is still trying to reform, then look down and see the soot-covered magazine that I slipped on. Looking at the magazine, I finally figure out how to get out of this.

Running out of the office, I yell for Sid to contact his ghosts and get them to delay this thing for as long as possible, and to look after Karen. I try to save our client. Scooping up the damned book, and grabbing Sam by the collar of his shirt, I hurry him out of the waiting room all the way out to my car. He gets in without much of a fuss, but once we're driving off he asks why we were leaving everyone else behind. Ignoring him and the question, I focus on weaving through the traffic, avoiding the few remaining obstacles still on the road at this time.

Arriving at a local hospital, I park near a side entrance used primarily by employees. "I hope Jose is working tonight. He's the only one that will let me in without any questions."

"Who's Jose? Let you in where?" Again ignoring his questions, I run past the security window, "Hey Jose! Just be a minute." And without losing a step I turn down a short hallway, and enter a double door.

"Why is it cold? Where are we? Are we... are we in the... oh

I think I'm going to be sick." I grab Sam by the front of his shirt and throw him to the floor and tell him, no I *order*, him not to move, and he complies. Searching the walk-in refrigerator, I can't find what I'm looking for and all of a sudden I hear Jose yelling, not as he would at someone trying to sneak into the hospital, but yelling as if he was being torn apart, and I think he just might be.

Just then I find the little black box I was hoping to find on top of a cabinet. Again ordering Sam, I shout for him to roll his sleeve up and hold out his hand. Clearly confused, still he does what I say with no qualms. I pull out the contents of the box and both of our stomachs retch.

I hope it's still fresh enough to serve our purposes. Grabbing the contents, I make a large cut on the bottom, and hold it above Sam's outstretched hand. I tell him to open the Necronomicon to a blank page.

As he searches for one, the creature crashes through the door. I reach a hose connected to a faucet and being to spray the creature, but it seems to have either anticipated this attack, or created a defense against it, because it isn't as affected as it was against the bottle.

"Hurry up, Sam; I can't hold this thing off forever!" Just then he shouts that he's found one. "Write exactly what I say with the blood on your hand: 'Still born baby!'" Giving up on the water, I grab a bucket of some liquid that's much thicker than water and toss it at Sakan Dubaba. This works much better than the water, and before it can fully reform, Sam finishes the inscription, and the ash flies disperse in a gray explosion of smoke.

Hoping all is well, I collapse on the floor worried about Sid, the ghosts, but mostly Jose. While still on the floor, I turn to look at Sam to see he's in the fetal position, with tears streaming down his face.

I can't help but think the image fits, knowing that his arm is covered in the blood of a stillborn child. Just then Sid calls from the office to let me know that they couldn't hold Sakan any longer. I laugh, just before I lose consciousness.

VI

I wake up in the office nearly eighteen hours later, but what feels like three weeks after the fiasco in the hospital morgue. Karen explains to me that Sam is all right, and paid the remainder of the fee, and the book is sitting on my desk. "We weren't sure what to do with it. Sid wants to burn it, but I don't want to let go of the infinite amount of knowledge contained in its pages." I tell her she sounds like what Sam must have before he began reading the book. At that, she turns and leaves my office. Before she closes the door, I ask her if Jose made it. "Who do you think got you back here?" That scream must have just been from fright, big baby.

I roll over to try and go back to sleep, and I see the magazine on the floor I tripped over during the fight, and reread the headline; *Rate of Stillborns Skyrockets in the United States*. Knowing I won't be able to go back to sleep, I sit at my desk and just stare at that book, that damned Book of the Dead.

Breaking from the Pack
From the Casebook of Detective James S. Peckman
By Alex Azar

Christmas time in New Jersey. Nothing worse than sunless days, freezing nights, and malls overpacked like an all-you-can-eat buffet next to a Jenny Craig. There was a time that I'd have been among the crowd. In fact it was on a Christmas Eve when I bought my two-year-old daughter, Sophia, her favorite teddy, London. I keep London's burnt eye in my wallet as a reminder of what I lost in that accident all those years ago. Today, it's a reminder that I have no one to shop for, even if I wanted to go to the mall.

I

It's Christmas Eve, and I'm alone in my office at Argus Agency. I pour myself a glass of Blue Label and light a cigarette, when I hear the front door open. Assuming it's one of the partners or secretaries, I stay quiet, hoping to avoid explaining my holiday plans, or lack thereof.

Suddenly, the light coming through my door frame is blocked, though not by much. Standing in the entrance is a silhouette that I can make out to be a less than average sized male, possibly a teenager.

Stepping into the room, I see he's considerably older, mid to late forties. He tries to spit out a greeting, but barely mumbles a whisper. Eager to get to my drink, I start the conversation for him, "Hello, I'm Detective James S. Peckman, how can I be of service to you?"

"You're... you're not what I expected."

"And I wasn't expecting any clients." That came out colder than I intended. He apologizes for the crudeness of his introduction; I leave mine where it stands.

"I'm sorry, it's just that I saw you on the news when you killed that sea monster; you looked bigger during the coverage." His scared mousy voice combined with me thinking about the drink before me cause me to barely grasp what he says.

I mockingly tell him that the camera not only adds ten pounds but three inches. "In person, I'm only five-nine." I'm not in a good mood and I'm taking it out on this poor guy, who looks like he's used to being walked all over.

"Uh, yes, I can see that, but you don't seem like a monster hunter."

Really, buddy? How many 'monster hunters' have you met? I take a sip of the golden brew before me, easing my nerves. "I'm not a monster hunter, I'm a paranormal detective, and you still haven't explained why you're here."

He apologizes again, shrinking his neck down, pulling his chin to his chest, and raising his hands up defensively. The pose combined with his five-foot frame covered in melting snow makes him look like a mouse begging for food.

"You need to help me; I'm being hunted by monsters."

"Okay, let's calm down." I pull out the bottle of Red Label I keep for clients, and pour him a small glass, sliding it over. "Helping is what I do, but start from the beginning. Who are you?"

He motions with a pale bony finger, silently asking me if he can have one of my cigarettes. I hate it when clients invite themselves to my cigarettes without me offering, but I guess that's what I get for leaving the pack on my desk, I nod approval. He tells me his name is Timothy Hunt. 'Timmy.' His name even sounds scared. He works for a company, doing some mundane job in a cubicle. I need another swig just to stay focused. "I know I don't have a chance with Janice, but I figured if I at least went to the bar for her birthday, she might notice me. Instead, she never even knew I was there, so I drank by myself at the opposite end of the bar. That's when this guy came up to me with his girlfriend and friend. I assumed they were either genuinely trying to be friendly or at the very least just took pity on me, but I'm not that lucky."

He's taking his time, drinking more than talking. Clearly wherever this story is leading, it's an emotional trip for him. "The female, Lucinda, said she could tell that I loved the birthday girl, but Janice didn't know I was alive. I could do nothing but nod in agreement. Her boyfriend, Josh, clearly the leader of the group, said that he didn't think she was attractive enough to even bother with, but that he could get her if he wanted to. He said it with such arrogance I already didn't like him. I'll admit Janice isn't as attractive as Lucinda, but Lucinda had a blank look in her. Seemed like she wasn't much more than arm candy for Josh. Glen, the other guy, didn't say anything, just agreed with Josh, clinging to him almost closer than Lucinda was, feeding off of Josh's bravado."

I don't see what any of this has to do with hiring me, which means that it's only keeping me from my Christmas celebration. "Josh looked at Janice again, then back at me, and said that he could give me the confidence to take her as my own. He said it like she was a piece of meat for a dog to claim, and I think that to him that's all she was. Not for a minute did I believe anything he could say or do would help me, but when Lucinda asked me to join them, I figured I had nothing left to lose."

I ask if he felt his life was so meaningless that he'd forfeit it for nothing. "That's the thing; Josh told me how he could make me stronger, faster, and more confident, and even though he was so cocky, he said it with such assurance that I began to believe him. We were in a dark area of the parking lot when from behind Lucinda started kissing me on my neck, and running her hands all over my body. She lifted my shirt and I forgot all about Josh and Glen standing right in front of me. I thought maybe she wasn't just for show, when suddenly I felt a burning pain in my gut like nothing I'd ever experienced. Looking down I saw Josh's hand stuck in me; he actually plunged his bare hand into my stomach." Timmy mimicked the hand thrust for emphasis.

"I fell to my knees and eventually keeled over, passing out as I watched them walk away. Last thing I remember is hearing Glen congratulate Josh.

I woke up the next morning in my bed, still in the clothes from the night before. The wound was completely healed and I'd never felt better, but for proof of the night, my clothes were bloody and there was a feather laid on my nightstand."

He tells me this happened three nights ago and that he tried to pretend that it didn't actually occur and that it wasn't his blood on the shirt. He had nearly convinced himself that the night never happened, until this morning. On his way to work, the wound from his stomach began to burn a dull heat that didn't hurt, but definitely wasn't comfortable. He got to the office without further incident. Unfortunately, as he was about to enter the building, he saw Josh and the other two waiting for him. "He told me that I couldn't ignore what happened, like he was reading my thoughts. He told me that I was feeling stronger, that I was more confident and that I would keep progressing until the next full moon. He said I better make my move on Janice before then because I wouldn't have a chance after that. I don't know why I know this, but he's going to kill me before the full moon. That's New Year's Eve!"

The whole thing reeks of werewolves, except I can't figure out why they'd choose Timmy, or why he has the feeling that they plan on killing him. I tell him that I'll take his case, but he needs to return in two days to fill out the paperwork and make the first payment. I assure him that I'll figure it out and protect him anyway I can. He thanks me and goes, finally leaving me alone with my thoughts... my thoughts and my drink.

II

I spend most of the morning of the 26th trying to recover from my nearly thirty-hour binge. Unfortunately, nothing is working. I'm surprised that Timmy isn't here waiting for me, but that's the only pleasant surprise I'll be getting.

"Hey boss, I called you yesterday; did you get my message?" Sara asks as she hands me the messages from the morning; two of the three are from Timmy, the third is to notify me that I may be eligible to receive a million dollars. I think I mumble some sort of response before I blurt out the word 'coffee' with dry bile. I instantly regret making the effort to speak. As I walk into my office, I remove the fedora that's hanging on the coat rack just inside the door and hang it on an identical rack outside my office: the office-wide symbol for 'do not disturb.'

I don't typically wear the fedora, except when it's raining. I wear the hat instead of using an umbrella because I feel umbrellas are a disconnect from nature, and rain almost always has evil behind it but people don't notice it because they shy away from the rain. Ironically, I only bought the fedora and matching trench coat when I first got into this line of work because they fit the look. But the long jacket just got in the way when drawing my weapons, and it gave people chasing or fighting me something to grab hold of. I much prefer my pea coat; at medium length it conceals most weapons and allows for unconstrained movement, and doesn't become a target for others.

My partner, Dick, ignores the 'do not disturb' sign, and wakes me up at two in the afternoon. He tells me I have to call Timmy, otherwise I can't take the case, and we don't get paid. Of course he's right, so I drink my mug of coffee quicker than recommended, and look up Timmy's number.

"Sorry I didn't call you earlier, but I was working on something. Come into the office and fill out the paperwork with Sara. I might not be in the office; I'll be following up on a lead." Normally, that would have been a lie, but this time I do have a good source for this kind of case.

III

Standing on the doorsteps of a Brooklyn brownstone I haven't been to in almost a decade, I offer a greeting before the door's fully opened. "Wow, Dean Samuel, good to see you buddy." Dean's an old friend that I've lost touch with over the years, but he's perfect for this case, being a werewolf and all.

"Buddy? James, you haven't talked to me since I helped you out with that little werewolf problem you had some years ago. Doesn't seem very 'buddy' like to me. And let me guess, you're only here because you need my help, again." In lieu of answering him verbally, I hand him the gift I was concealing behind my back. A bag of imitation bacon strips meant for pet dogs. He looks at me with his head hung low, and eyes burning with anger "I hate you," he says as he takes the bag from my hand, and leads me into his home.

Nearly ten years, and the place hasn't changed at all. He sits down, chewing on one of the bacon strips, and picks up a bottle of beer. My stomach does a back flip at the sight of the alcohol, and I need to physically keep myself from vomiting.

Dean motions for me to sit across from him, still chewing away.

"I've got a case that I need your expertise on."

"And let me guess, you only have a week to solve it." Obviously he's going to know when the next full moon is, but before

I consider requesting his aid in a physical manner, I need to know if these are run-of-the-mill werewolves or something I haven't come across before.

I tell Dean everything Timmy told me, about the three's attitudes, their pack mentality, the gut wound, and its miraculously healing the next day.

"That all seems like your typical werewolf fare, but if what you're telling me of this Timmy guy is true, he doesn't seem like a likely choice to add to their ranks. Combine that with the feeling he has about them wanting to kill him, there's something off about it." He lets me know that he won't be able to physically help me with this case, because he has a 'suckling' that's experiencing his first full moon.

"I can tell you this, I don't think this is your average werewolf pack. There's traces of an African therianthropic tribe, even a cannibalistic pack in Asia that fit the description you've given me, but as far as I know, they haven't migrated to the States." We agree that the Asian pack that eats their young is the likely choice. We shake hands at the door, and he tells me that he'll call the office in a few days after he's gathered what he can.

IV

It's nearly four in the morning and I'm startled awake from a dream. Not a nightmare, but a very innocuous dream, that's nagging me more than it should. All I can remember from it is a white piece of paper with jumbled letters cut out of magazines and newspapers like a ransom note. It looks like a list, but I can't make out any of the words, but halfway down the words I stop and in handwritten jagged pencil is the letter 'r' three times over.

I have no idea what it means but I've always been a big believer in the meanings behind dreams. It has to mean something, but I can't for the life of me figure it out, and it's bothering me. Making it worse, at four in the morning, I've got no one to call.

Unable to go back to sleep, I fall into my old trap of looking through my memory box of Talia, my wife. I have all the letters exchanged from when we were dating, our wedding photo album and countless other memories.

Sadly, I can never bring myself to open up Sophia's memory box. The pain is unfathomable, and it's because she's been dead longer than she was alive. The memories in the box are all that's left of her. Talia's death was tragic and there isn't a day that goes by that I don't miss her, but the pain of the loss of Sophia is on a whole different level.

V

Before I even realize it, it's six o'clock and I'm on my way to the office, the first in. Walking into my office, I see the stack of papers that Sara printed last night on everything she could find on the Asiatic cannibalistic tribe of werewolves that Dean pointed me to, even a little on the African tribe.

From the looks of it, Cereal has gone through the pile, probably enticed at the prospect of fighting werewolves. Maybe I should let him tell me his take on this; he is our resident hunter after all. I'm just too tired to think clearly, and every word I read looks like it's cut and pasted in that same ransom note format from my dream.

Quarter to eight and Sara walks in. The first in and last to leave every day; I've got to show her my thanks somehow. By this time I've fully woken up, which surprises Sara more than just my presence at this hour; what she doesn't know is that I've had the help of an entire pitcher of coffee.

I tell her my dream, but she's not much help in that department. She offers to look it up online, but I dismiss my own urgency as childish. We discuss her thoughts on the research she did on the werewolves. She admits that she didn't find anything conclusive, but parts of Timmy's story fit into all the different mythologies she was able to find.

"It's possible that he's encountered a new breed of werewolf that my typical resources haven't come across yet." We agree that he has that kind of luck, but I don't buy it.

"There has to be something we're not seeing."

"Well, let's go over his story together. You tell me everything he told you, and I'll search all things of significance."

We go over his entire story, starting before he even meets Josh and the two. Beginning with his menial job, infatuation with Janice, his timid attitude and complete lack of initiative. We get to the night in question and begin the circle I've been rounding since I took the case.

"He gets attacked by what we are sure are werewolves, but he doesn't fit the profile of a typical recruit and he 'knows' they plan on killing him before his abilities can fully mature during the next full moon, which is only five days away."

"Correct, and from what we know, and what Dean confirmed with you yesterday, leaders of average packs only choose to convert those that can contribute to the pack. They never kill their own." And we're back to where we started.

As we're discussing alternatives for Timmy's safety, Arnold walks in with a dusty old book under his arm. Without pleasantries whatsoever, he says, "Quit your prattling, I've got your answer right here." But instead of sharing this information, he decides to bitch about there being no coffee in the pot, and blames Sara for not doing her job. Unfortunately, me explaining that I drank it all only leads to a new string of questions of why I'm in so early.

Arnold is a researcher on staff, versed in all things arcane, and has encyclopedic knowledge on many of the things the other detectives and I encounter. On the few occasions we come across something he hasn't learned about, he can find out about it along with Kelly, our other ancient researcher, and Sara, our secretary-slash-web researcher. I tell him about the dream and that I couldn't go back to sleep.

"Bah, dreams don't mean nothing, this means something!" Holding up the book again, he pats it with his hand, making a puff of dust. He opens it to a bookmarked page with what looks to be Chinese writing on it. He waves the book in front of my eyes with an eager look as though I was supposed to understand what I'm reading. When he notices my dumbfounded expression, he curses me.

"You haven't learned to read Pinyin yet? What do you do all day when you're not chasing down rebel gods and the Necronomicon?"

I tell him that typically takes up most of my day, but he doesn't hear me. He's already moved on to his explanation of the page. Arnold says the page dictates the method in thwarting the wolf people of ancient times. "Earlier passages cover the basis we already learned about the Asian tribe and their cannibalistic ways, and they seem to confirm the theory that our client is indeed going to die during the next full moon." He explains that this bloodline of werewolves feed on their weak, adding to their own power.

I ask him how we stop these things, and he tells me it's

simple: "The ringing sound of bronze."

Sara asks my next question for me, "What the hell does that mean?"

"I thought I was the old one; why are you two so slow? In most cases a wound of silver, preferably to the heart, kills a werewolf, right?" Without waiting for an answer, Arnold clarifies for us. "This particular tribe of werewolves isn't susceptible to silver, but the ringing sound of bronze; the ringing of a bronze bell, the banging of a bronze gong, or even bronze pipes."

Cutting my thought process off again, Arnold continues, "I even looked up on one of Sara's fancy computer boxes and found that most novelty magic shops sell bronze bells for some idiotic Wiccan ritual for around $100."

Too shocked that he was even able to use a computer, Sara didn't cut me off this time, "I'm pleasantly surprised with you, Arnold. We'll have to test the metal to make sure it is in fact bronze but we have enough time for that."

Before I head back into my office, I ask both Arnold and Sara to continue searching for info on the African tribe. Despite how easily Arnold was able to toss my dream aside, and how hard I've been trying to do the same, something keeps nagging me about it.

VI

By nine in the morning most of the staff has arrived, Karen, our other ancient researcher, Dick, another detective and my business partner, and Cereal, our resident hunter. Sid, the last detective, is away on a case in Canada searching for the missing link: Yes, someone hired us to locate Bigfoot.

Without a family of my own, the staff of Argus has become my surrogate family. I think that's why the dream is bothering me so much. I've lost too many people already; I can't lose anyone else. Werewolves at face value are nothing new, dangerous but manageable. But if we're dealing with a new breed none of us have encountered before, I can't guarantee I can keep the client safe, or my own staff for that matter.

VII

Sure enough, just like Arnold said, I was able to find a

bronze bell in a cheap magic thrift shop, but this doesn't answer how the ring of a bronze bell is supposed to stop a cannibalistic werewolf. Then again, why does silver work where every other metal falls short?

Getting back to the office, Karen tells me, "The African tribe you asked about seems to have similar weaknesses as the werewolves we're used to." But she can't find any confirmation of that or any descriptions with concrete details.

I fight the urge to snap at her, and instead storm off and slam the door. I've never yelled at an employee, but I was extremely close this time, and for no reason. Unfortunately, my actions speak louder than my words ever would have and I can hear Karen sobbing through the door.

By the time I make up my mind to apologize, Dick comes in the office and places a hand on my chest to keep me from leaving. "Don't say anything to her yet. You've put a fire under her and the others. If anyone can find what you need, those three will do it. But what the hell's wrong with you?" He asks if this is leftover depression from Christmas. I tell him that I honestly have no idea.

"I've barely done anything on this case, and if we go into this blindly I could get every one of us killed." He suggests I let the researchers do their work, and assures me they'll update me on anything they find that might be relevant. He also wants me calling Timmy, and checking on him daily, to see if his condition worsens or if he has any other run-ins with the pack. All of which is typical procedure for us, but I'm too clouded to focus.

VIII

After a couple days I've mellowed out a bit, but making matters worse, I've had that stupid dream twice more, and we're now two nights away from the next full moon.

Taking Dick's advice, I met with Timmy yesterday and am currently on my way to have lunch with him. He's had no new encounters with the pack, and his transformation has progressed as expected. His senses are heightened; he has an increased appetite for meats that are prepared closer to raw.

Spending more time to get to know Timmy, I have to admit he's more than what I first pictured him to be. I won't retract my original thesis of him being a very mousy timid character, but there's something more to him. Although he does a menial job, typically reserved for youngun's, he takes pride in what he does. He's very shy and reserved, but he carries himself with honor when he's not pining for a girl out of his league. And the way he talks about her with such respect and admiration, he might have a chance if he could convey that to her, instead of cowering away whenever an opportunity presents itself.

In an attempt to get a clearer picture of the situation, I call everyone into my office with Dean on speakerphone. "Dean, our research has shown that this Asian tribe of werewolves, the ones that feed off each other, have a weakness to the ringing of bronze. Does that make any sense to you?"

"I've never heard of anything like that for werewolves, but it's as plausible as anything else. Weaknesses for werewolves seem to trace back to original transformation for the tribe. Rituals done under the full moon, blood sacrifices from wounds created by a silver dagger, it all has some origin. The same has to be assumed for this tribe."

"I don't like risking my friends' lives on assumptions. You have your ear to the ground on this sort of thing; have you not come across anything like this before?"

Cereal chooses now to chime in. "Easy, Warrior, the man's doing all he can." He's right, so I excuse myself from the group to catch my breath.

I leave the building just in time to greet the next snowfall of the season. In Jersey we always get snow during the winter, but almost never on Christmas Day, robbing us of a white Christmas. We're usually stuck with three-day-old snow, more closely resembling a gray Christmas, probably adding to my not-so-sunny disposition during the holiday. Ironically, since Christmas it's snowed every day. It feels like it's been one constant snowfall, never strong enough to be called a storm, but just the right amount to keep the roads slick, backs aching from shoveling, and a somber light reflecting off all surfaces.

It's because of this glow that I notice Timmy walking towards me from a distance. A car passing by splashes sludge, covering him in a fresh coat of gray snow, and as he gets closer all I can think of is that at least it's not yellow snow.

The first words out of his mouth as he gets to a comfortable conversation distance, "At least it wasn't yellow."

Wiping as much of the sludge as he can, Timmy looks like a man that's used to brushing other people's crap off, but he's doing it with a smile. As if no matter how many times life stomps on him, he keeps getting up.

He complains of feeling the familiar burn in his chest, but more intense than it has been. I go to shake his hand, when I notice for the first time that he's out in this weather with no gloves or hat. I question him about it, and he tells me that he forgot them on the bus. He says he doesn't like to drive in the snow, because he got in a terrible accident when he was younger while driving in the snow. The doctors didn't know how he survived. He says the same for the airplane accident he was in. I ask him how many lives he has, and before he can give the expected answer, a car hydroplanes to a stop right next to us.

"Oh no! Mr. Peckman, those are the people. They're the ones who attacked me!" And out the passenger side window leans a clean-looking Hispanic man. He's wearing a navy suit, and from what I can tell, it seems to be expensive. If these are the characters from Timmy's story, this must be Josh, although he doesn't look like what I was expecting.

And if he's Josh, the trophy wife clinging to him over the back of his seat must be Lucinda. She's got big hair, and is popping her gum every time she chews. I have to agree with Timmy on his assessment of her; she truly is North Jersey attractive, but has the vacant eyes of South Jersey.

All of that makes the driver of the car, who's leaning close to Josh so he can see Timmy out the window, Glen. He looks exactly like I imagined: short, fat, and balding prematurely. He looks like the kind of person who in high school didn't have many friends so he clung to the few he did have, or in this case, his one friend.

I pull Timmy behind me, placing the bulk of my body between him and his predators. "You can hide behind your bodyguard, or whatever this guy's supposed to be, all you want tonight, but we'll be back for you tomorrow night. The full moon's coming, can't you feel it?"

I begin to pull Stacy, my Glock 9mm, from her holster, but Lucinda is out of the car and has me off the ground by my neck quicker than I've seen anything move. She slaps Stacy out of my hand with so much force that I think she breaks bones, and slams me against the wall of the building. Josh continues to speak from the window of the car, "Timmy, keep the bodyguard with you tomorrow night. I'd like to see his face as I kill you, and rip his insides out from his ass."

Lucinda gives me a wet sloppy kiss on my cheek, surely leaving a mark of her lips, before dropping me to the ground. Before I can even regain my footing, she's back in the car and they're driving off.

I scramble to pick up Stacy, but by the time I get her in my hands, they're out of range, and there are too many people to attempt throwing Gwen, my tomahawk. Even though Gwen is enchanted to strike whatever I throw her at and return to me, I wouldn't be able to take out the driver through a closed window, and I can't guarantee I'll be able to take out a tire with one hit. Additionally, seeing how shaken up Timmy is over the whole ordeal, I know I need to tend to my client.

Back inside, I recap to the staff everything that happened, and stress how quick and strong Lucinda was. This even more firmly assures me that we're on the right trail with the cannibal tribe. If she's this strong when the moon isn't full, she must have fed on a good amount of werewolves, which leads me to believe that Josh, the head of the pack, has fed on even more, making him more powerful. Not a heartwarming prospect.

IX

After nursing my wounds, and my pride, we all go over the plan for tomorrow night. "We each have a bronze bell, right? Timmy, even though you have one I don't want you using the bell unless absolutely necessary. The ring has no effect on you now, but we don't know how you'll react tomorrow night when the moon is full. And because of that, you are to stay behind me wearing these earplugs at all times. You and I are going to literally be tied at the hips. Since you won't be able to hear me, I need you close enough to be able to follow my commands, and if I run, you better run just as hard, and exactly where I run. I'm not about to die, because you decide to run around the wrong side of a light post."

I dig into him for so long, and so much, I can see him physically getting more scared. Deciding it's best to lay off until he can regain whatever composure he normally has, I remind Cereal and Dick to keep silver rounds on them in case things aren't what they seem. Arnold's not in the office, but he'd tear me a new one if I didn't plan for every contingency.

We agree that Timmy is going to stay the night in the office with me. Cereal and Dick will meet us here, and rehash the plan one more time. I trust the guys to know what to do and how to handle themselves, but I don't trust our client; and if he deviates from the plan it could cost more than his life. We also decide to set up camp for tomorrow night in the underground parking deck of the building the office is in. There are some rumors that direct moonlight increases a werewolf's strength. It might not be true, but this isn't the time to gamble.

With everything squared away, I send Cereal and Dick home to rest up for tomorrow, and pull out the sofa bed for Timmy. I can distinctly remember the two other times it's been used as a bed, and if Timmy knew, he might opt to not sleep on it.

After getting him settled for the night, I give a last check-in call to Karen, Sara, and Arnold to see if they've dug up any other useful knowledge. They hadn't.

X

The following morning, it's New Year's Eve, and I've never detested this time of year more. Timmy kept me up all night, saying that he hasn't been getting tired at night as often, another side effect of his lycanthropy. He asked me about my life, and of all the clients I've had, he's the only one to seem to generally care about my personal life, not just the weird cases I've had. Telling him about Sophia and Talia, I must have gotten noticeably upset, because he quickly changed the topic to Cereal.

Cereal is like a favorite book you just have to tell others about. "I never fully understood Cereal, until we had to destroy the reanimated corpses of thirteen dead presidents together." He spent his entire adult life hunting down the monster that slaughtered his parents after the police told him it was this serial killer they'd caught the next day. That's where he got his name from, mocking the police's 'serial' killer. We met while we were each hunting for the same wendigo in northern Michigan. Since then he's been on the Argus Agency payroll, although granted for insurance purposes, he's listed as a detective.

Throughout the story Timmy is captivated, and I have the

sneaking suspicion that I just made Cereal a new fan; something he's not going to be happy about. He doesn't mind people knowing his story, he just doesn't like talking about it; something I left out when telling Timmy.

As soon as Cereal walks into the office: "Hi Cereal, can I see the tattoo on your back?"

He gives me a dirty look, and then begins unbuttoning his shirt. Dick walks in, and before he can even ask what's going on, I ask him into my office, leaving the two new buddies alone.

"This guy kept me up most of the night. If I don't get some rest during the day, I'll have to call an audible and have Timmy tethered to either you or Cereal. I don't like it, but it's for the best." Dick agrees, and nominates Cereal based on their new friendship.

I call Cereal and Timmy into my office, and relay the plan to them. Timmy surprises me. "No offense to Cereal, but I would feel more comfortable if I were with you, James, during the final hours." It's sad that such an insignificant gesture pleases me, but it does, and since he's the client his comfort is paramount.

I tell Dick and Cereal to stick with Timmy, test the bronze bell on him again, feed him and take care of any other amenities, while I go home and get a couple of hours of rest.

XI

I return to the office well before dusk, but get a little worried when I realize the full moon is already visible with the sun out. Sara, Karen, and Arnold were all told not to report to work today, and after checking on Timmy, I call the super of the building. Gustav doesn't really know what we do, but he lets us be and tolerates a lot. When I tell him we're going to need the parking deck closed off, he thinks it's because we're planning some New Year's party. I let him believe what he wants, and he agrees. I tell Dick to have Sara order Gustav a gift basket for thanks.

Heading downstairs, Dick and Cereal place guns in various positions throughout the parking deck, and an accompanying clip of silver bullets for each gun. I tether Timmy around the waist with a length of bungee cord, and fasten the other end around my waist. "The sun is going down in a few, so from this point on you do as I say, and stick close to me."

During the day Dick had picked up bronze Christmas bells

and affixed them near each entrance. Cereal, on the other hand, brought a bronze dagger, and two large three-gallon water jugs filled with a yellowish liquid. Scared to know what was in the jugs, I was content letting the hunter do his thing. Timmy, on the other hand, wasn't as comfortable. "What is that?"

As he pours some of the liquid along the edge of where the floor meets the wall across the entire length of the parking deck floor, Cereal tells him, "Elephant piss, it'll throw the scent off for our guests. You might want to pour some on yourself, Timmy."

I can almost see the large floppy ears and droopy dog's eyes as Timmy looks at me, and silently asks if Cereal is serious. I pat him on the shoulder, "Sorry, he's right; anything that'll work in disorienting them will help. They obviously can track you, and that puts us at a disadvantage."

In a complete surprise, he doesn't revert to his mousy position, but he puffs his chest out, puts his shoulders back and stands tall... well, as tall as his small frame will allow.

With a smile that reveals he's enjoying this too much, Cereal drops the newly emptied jug of elephant piss, and pours half the contents of the second one on Timmy. All I can think is that this has to work. I don't have a heightened sense of smell, and I'm ready to vomit.

XII

After tearing away the sheet metal gate leading to the street, Josh, Lucinda, and Glenn saunter in like the cool kids in high school walking through the halls. The noise of the bent metal was so loud it must have overtaken the ring of the bells.

Cereal and Dick circle around, holding their bells out in front of them, readying so the three of us can ring at once. The wolves in fleshy clothing seem to be unable to focus on Timmy, and keep darting their heads from side to side trying to hone in on him. With her frantic jostling, Lucinda works her necklace out from her shirt, and it begins flailing around. She's moving so fast I can't make out what it is until just before we ring the bells. She's wearing a peacock feather.

I grab Timmy and dive behind a car, as Dick and Cereal ring their bells to no avail. "Timmy, did you mention anything about a feather? The first time, right? Why didn't you mention it again?"

"Well, I didn't think it was important, not if I'm becoming a werewolf." Damn it, how could I have overlooked that? Dick keeps ringing his bell, hoping it will finally work; Cereal, on the other hand, is used to thinking on his feet during a battle, and shouts out "Silver rounds!"

I grab a clip of silver bullets from behind the tire of the car, but before I can load it, Glen is standing over Timmy and me. "You sweat too much, newbie."

What happens next is something I'll never be able to purge from my mind. Glen's mouth opens impossibly wide, and his teeth begin to fold outwards, so much so that his mouth is now the majority of his face. Once his teeth settle into their perfect circle of tiny fangs, they're joined with several more rings of teeth, resembling an inside out shark's mouth. Then, instead of fur sprouting from his skin, a clear black sheen covers his entire body. His body has absolutely no definition, just a slick black form, similar to a biped with no visible joints.

However, in lieu of attacking us, this Glen-creature calls to Josh saying he found the prey and the bodyguard. I take comfort knowing I'm not the one referred to as 'the prey.'

Before Josh makes it to us I hear gunfire and Lucinda screaming, and I think to myself maybe silver will work on whatever these things are. I silently load Stacy out of Glen's view, but as soon as I try to draw her, Glen is on top of me, pinning me to the ground. From this angle, and unable to see his limbs, I figure out what he is, a leech. Which explains why they're so strong; they 'leech' their powers from others.

I'm proud of myself for figuring it out before I die, but upset I won't live long enough to gloat. "rrr" Just like that, the image from my dream pops back into my head. Timmy picks up Stacy, and fires her at Glen. He somehow manages to miss both of us from four feet away, but it works at getting Glen off of me, and giving me enough time to chop at Glen with Gwen. She sinks into his chest like a fork cutting cold tofu, but I know it's not a lethal blow. Kicking Glen away from me, I yell at Timmy to shoot. He hits a couple of times, but nothing that drops Glen.

Throughout all of this I hear gunshots, but no communication from Dick or Cereal. Pulling Timmy to safety, I cut the tether between us and find Cereal being pinned in a corner by Lucinda from atop a car. She turns to me in all her beauty and rips her shirt off, revealing the most beautiful blue and green feathers that shimmer with each ray of light that hits them.

She jumps off the car and walks towards me. As she does so, a large plume of peacock feathers sprout from… somewhere, and her neck triples in length. By the time she reaches me, she's a full-blown peacock, with feathery arms, and wings, not to mention a wicked looking beak.

Cereal and I start shooting her from each side and everything seems to going in our favor until Josh dives over the car Lucinda was standing on and knocks Cereal out against the concrete wall. I yell for Dick, who responds in moans of pain, saying his leg is broken. If Dick drinks some blood, he'll heal fine, I have to worry about Cereal and Timmy. Apparently, Josh doesn't see me as much of a threat.

I decide to show him how dangerous I can be, so I throw Gwen at Lucinda while running to Glen. Gwen takes a wide arc, going out of Lucinda's visual range, circling back, and hits her from behind, slicing her long slender neck with ease. Her limp body drops to the ground with all the glory of a drugged up supermodel… if that supermodel were headless, of course.

Gwen returns to me, as I reach Glen, and I chop at his leg, keeping him from reaching Timmy. I empty the rest of my clip into what would pass for Glen's head, but clearly silver isn't having an effect on them, just like the ring of bronze didn't. As I contemplate what other methods could be used against them, Glen reaches for me with an inky hand and grabs my shirt. His hand reverts to human form, and he pulls it away in obvious pain.

Searching my chest I find nothing unusual, except my rosary beads. Whatever form of therianthropic were-creatures these are, they seem susceptible to religious artifacts. People always ask me how I could still believe in God with everything I've seen, and I always tell them it's all the shit I've seen that assures me there has to be something better for us out there; this were-leech is just an example of that.

Unfortunately, we didn't prepare for this, and the only cross we have is mine. Holding the beads, I shove my hand into Glen's throat, causing him to completely revert to his human form. I try to cut his head off, but he's still too quick for that.

Remembering a vampire movie with George Clooney, I realize there are tons of crosses around me; I just have to make the shape. I start by cutting a cross into the palm of my hand with Gwen. Leech grabs me in a bear hug. Timmy runs to the corner, and I can see from the corner of my eye Josh is holding Lucinda's body in his arms, looking at her head. "Hey Glen, looks like your boy needs help." Turning his attention to Josh, Glen lets his grip loosen just enough for me to wiggle my arm free and place my bloody palm on his forehead, leaving the mark of the cross. He drops to the floor convulsing, but not dead.

"Josh, it's just you and me, the 'bodyguard,' come get some." Instantly, I wish I had thought of a plan before taunting the were-creature. God knows what he's going to turn into. I don't have to contemplate for long, because Josh jumps over several cars, and in midair, his body contorts and grows, shredding his clothes and shoes before he lands, with scaly yellow clawed feet, short stumpy wings extending from his arms, dark brown and black feathers across his entire body, and that gobble hanging from under his short beak. "So this is what roosters would look like if Jim Henson was God." Apparently, Josh is still upset about Jim Henson's passing, because he didn't laugh; in fact, he tried knocking me out like he did Cereal.

Josh tries wiping the blood off of Glen's forehead, but his foot reverted, temporarily throwing him off balance. I didn't have enough energy to mount an attack, and stood up only in time to watch Josh drive his beak into Glen's chest, ripping out and eating his heart. All the while he looks at me with his beady bird eyes.

Still a little wobbly on my feet, I need to keep Josh's attention on me and not Timmy. "So now I get it; you're clearly not werewolves, but your changes reflect your personalities. Glen was a clingy little prick who fed off your coolness, and Lucinda was the perfect trophy wife, dumb with big tits. That leaves you, the cocky son of a bitch who plans on eating the heart of mousy little Timmy."

Speaking of the devil, Timmy places a hand on my shoulder, easing me against a truck; letting me know it's okay to rest, he's got this. Right away, Timmy grows nearly a foot in height, tearing through his clothes much like Josh, but instead of wiry chicken legs, Timmy is standing on golden brown muscular legs that end in large powerful looking paws. And in place of Josh's wattle, Timmy grows a flowing brown mane of fur circling his entire head. He lets out a growl so loud, car alarms from two decks below are set off.

"Everyone talks about shy, mousy Timmy, meet Timothy Hunt, and it's time to prey." Now that's how you trash talk.

"Wait, wait, wait. You're not supposed to be a lion. You're a mouse, a fucking pussy cat at best." Josh is so scared, he actually begins shedding feathers. He's not talking or even looking at Timmy, but instead directing his questions to me. "*You* did this, didn't you? You're not a bodyguard, who are you?"

"Me? I'm Detective James S. Peckman, and that's not the Cowardly Lion." Damn, I should have said 'ain't'. Ain't is always more bad ass trash talk.

Josh turns to Timmy, who I see is looking at his paws, fascinated at what he's become. Seeing this, I realize, if he's not used to his new body, Timmy's transformation isn't the advantage I thought it was. I stumble towards Gwen, completely oblivious to Timmy and Josh.

Aiming Gwen at the back of Josh's neck, I see Timmy's cat eyes, and the anger raging in them. I know if I take this kill from him, he'll never stand up for himself again. I lower Gwen, but keep her handy, in case she's needed.

What happens next, makes me laugh at being worried about a lion against a chicken. Josh pecks his beak at Timmy, who is able to catch his entire face with one hand. Timmy knees Josh in the gut, doubling him over, before he falls completely. Timmy then grabs Josh by one of his scaly legs, and swings him overhead to crash him into a car. "No! That's my landlord's car." Timmy changes direction in mid-air and slams Josh against the brick wall. Lying on his back, I can see Josh's beak cracked in half like a crab claw after meeting a nutcracker.

I'm not sure if I could check for a pulse under all those feathers, but I know there wouldn't be one anyway. With all the blood he's lost, Josh won't have to worry about how bad of a judge of character he was ever again.

XIII

After Timmy... I mean Timothy was able to calm down, he finally turned back to human. In the meantime, I gave some of Lucinda's blood to Dick, who healed up nice and quick. Cereal came to, a little after, mostly embarrassed with his short-lived performance.

As we're gathering all the guns and other tools, Timothy lets us know that his transformation has imparted the knowledge of his tribe with him. "This particular African Khoisan tribe my bloodline is from melded their beliefs with some Judeo-Christian notions of the body being the temple of their animal gods, and the results are what the rest of them and I have become." He's unsure how the tribe has worked its way to the States, but vows to find out, and stop any others there may be.

We get outside onto the streets just in time to catch the finale of the fireworks display, and all in all I have to admit it's a fitting ending.

Dick mentions how pissed Gustav is going to be that we trashed the garage.

Cereal laughs. "Or he'll just be upset the boss didn't invite him to the party. Well, good hunting, gents!" He pats me on the shoulder.

What Cereal says reminds me of when I first met Timmy on Christmas Eve. He called me a monster hunter, but I had to correct him. 'I'm a paranormal detective' I answered, but he was right. I didn't do any detective work on this case, just followed the trail before me. I thought it'd lead me to werewolves, but instead I blindly led Dick and Cereal into a confrontation with creatures we've never even heard of.

I've become too reliant on the people I've surrounded myself with. I need to start doing the legwork myself again. This year, I'll be sure to put the 'detective' back in my title.

Getting back to the office after we've clean up, Dick asks Cereal where he got two jugs of elephant piss. "If you know the right circles, you can get some, but it was so expensive I was only able to afford one jug."

Timothy, with trepidation in his voice, asks what the second jug was. All he receives for an answer is Cereal shrugging his shoulders and looking down. Disgusted, Dick asks if that was why Cereal ate asparagus for lunch the whole week.

Timothy, still unsure if he wants to know the answer to his questions, asks which jug Cereal poured on him. Once again, Cereal shrugs his shoulders: "Sorry".

About the Author

Alex Azar is an author born and raised in New Jersey. He made the courageous decision to leave the glamorous life of an electrical engineer student behind and concentrate full time on his life long passion of writing. He is now a happily struggling author. This is his first full length publication.